HEAVENLY VISION
By Koos Verkaik

About the cover
The cover was drawn by Doriano Strologo, an illustrator in
Numana, Italy, depicting the main character in the book, the
mysterious Raso, the man who had the heavenly vision.

Outer Banks Publishing Group
Raleigh/Outer Banks

SECOND EDITION – September 2018

Library of Congress Control Number: 2018909428

ISBN 13: 978-1-7320452-4-8
ISBN-10: 1-7320452-4-0
eISBN – 978-0-4639702-7-0

All these strange people
In strange circumstances
Puppets in a crazy play
Part of a cruel plan

The Cape of Good Hope
Around the Year 1745

How harshly a lie will be punished depends on a number of facts, of which place and time probably are the two most important. As far as that is concerned, luck seemed to be against skipper Adriaen Kalf, for he had lost his ship under suspicious circumstances off the coast of the Cape of Good Hope, around about the year 1745. There were few survivors, and the valuable cargo—spices, mainly cinnamon from the isle of Ceylon, present Sri Lanka—had disappeared into the ocean. A captain was responsible for his ship.

Adriaen's statement about what had taken place was so fantastic that it was hard to believe that he hadn't made it all up.

When he reached the shore in a small yawl, together with surgeon Cornelis Swart, boatswain Pieter Post, and the sailors Gerard Houtman and Stijn van de Ende—the only survivors of the catastrophe—he was already a ruined man. What was hanging over his head could vary from a prolonged imprisonment to death by hanging.

And still, he told his improbable story.

They brought the remains of Allart Vroom on land. He was the ship's cook, who had died in the yawl. All that remained of him was wiped together from under the rowing benches of the small boat and hardly covered the bottom of a wooden bucket.

"Allart Vroom climbed down from the ship, and we stood ready to catch him," wrote Adriaen. "His clothes, his flesh, his bones pulverized in our hands. He formed a small heap of powder at our feet. Please, believe me—it is not, like someone suggested, the contents of broken hourglasses."

The jolly boat was still lying half in the water. Along the sides floated large amounts of dead fish. That day many hundreds of other fish would be washed ashore.

The name of Kalf's ship was the Starfish—in Dutch, Zeester, a name that could not be found in the history of the East India Company.

Lots of ships with names that referred to the sea were listed—Sea Gull, Sea Horse, Sea Wolf, Sea Lily—made lucky trips to Asia or went down, but the Starfish was not one of them. That was surprising. For a ship with a Dutch name and a Dutch crew that came back from Ceylon should have belonged to the East India Company. It is also not clear whether the Starfish was a big return ship (the favored type as it could hold the most cargo), a pinnace, a flute, or a frigate.

Anyway, Adriaen was jailed under the authority of Hendrik Swellengrebel. Adriaen mentions this name in his report, and that is why I was able to determine the time of the events, for Swellengrebel was governor from 1739 to 1751.

The ocean near the Cape of Good Hope was notorious for the terrible storms that had set many a ship adrift.

What the governor and his police officers wanted to hear from Adriaen was how his ship could go down on a day when the sea was calm and there wasn't a breath of wind.

They probably believed it was much more likely that Adriaen had sold his ship and had gone ashore himself because the destination of the Starfish would no longer be a Dutch harbor; and that he was he planning to leave the Cape of Good Hope and head for home aboard another ship.

His detainers found forty silver rix-dollars in Adriaen's leather pouch. "Who would sell a ship and cargo and sacrifice his crew for a low price like that?" wrote the captain. "I earned the rix-dollars by rendering someone a service that I will describe accurately. I kept my own money in the captain's cabin. I was forced to leave it all behind."

To which the police officers likely answered, "It is enough to make a pleasant living here until you could step aboard another ship—no doubt the final payment would have taken place somewhere in Holland."

Piracy was out of the question. No pirate ship would dare to come that near to the coast. And why should one have allowed only a few men to go and take all the others along with them? Besides, if it had been piracy, Adriaen would have said so immediately; instead, he wrote:

"Did no one see my ship disappear? We had set all sails to make the most of the soft breeze. We could still see the Table Mountain behind us; from the land, our ship, with full sails, still must have been a big spot on the horizon..."

)))

There have been lucky dogs who have bought an old book at a rummage sale, riffled through, and found a valuable etching by Rembrandt that someone had placed between the pages. Jan Glas bought an atlas from the year 1901 in a second-hand bookshop, but he would be the last to say that it brought him luck.

Old books had always fascinated him. He was a little collector who spent all his savings every now and then to buy the first printing of a special book.

Several booksellers in his place of residence, Amsterdam, had his business card: Jan Glas, Publicist, Translator, with his address and different ways to get in contact with him, and at the bottom right in small letters, Looking for interesting old books, all kinds of subjects.

The atlas was part of a small set of books, and actually, it was the most uninteresting part of the bargain. Only after a couple of days had he picked it up and thumbed through to check that it wasn't damaged and no leaves had been torn out, which is often the case with atlases. Everything was all right. Some of the plates unfolded. Folded up they formed a perfect place to hide important papers. By the force of habit, he started to open them one by one. In order to make the map of Asia completely visible, he had to unfold a double left page to the left and a double right page to the right. Here he found a number of loose sheets of paper. He saw immediately that they were much older than the atlas. Carefully he picked one up and looked at it closely. It was inscribed with elegant handwriting in black ink. The text was in Old Dutch. The fact that he discovered that, didn't mean that he was also able to read it. It had nothing to do with altered methods of spelling or words that had fallen into disuse; it was more the handwriting itself, with curls and loops that made it almost impossible for him to read it. Besides, there were ink spots and deletions, and the letters were shaky as if the author had been nervous. Jan looked at the other sheets as well, and then he put them back again in the atlas and refolded the pages and closed the book.

In retrospect, it might have been better never to open it again.

But the next day he was sitting with it at a table in a pub at the Rozengracht and handing it to his friend Robbert Goudriaan, a historian.

Jan expected that they would meet again a week later, in the same pub, and that Robbert would return the atlas to him with his comments hidden somewhere between the maps of England

and France, but the historian called him after only two days and asked Jan to come and visit him that evening. His voice sounded excited over the phone and still was when Jan had sat down opposite to him in his big study.

"It's all rather confusing, my friend. Let me put it this way—if what Captain Adriaen Kalf asserts is true, we'll have to rewrite history. For then there should not have existed something in his day that could..." he searched for the right words and then said, "pulverize a ship entirely!"

Jan looked at him in a dazed sort of way.

"Adriaen Kalf..." he repeated.

"Ah, of course," said Robbert. "You still don't know a thing about the contents of your discovery. I suggest that you read it all at your leisure. Adriaen Kalf was the captain of a ship called the Starfish. He was returning from Ceylon and called at the Cape of Good Hope. The Starfish did not come much farther. The ship went down in broad daylight, right in front of the coast, when the sea was calm. Adriaen explains in a lengthy argumentation what happened in his opinion. I think he first drafted the story, with the intention of reading it through closely later and making a fair copy of it. He hoped to become a free man again with this, for he was being kept in prison. It is not a parody, I'm sure of that. No doubt you know an editor-in-chief of a magazine who would love to publish something like this. Otherwise, I have some interesting names for you. You have something very special here, Jan- you'll understand that soon yourself. I would highly appreciate it if you would keep me posted. I cannot say it often enough if this captain has written down the truth..."

"Can you guarantee the genuineness of the document?"

"Without much consideration. The middle of the eighteenth century. When Hendrik Swellengrebel was governor. I found that name only once, but of course, that's enough to know when the text was written."

Then Robbert again suggested that Jan first should read the text thoroughly. He had made copies of the original and of his own version. He took the papers from his desk drawer, put his version on top, and said, "I'll read it to you. Listen..."

It was dark in his study.

Robbert bent over the papers on his desk, and the only lamp that burned shone mercilessly on his bald crown.

Jan was in his early thirties, and Robbert was twice as old.

Jan, with his dreamy green eyes, narrow face, and lank, dark hair, had the looks of a mystic, while Robbert, with his deeply lined face and investigating eyes behind thick glasses, seemed to be the personification of the true scientist.

The voice of the historian sounded hoarse and monotonous. But the emotion that came up from the words struck Jan deep in the heart.

And he was right.

This couldn't be true.

And if it was true after all, history had to be rewritten.

Robbert had done more than translate the text into modern Dutch. Being a historian, he knew much about the part Holland had played during that period of time, and he had consulted many books and done a lot of research. He told about the South African Cape of Good Hope, where the Indian Ocean and the Atlantic Ocean come together.

During the long sea voyages to Southeast Asia, sailors faced a number of horrors, of which scurvy—caused by the lack of vitamin C in the food, which brought on the loss of teeth, subcutaneous bleeding, festering wounds and total weakening of the body—was one of the most feared diseases. Death traveled along on each and every ship, looked with a grin into everyone's eyes, and struck in all ranks, from cabin boy to captain. Scum covered the dirty water in the butts, the food swarmed with maggots, rats, mice, and cockroaches were everywhere around and everyone had lice. Each wooden ship, little floating isles in the infinity of the oceans, formed its own little world, and the longer the voyage lasted, the fewer sailors remained—the dead bodies, wrapped in sailcloth, disappeared into the deep water where the hungry sharks waited.

Under the leadership of Jan van Riebeeck, the Cape of Good Hope was used as an intermediate station in 1652; the ships could drop anchor in Table Bay and take on fresh water and food. The sick were brought ashore. Damaged ships could get repaired. A fortress was built, the Castle and the government settled between its walls.

But a good hundred years later, in the time of Adriaen Kalf, the Cape had grown into a colony that accommodated all sorts of men; soldiers, farmers, winegrowers, cattle breeders, adventurers, slaves, whores, sailors, smugglers, merchants, laborers, landlords, surgeons, and tramps.

As soon as a ship had come in, the sick were taken ashore and brought to the hospital, where many of them died. Those who managed to stay alive would later go aboard another ship where new hands were needed.

The Cape of Good Hope was a notorious place; everyone who arrived longed for women and liquor. A man who finally found himself on firm ground again after a long voyage wanted to get everything out of life that his money could buy him before the signal came that he had to get on board again and proceed on his voyage. The innumerable taverns were always full. And it was in one of these taverns called the Mutineer, that Captain Adriaen Kalf came across someone who made the most peculiar request.

Making use of the writings of the captain himself, that Robbert Goudriaan had put into modern Dutch for him, Jan wrote a report of the events. He filled in the gaps to make it an understandable work. But nevertheless, no one would ever know what it had been like in the Mutineer and who was present at that time.

The Starfish lay at anchor in Table Bay, the sick had been brought to the hospital, the crew had hived off, and Adriaen had arranged his affairs; he had put his ship under repair, and he had left a couple of grumbling sailors on board to watch over the cargo. He had taken a bath, had his beard trimmed, and put on clean clothes. He took a stroll and picked up all kinds of nice smells that made him forget about the stench of the ship.

Black, brown, and white people talked in all possible languages; a wonderful crowd was packed together here in the safe enclave between the infinite ocean and the infinite hinterland.

Adriaen entered the Mutineer and ordered wine.

A captain who gave his crew a shot of liquor on an empty stomach, every morning, as was the practice in those days, who never dined in the captain's cabin without wine, and who had the liquor supplies at his disposal didn't need a visit to a tavern where he had to pay to get drunk. He wanted to be among the people, see strange faces, and make conversation, but the main reason for entering the Mutineer was a good, healthy meal.

He found a place at a big table. Those who were on a return voyage told stories about his events in far-away countries, while those who were on the outward voyage brought the last news from the home front. Adrian talked with compatriots and foreigners.

As he listened, talked, ate and drank, he noticed that someone was watching him. At another table sat a middle-aged man. He was all skin and bone and looked as white as a ghost as if the sun had evaporated most of his lifeblood. As soon as he understood that he had caught the attention of Adriaen, he made an inviting gesture with his right hand.

Adriaen first cleaned off his plate. Then he stood up and went to him.

"Do we know each other?" he asked.

The man reached out his hand.

"No. But I know that your name is Adriaen Kalf and that you are the captain of the Starfish. My name is Colton. Samuel Colton. Just call me Sam."

He spoke English. Adriaen had a thorough command of that language.

"That's right. I arrived not long ago. Who told you my name?"

"I've seen different ships come in. I am looking for a reliable captain. A sailor on board the Starfish said your name was Adriaen Kalf."

Adriaen nodded yes. "I think we understand one another, Sam. There is a place for an extra passenger in my ship. But do you have any idea where I'm going to?"

Sam shook his head.

"No, no, you don't understand at all." He pulled at a wisp of his long, thin, white hair. "I'm too old to leave here ever again. I wouldn't survive a long voyage. I don't have the strength for it anymore. Captain allow me to order some good wine for you. Then we can go and sit in a corner, where no one can hear us."

He rose to his feet slowly and leaned with a hand on the tabletop. "In the meantime, try to think of what you could do with forty silver rix-dollars. For that is what I will pay you for a relatively small favor you can do for me."

He shuffled away. Adriaen looked at the other men who sat there at the table and addressed the first one who looked up at him:

"Samuel Colton. Do you know him?"

The man's grin showed that scurvy had cost him his incisors. He said something in Portuguese.

Adriaen kept silent until Sam came back with a jar of wine and two cups.

They found a place by one of the windows. The shutters were closed. A harsh beam of sunlight fell inside through a small, heart-shaped opening in them. Sam poured wine from the jar.

"This is all a matter of trust, Captain. I hope you are willing to cooperate and save us from a huge danger."

Adriaen raised his eyebrows. Sam leaned with his elbows on the table top and bent forward. "It's all about a wooden chest. Take it on board. Promise me that you will watch over

it personally and that you will keep it in the captain's cabin. And swear to me that you'll never open it. Forty silver rix-dollars..."

Adriaen kept silent.

"Do you want more money?"

"I was thinking. Saving us from a huge danger...What's inside of that chest? Where should it get delivered?"

"I will not answer the first question. About the second one—the final destination of the chest is the bottom of the ocean."

"Do you want me to cover up a crime, to hide a dead body? Did you kill someone?"

Sam waved with the long, bony fingers of his left hand.

"If it were only about a dead body, I would have dug a hole somewhere on a spot in the Godforsaken wilderness where no human being would ever come to search."

"Dig a hole for the chest, and you'll be well rid of it."

"Please, believe me, you'll have to throw the chest overboard. Far away from here, where the water is the deepest. Are you willing to help me, Adriaen Kalf?"

Adriaen could read the fear in the pale gray eyes of the man. But he shook his head resolutely.

"No, I can't help you, if I don't know more about the contents of the chest. Will, it put my men in danger?"

"Absolutely not. As long as the chest remains locked, there'll be no danger at all. It's as simple as that."

With the forefinger of his left hand, he touched the fingertips of his right hand one after the other, while he explained in short sentences what had to happen.

"Take the chest on board. Keep it in the captain's cabin. Never open it. Throw it into the deep sea. Forty silver rix-dollars."

"The answer is no."

The thin man drank his wine thoughtfully.

"There's no other captain who can do this for me. I trust you, Adriaen. It is of great importance that the chest disappears."

"How can you say that you trust me? You don't even know me!"

"Then let me put it this way. all other captains who have called at the Cape of Good Hope are unreliable."

He put down the cup and tried with a smile to make the captain smile as well. Adriaen only shrugged his shoulders. "Come, let's go outside," suggested Sam. "I'll explain a few things to you, without the chance that someone else will overhear."

A few moments later they stood in the shadow at the side of the Mutineer.

"I'm listening," said Adriaen, "but please keep it short."

"About the contents of the chest: The best way to describe it briefly...I could say that it has to do with devilish powers."

Adriaen took one step back, pulled a little amulet from one of his pockets, and stroked it softly with his thumb.

"Don't you ever talk of the devil in my presence. Keep in mind that it is my task to bring a ship home safely."

Sam sat down on a solid little bench.

"A captain like you...You know all about the feeling of humility that can possess you when you go on deck on a bright night and look up to the sky. How big is the universe? Unimaginable powers are in operation. The energy of the cosmos. It's all around—on our world as well. Invisible, but not elusive! I did research in England, traveled through Europe, made sea voyages. Talked with Arabian scientists, with African magicians...Slowly but surely I began to understand that the cosmic energy really exists and that there has to be a possibility of catching these powers and saving them.

"I devised a system of hollow cylinders, solid cylinders, and filled cylinders, three times three of them next to each other. I tried using copper for the connections, but that was not sufficient. I had to use gold. A ship brought me to the Cape of Good Hope. I went inland, all by myself. The ox that pulled my cart was my only company. I searched for gold and found it. Finally, the work could be completed. The machine sucked in cosmic energy like an exhausted horse fills its lungs with air. But after the cylinders were full, after the powers had built up, I witnessed the effect of the first outburst. Horrible! I was terrified. I was able to avert a disaster by closing the cover of the chest that contained the machine— there was no second outburst. It almost cost me my life, Captain. Look at me, as I'm sitting here! When I was searching for gold and hacking myself a way through the hardest stone, I was in radiant health and as strong as the ox that pulled my cart. Now I'm fit for nothing.

"I hope you understand now why I chose you. You have a valuable cargo, you have made quite some profit. And I strongly believe that you're an honest man and that you know how to control yourself. Open the chest and look at all that gold—it's worth a fortune, but as soon the chest is opened, you're doomed. It will release the powers. Help me to stave off disaster and do me that one big favor - take the chest with you and let it sink into the deep ocean. I beseech you. I didn't dare to ask other captains, and I don't want to trouble our governor Hendrik Swellengrebel with it; he simply will not believe me."

At this point the captain interrupted him. "And what about me? Should I believe you?"

"I beg you to. Please believe me. I have built something that should never have been built. I have broken certain cosmic rules. I have caught something that should never be set free again."

Adriaen looked into the eyes of Samuel Colton and believed that he had spoken the truth.

He heaved a deep sigh and said, "Very well then, Sam. I'll help you."

Sam jumped to his feet and gripped both of the captain's hands.

"Thank you, thank you so much. You're doing me a big favor. Let's go inside again and order some more of that wine. I'll pay you and see to it that the chest is brought on board the Starfish."

Right before the Starfish sailed out, Samuel Colton appeared on the quay. He walked next to an old, thin ox that pulled a rattling cart. Four strong sailors were needed to lift the chest from the cart and bring it on board. It is possible that someone saw Sam hand the captain a leather money bag. And the weight of the chest must have excited the curiosity of the crew. Adriaen had explicitly ordered the chest to be stowed in the captain's cabin—he remained on deck himself to watch how the ship was made ready to sail out.

"There wasn't much wind, and I had ordered my boatswain Pieter Post to hoist all sails. I had renewed most of the rigging and inspected everything to make sure it was in order. We had already left the port when I went to my cabin and looked around for the chest. I was surprised when I didn't find it there. The moment I decided to leave the cabin again to look up the sailors concerned and ask them what they had done with it, the ship suddenly started to shake and pitch, as if we suddenly had come into bad weather, and the Starfish was lifted up by high waves. It happened so unexpectedly that I lost balance and fell down. My head bumped up against a table leg, and I lost consciousness."

He couldn't tell how long he had lain there.

"Someone hit me in the face. I opened my eyes and saw the boatswain standing over me. What he said sounded so strange, that I thought that I was dreaming or hallucinating.

"'Captain! The ship is wasting away!' I read panic in the eyes of Post. Next, to him, a sailor popped up, Stijn van de Ende. Together they lifted me up and carried me outside the cabin."

Adriaen was dizzy and began to feel sick. There was screaming all around him. He looked up at the blue sky. Then, all of a sudden, he realized that something was missing.

"Where were my sails, where were my masts?"

He ordered the boatswain and the sailor to let go of him. He stood up and immediately fell forward.

"The ship—or better said, what was left of it—listed. The bow had disappeared, and we took on water. I saw men run across the deck, and the next moment they'd disappeared! Post and van de Ende caught hold of me again and dragged me away. Someone had launched the yawl. They tied a rope under my arms along my chest and then they hoisted me down into it. Cornelis Swart, the surgeon, was there already, and I also saw sailor Gerard Houtman. Pieter Post and Stijn van de Ende climbed down. Right behind them was Allart Vroom, our ship's cook. I was lying on the bottom of the boat, rigid with fear. The surgeon shouted at the cook that he should let himself fall. I stumbled to my feet to lend a helping hand and break Allart's fall. And in the meantime, more and more of the ship was disappearing, as if an invisible giant was taking huge bites of the wood. We caught the cook. His clothes, his flesh, his bones pulverized in our hands.

"Not much later the Starfish had completely disappeared. We rowed the yawl to the port.

"I don't think," wrote the captain, "that Cornelis Swart, Pieter Post, Gerard Houtman, or Stijn van de Ende have ever set eyes on the chest of Samuel Colton. Please, don't hurt them to make them say things that are not true. I am the only survivor who knows about the chest. Samuel Colton had been talking about horrible powers... He had, as he put it himself, built something that should never have been built at all, he asserted that he had broken certain cosmic rules. That's all I know about it, for I've only seen the outside of the chest. Someone must have been so curious that he broke the chest open. The results were disastrous. I'm a broken man. The only one who can explain everything is Samuel Colton. Someone has to find him and call him to account!"

There were more mysteries. When the jolly boat had rowed safely back to the port, Adriaen looked back for one last time and stared at the spot where the Starfish had disappeared.

"Something was moving there, right above the calm water. It was thin, it knit together, it became shape and color. Two fiery eyes stared at me. Then it sank back into the water. The moment the eyes disappeared, I thought I heard a hissing sound, and two narrow pillars of steam rose up from the ocean. I turned my head and looked toward the landside again and didn't dare to look back a second time."

The report of Adrian was incomplete.

Jan went searching in the National Archives in The Hague and consulted lots of other sources, without finding anything. The Starfish and Adriaen Kalf were mentioned nowhere; neither could he find the name of Samuel Colton. Together with Robbert Goudriaan, he rewrote the report of the events, to which Robbert's primary contribution was important details from the time around 1745.

They sold the story to different domestic and foreign magazines.

It brought in quite some money.

The sensation was of short duration.

Not a single scientist took the matter seriously.

2

Harwich - Present Day

Jan Glas sat comfortably in an easy chair in the lobby of a hotel in Harwich and listened with amusement to the conversations of the people who sat around the same coffee table. He had arrived the other day—he had gone from Amsterdam to the Hook of Holland, where he had put the car on a ferry that had brought him in six hours and fifteen minutes across the North Sea to the English port.

The article about Adriaen Kalf had earned him an invitation to attend a symposium in Harwich, which should last for several days, at the expense of the Third Eye Association, a society that investigated paranormal events and supernatural phenomena. Everything was paid for him, under the condition that he would make a speech about his extraordinary article. The symposium was sponsored by the big American. English publishing company Arnold McKay Publishing, or AMP, which had put a new magazine on the market under the daring, intriguing name of ParaPsycho—Was it short for parapsychology or parapsychologist, or did psycho literally mean psychopath?— and it featured news and background stories about all possible alternative views.

The hotel, a big old building in the town center, had been booked up by the society, and all persons present in the lobby were invitees. It was early in the morning. The hotel guests had gone to the dining hall for a heavy English breakfast and then gathered in the lobby, where they waited for a coach that would bring them to the conference center.

Someone sitting right next to Jan knew a very special medium:

"She goes into a trance by reading a book aloud. At a certain moment, her eyes fall shut. Still, she goes on reading. After a while, you can take the book away from her. Then you can follow the lines with your own eyes while she recites them, and when you do nothing to pull her out of her trance, she will continue to the last word of the last page. I gave her an unpublished essay written by myself. She didn't even stumble over the most difficult words and read everything blind from A to Z."

Nobody questioned his assertion.

"The mind sees without eyes," a woman stated.

A man said that he could make any person react by staring long enough at his or her neck:

"I look at that particular part of the neck, right under the back of the skull, where we find the brain stem. Then I force the person in question to do something—to shake the head, to raise a hand, to rise up."

One asked him for a demonstration, and he expressed a willingness to do so, immediately adding that not everyone would believe him. "For it could be rigged, couldn't it?"

Right at that moment, a woman entered the lobby. She looked around, found an empty easy chair facing away from the group, and sat down. The back of her head and her neck stuck out above the back of the chair.

"It would be very coincidental if you knew her," said someone, nodding in the direction of the woman. "Make her pull her ear. Her left ear."

The man leaned forward and stared at the neck of the woman. Not even ten seconds later she brought her left hand to her left ear and pulled it, after which she stood up abruptly and turned around. She rubbed her neck with the same hand as if the compelling look of the man had caused some kind of an irritation there. In the meantime, another discussion had started. Jan listened eagerly.

"No one would accept that life on earth began following an extraterrestrial visit," said a man with a snow-white beard, while he stared attentively into a plastic cup as if it contained primeval soup. "No one would believe that the aliens had left something behind after a picnic. But now one begins to think differently since NASA accidentally brought the bacteria Bacillus safensis to Mars. It is a fact that the bacteria were able to survive the dangers of the journey, and when the little vehicle drove out of the landed capsule, Bacillus safensis probably sneaked off as well." He stirred his coffee with a plastic spoon. "Give the bacteria some time...Two, three billion years, for instance. And what will we find when we visit Mars?"

The reaction came promptly.

"Bacteria are not earthbound. They can be found in the upper strata of the atmosphere. And tiny parts of our atmosphere disappear into the universe. That way bacteria travels through space, and their chance of survival is huge."

Jan leaned back and waited on more reactions from other people when he suddenly heard someone say, "Mr. Jan Glas?"

He looked up. A woman about twenty-five years of age reached out her hand to him.

"Hellen Derringer from the Third Eye Association. We've talked regularly on the telephone."

Jan jumped to his feet and shook hands with her.

"Hello," he said. "Nice to meet you."

After she had let go of his hand, she took two steps back and formed a rectangle with her thumbs and forefingers and looked through it as if she were using a camera.

"What a beautiful, eccentric face," she said. "And then those green eyes...You're perfect to be on the cover of ParaPsycho."

"Then I'll have to write an article for the magazine first."

"But of course you will. I will introduce you to the editor-in-chief presently, Pamela Mitchell. She's very interested in you. In fact, everyone is, after having read your story about Adriaen Kalf. The conference center is not far from here. Shall we walk to it, or shall I ask someone to take us there by car?"

"I prefer to walk. I'm here in Harwich for the first time."

"Fine," said Hellen. "That gives me time to explain a few things about the state of affairs."

They left the lobby and went outside.

"The interest in the mystery of our existence has never been as great as nowadays," Hellen said. "The press will be omnipresent at our symposium, and we have thrown two additional big halls open to the public. All speeches can be heard there, and one can see the speakers on a big screen. Stands have been put up in the same halls by different businesses, who form a wide range of interesting things together: paranormal affairs, alternative therapies, life after death, original philosophies, the riddles of the universe, and so on. Now that ParaPsycho is being launched on the market, the interest will grow even more. Everyone seems to be searching for his personal truth."

"Exciting times," responded Jan. "I always try to get as much information as possible about new trends."

"How about your personal philosophy of life?"

"I don't know. I never succeeded in bringing all I know and believe, together into one theory that seems logical to me. There had been a time that I thought life was just a mean joke."

"Not any longer?"

"Still mean, but no joke?" Jan asked himself aloud. "I just don't know."

He met Pamela Mitchell in an office at the conference center and went through his speech with her and Hellen Derringer.

A few hours later Hellen opened the symposium. Jan was the fourth speaker.

"I am Jan Glas from Amsterdam," he started, in his best English. "Publicist and translator. Once I translated an encyclopedia about everything that acts outside the domain of the regular sciences and became interested in the original ways of thinking of my fellow men. I started to write about different subjects myself, about the origin of black magic, the effect of placebos, telekinesis, and so on. I started to collect old books to find out how earlier generations thought about certain subjects. The fact that I'm standing here in front of you right now is purely by coincidence. As you know, the Third Eye Association wants to bring some important things to your attention. Special powers, hidden energies, undiscovered sources.

"Mother Earth is tired, her reserves are almost exhausted. What are the alternatives to electricity and nuclear power? Allow me to tell you about a marvelous appliance, that has become known—as soon as one has read the article I wrote about it—as the Machine of Colton, which was obviously so powerful that it could make a ship, together with crew and cargo, disappear. My story begins in Africa, and it is, very appropriately, about a Dutchman and an Englishman... ."

Jan told the story of Adriaen Kalf and Samuel Colton.

The audience listened attentively, and after his speech, he received a standing ovation. He left the stage and went into the hall, where he sat down on a chair in the front row that was reserved for him.

Pamela Mitchell took the stand.

"A different view on different affairs—that can be refreshing. All the alternative thinkers all over the world together form the sharp little stone in the shoe of the giant named Science. Slowly but surely one begins to realize that there are other truths. Being the editor-in-chief of a new magazine, it is an honor to be able to work in a new world, full of new ideas. Just like you, I've listened with astonishment to everything Jan Glas had to tell us. Ladies and gentlemen, his words have only been the introduction to the sensational contribution of a scientist who goes further into the matter that gives color to this symposium, who goes further on the road we've set about together with Jan Glas. Please give a warm welcome to an indefatigable researcher from London; here is Professor Mary Landock."

Jan watched Mary Landock come on stage and walk up to the lectern. She put down some papers, placed a little metal box behind them, and leaned over to the microphone. Her face appeared on a big screen. Jan saw her lips moving as she seemed to look intently at him. He didn't know her and had only read her name in the symposium program. He sat up, clasped the armrests as if he were afraid to slip down from his chair, and stared as if hypnotized at the woman's huge head on the screen—never before he had seen such a beautiful, attractive woman. The force of her personality impressed him so much that he remained deaf to all sounds for quite some time. But then, all of a sudden, her words hit him straight in the heart.

"...unsolved mysteries are like unfinished literature. Like The Narrative of Arthur Gordon Pym of Nantucket by Edgar Allan Poe, which stops abruptly and inspired Jules Verne to finish it. Pamela Mitchell just said it: I will continue where Jan Glas stopped. Besides men of consequence like Poe and Verne, I will mention another important person—Charles Robert Darwin. I admire Poe and Verne, and it would never enter my mind to criticize a man like Darwin. As far as I'm concerned modern evolutionism, to which he laid the foundation, will remain a guideline for the development of all life on earth. Mind, I am not mentioning the extraterrestrial life here..."

Jan gasped for breath.

He had never realized that such a thing would ever happen to him, that he had managed to control himself giving a speech to a large, foreign audience and yet felt quite disconcerted shortly afterward merely by looking at an unknown woman. She was unquestionably the woman of his dreams!

"The cosmos is a creating brain. It rains life on all planets," he heard her say now, "and sometimes that life falls into fertile soil.

Then evolution can begin. In our case, it produced a procession of bizarre creatures of which we, human beings, probably have been the most unlucky ones. Sometimes I compare the universe with a huge kitchen where all the ingredients are present to cook the most exquisite dishes. But what the cooks love the most is to experiment, and more often than not, something's burning or something is served that no one ever would like to find on his plate. And here we are. We, human beings. With our limited brains. We understand so much, but not everything. We call our mortality a punishment or a blessing, depending on religion or philosophical ideas. We're the cook in our own kitchen and eat everything, vegetable or animal, in order to survive.

"Restaurant Earth is open both day and night. Still, our time is short. All earthbound life is doomed to die early. If life had developed in another way, if our evolutionary history had led along other paths, we probably would have become creatures who counted not in years, but in centuries... ."

Behind Jan a man jumped up from his chair and raised both arms.

"This woman is blessed!" he shouted out loud, his voice cracking.

Jan turned his head. The man was long and thin, and his dark eyes were fixed intently on Mary Landock.

He suddenly seemed to become aware of his strange behavior. He dropped his arms and sat down again.

Mary chuckled softly, but everyone was able to hear it because she was standing so close to the mike.

Everyone in the hall had to laugh.

On the big screens in the other halls, the grin slowly disappeared from the grotesque close-up of her face.

"To be born and never die. How different the world would have been if evolution had taken that turn. A body that repairs itself; a third, fourth, fifth set of teeth; wounds that heal themselves- diseases getting no chance to do their destroying work."

Her hands showed on the screens now, picking up the little metal box and opening the lid. She took out a round object. It looked like a white stone with black veins.

"Now, pay attention, please!" she advised her audience.

She broke off a little piece of the object and rubbed it between her thumb and forefinger. It pulverized. It disappeared. Now there was a hole on the outside of the object, the size of a fingertip. A muttering rose when the hole slowly filled up until the stone looked exactly the same as the moment she had taken it from the metal box.

"Don't ask me about the value of what I'm holding here in my hand," said Mary. "But it exceeds the price of gold many, many times. It is alive, I'm sure about that, and it is unique. It repairs itself, it is immortal! And I want to add to this, that I think that there is more here than we are able to see with our human eyes. This is a concentrating of cosmic powers unknown to us!"

It gave Jan a shock. Immediately he had to think of the experiences of Captain Adriaen Kalf.

The tall man behind him remained sitting now, but he made himself heard for the second time:

"Praise this day! Praise this day!"

Again there was a muttering and here and there people entered into discussions about what they had seen a moment ago. It only became quiet again after Mary raised her hand. It waved grotesquely to and fro on the big screens, and then leaned over to the mike and produced a hissing sound.

"Before I continue," she said, "there's something I want to emphasize. Actually, I should apologize to all of you, and especially to everyone from the Third Eye Association and ParaPsycho. One might say that I have switched to what we call the alternative sector. Being a scientist, I was not taken seriously by my colleagues at all. Or, putting it more strongly, there was no one who really wanted to listen to me when I tried to explain my special research and discoveries. And that is why I'm standing here, in front of people who are willing to listen and at least give someone the benefit of the doubt. I thank you all very much for that."

She received a warm applause for her words.

Then she started a lecture about the proven boundaries of the universe, its genesis, the twenty-two existing elements of which everything is composed, solar wind, electromagnetism, and powers still undiscovered.

She made the heads of her audience swim by enumerating unimaginable truths.

"The earth turns around the sun at a speed of 65,000 miles per hour, while our entire solar system races through the universe at a speed of 47,000 miles per hour...

"When a star dies by sinking in under her own weight, she squeezes herself together and becomes a white dwarf; one cubic inch of her matter can weigh more than a thousand million tons...

"If you feel like taking a sunbath, dive to the center of a star and experience the sensation of the atomic fire that reaches a temperature of fifteen million degrees Celsius...

"If it is true that the universe came into being in the Big Bang and expands through that power, once the limit of growth is reached, all matter will fall back again and will be reduced to nothing—and then there will be another Big Bang, which will ring in the birth of a new universe with the most imposing fireworks ever. A new universe that will exist for many, many billions of years. We cannot imagine the powers this involves. Our brains don't allow us to picture anything like that...

"Energy is the keyword. There is matter, there is antimatter, there are powers active in the universe that we want to discover and use for all different purposes. Invisible powers. They do exist. Even the layman understands that. Everyone knows about the different kinds of radiation the human eye cannot see. Just as clear is the fact that you can't buy a pound of current in a paper bag somewhere around the corner. Everyone works with electricity, but can we see it, feel it, smell it? We have found a new power that we don't understand yet, but we're already able to use it."

The tall man had risen to his feet, this time to stand behind Jan and tap him on the shoulder.

"I would like to have a talk with you. This very day, if possible." He talked with an American accent, and his voice was trembling with emotion. "Is that possible? My name is Wesley Dunn."

A hand slid over his upper arm. A business card fluttered from long, bony fingers. Jan took it, nodded yes, put the card in the pocket of his jacket, and concentrated again on the speaker. He was surprised to hear Mary mention his name again.

"In the article by Jan Glas, we can read a short description of the contents of the wooden chest that was brought on board the Starfish. No more than a couple of lines, but they contain some interesting clues for the insider. The Machine of Colton was made of hollow cylinders, solid cylinders, and filled cylinders. Three times three cylinders, next to each other. Not everything we know can be found in libraries or via the Internet. Few people know anything about the Heavenly Vision of Manuel. I have understood that Mr. Wesley Dunn will tell us all about it tomorrow, and I really look forward to that."

Jan heard a murmur of approval behind him.

"The Machine of Colton, the Heavenly Vision of Manuel," Mary continued. "Take a look at this."

She pushed the button on a remote control. Her face disappeared from the big screen behind her and was replaced by the image of a little machine.

"Thanks to the powers that were withdrawn with this from the immense universe around us, the bizarre form of life that I've shown you materialized—and you know now that it is able to repair itself, and that's something evolution didn't provide us human beings with fully. Although I'm not able to explain to you how it was possible, I have just shown you, for the first time, something that is so unique it will change everything! A living...something, a living organism, so totally different from us, yet sprung from powers that surround us, feeding itself with those same powers."

The machine was smaller than the remote control she held in her hand. Enlarged on the screen, everyone could see that it existed of three pairs of little cylinders, connected by gold-colored wiring. The little case was of shining steel, the upper side was of glass. When Mary turned the case, a little, ruby red eye became visible, sparkling in the center of one of the sides.

"This little machine can cause a lot of damage- therefore I put it out of action before I came to Harwich. A part of the wiring has been taken away."

"Help me!" suddenly sounded the voice of Wesley Dunn.

He had risen to his feet again. His left hand leaned on the backrest of a chair in the front row, while he pushed his right hand on his chest at the height of his heart.

"No!" he cried out. "I cannot die this way, there's still so much to be done! Help me..."

He collapsed and was caught by the man and the woman sitting on either side of him. Someone called for a doctor. Dunn was carried between the rows to an aisle and laid on the floor. Someone from the security service appeared and knelt down next to Dunn, loosening his tie and opening the upper button of his shirt. He confirmed a cardiac arrest and started CPR, breathing into the man's mouth and pushing with both hands several times on the lowest part of his breastbone.

Medical assistance came quickly. A doctor shoved through the crowd that had gathered around Dunn. Not much later an ambulance arrived. Male nurses brought in a respirator and continued the resuscitation efforts as they moved him to a mobile stretcher.

Pamela Mitchell followed the stretcher, talking nervously to one of the nurses.

Mary Landock had left the stage, and Hellen Derringer had taken her place.

Hellen tapped her nails on the mike.

"On behalf of the Third Eye Association I express the fervent hope that everything will turn out all right with Mr. Dunn—he was here at our invitation! Of course, I also speak in the name of everyone at ParaPsycho. Maybe you have noticed Mrs. Mitchell accompanying Mr. Dunn. She's going with him to the hospital and will keep us posted on all the details."

She cleared her throat and raised her hands in despair.

"What Ms. Landock told us and showed us is sensational. But I never expected Mr. Dunn to—well, perhaps the best thing to do now is to go on. If everyone agrees, I would like to announce the next speaker. After the speech, there will be a short coffee break. Following that, everyone is welcome in the big meeting room to discuss different subjects. If you don't want to join in, you can listen to other speakers or pay a visit to one of the other halls to take a look at all the different exhibits. Now I ask your welcome to Mrs. A. J. Cooper, who will talk about the special powers that hide inside of you and me, in every human being..."

Jan was disappointed not to find Mary Landock during the coffee break in a bar that was only open for the members of the symposium. He longed to see her again and have a talk with her. When he saw Hellen, he walked up to her immediately and asked, "Where did Mary go?"

Hellen smiled.

"We should have told you earlier. Pamela Mitchell has arranged everything perfectly. In the second issue of ParaPsycho, Mary will give an explanation of her special discoveries. Her picture will be on the cover. It will produce a sensation, I'm sure about that. I believe they want you for the cover of the third edition, plus an article about your personal experiences and the resemblance between your story and the little machine that Mary showed us."

"I didn't know about that."

"I suppose that Pamela will talk with you about it soon. It was a smart move for her and her team to promote her magazine via a symposium of the Third Eye Association and we, of course, are very happy with all the extra attention. When Mary held her speech, there were journalists present from different newspapers and weeklies. And now everyone wants to arrange an interview with her. But no one will find her! On the last day of the symposium, there will be a press conference, and Mary will be present for twenty minutes only to answer questions."

"That way ParaPsycho pulls the strings and will be the only magazine that comes up with a big article."

"Exactly. And it will sell very well, with the beautiful Mary on the cover."

Jan nodded. He turned on his heels, lost in thought, and walked away. Hellen, who misunderstood his reaction, hastened to call after him, "Number three will have a beautiful cover as well—with your handsome face on it!"

Jan attended the discussion in the meeting room. Although he normally would have found the subjects being discussed there very interesting, he caught himself thinking constantly of Mary Landock.

Again and again, someone would bring up the odd white object that Mary had showed to the audience and which she had asserted was alive.

"It sends shivers down my spine," said a man, whose eyes looked twice their actual size behind thick spectacle lenses. "If it really is a form of life, originating from and feeding itself with unknown powers from the cosmos...then we're talking about the discovery of the century!"

"And it all fits in perfectly with your article, Mr. Glas," remarked someone.

Jan heaved a deep sigh.

"Yes," he said, "and believe me, I shudder to think of it."

Pamela Mitchell showed up at the end of the meeting, with news about Wesley Dunn:

"Of course, as we all guessed, it was a heart attack. But fortunately, it all appears to be less serious than we thought. Mr. Dunn is out of danger. He has regained consciousness. The doctor in attendance supposes that Mr. Dunn got very excited over something—which I could confirm immediately."

At the end of the day, Jan unexpectedly had the chance to shake hands with Mary.

ParaPsycho had organized a photo shoot and had gathered a number of people in an improvised studio on the top floor of the central building of the conference center. The roof was of glass, and a blood-red setting sun bathed the room in a mysterious light. The photographer wanted to make use of it as quickly as possible.

There was an enchanting atmosphere, thought Jan, and he didn't realize that the presence of Mary was the main reason for it.

Long, blonde curls; wise, blue eyes in a pale face; a tight, green dress emphasizing the slightness of her figure gave her a fragile and at the same time strong charisma—this contradiction of brittleness and power made her a very special woman.

The photographer invited everyone to stand at a roundtable.

"Hold each others' hands and look up at the ceiling," he suggested. "Then you'll show with self-mockery how so many people still think about you all—vague thinkers who call in the help of supernatural powers..."

Jan sat at the left side of Mary and took her hand. She gently stroked his skin with her thumb.

They squeezed up closer to each other while the photographer shot a series of the two together, and not much later they stood together for a moment near a window in the red sunlight.

After that Mary left the room; he had hardly exchanged a word with her.

ParaPsycho entertained the members of the symposium at dinner, but Mary didn't
show up.

Dinner ended around nine o'clock. Jan didn't feel like going back to his hotel room. He decided to visit the halls that were open to the public. He searched his way through long corridors and entered one of the halls. A ticket inspector noticed the little card on his lapel, indicating that Jan was a member of the symposium, and gave him a friendly nod.

The place was crowded. Jan had to smile spontaneously when he thought about what the photographer had remarked about vague thinking and supernatural powers—the stands, set up in long rows, showed all sorts of alternative possibilities for the searching mind.

There were healing stones and predicting cards. Men dressed like Celtic druids sang the praises of ancient views. Serious information was offered on everything from the latest DNA research to the boundaries of space travel, and attention was still given to the doubtful opinions and publications of H. P. Blavatsky and Aleister Crowley. Demons and aliens were on sale as puppets, magicians and skeptics shouted each other down and one handed out flyers that recommended the newest books about subjects as psychokinesis, spiritualism, hypnosis, dream interpretation, levitation, and life after death. There were smiling girls everywhere, passing out the first issue of ParaPsycho.

Jan was in his element here.

He thought that everyone was a little right and a little wrong and that the mix of all opinions would form the most bizarre philosophy of life possible.

He knew that he would never stop wondering about people who felt confident that they knew the Big Truth and devoted an important part of their time to preaching their personal opinion.

All of a sudden he saw Mary. She was wearing sunglasses now and had hidden her blonde curls under a silk headscarf, but he recognized her immediately. She held the strap of her handbag tightly as she walked from one stand to another and looked at everything over the top of her sunglasses.

As if she could feel that someone was watching her, she stopped, straightened her back, and looked in Jan's direction.

"Jan Glas!" she cried out in surprise. She walked up to him, took him by the arm, and dragged him along with her. "I'm so glad to see you."

"Hello... What's the hurry?"

"Let's go to another hall. I have the feeling that someone is pursuing me. Several times someone knocked into me. Very scary..." They pushed their way through the crowd and reached a broad corridor.

"If it were up to Pamela Mitchell and Hellen Derringer, I'd sit all by myself in little offices all the time to hide from the press. My hotel is not far away from here, but they pick me up or bring me there in a car with darkened windows."

"I tried to get in touch with you before- I would like to have a talk with you."

"I understand. There's so much we have to tell each other. Your story about the captain and my discoveries bear so much resemblance."

"The Machine of Colton. You have one yourself."

"I hadn't found a name for it. The Machine of Colton. Sounds good. You've seen that it's just a very little machine, much smaller than that thing in the chest of the captain. But the powers that you can set free with it are frightening! It really is a thing to fear."

"Did you build it all by yourself?"

"I'll explain all about that later. Then we'll take all the time we need."

"I look forward to that, I really do."

They entered another hall. Here it was also crowded. They started to walk slower, Mary still holding his arm. She pressed closer to him.

"The object you held in your hand intrigues me," said Jan. "Especially because you think that it's alive. You used the Machine of Colton to—how do you say that?"

"To make it materialize, to make it appear. Yes, it is alive, it is able to repair itself, it is unique!" "Did you build the machine yourself?" Jan wanted to know.

Mary stopped and turned towards him. She shoved her sunglasses up onto her head and looked at him with her bright blue eyes.

"Jan, this has been a huge and expensive research project. You can't do a thing like that just by yourself. The most difficult part of all was getting the necessary funds together. Who wants to invest in a team that searches for something no one has ever seen? What helped was the common understanding that our sources of energy aren't inexhaustible. We're running out of our fossil fuel, that's a fact. Now imagine being able to get our energy from the cosmos. It would be the solution for all worldly problems. Forever. And thus we got our lab, and there I worked together with a great number of people."

She smiled at him and dragged him along again.

Just as Jan started to ask her another question, someone pushed vigorously against his back. He stumbled forward and spread his arms in an effort not to lose his balance.

Someone caught hold of his wrist and spun Jan around in a wide circle.

"Be careful!" sounded a voice.

Jan stopped himself and looked for Mary.

She was being attacked by a tall man in a pitch black tracksuit and white sneakers, undoubtedly the man who had pushed him.

"He has a knife!" shouted someone.

The man in the tracksuit had put his left hand round Mary's neck and pushed her down. He cut the strap of her purse with a knife that he held in his right hand. Then he quickly let go of her neck to catch her purse. He pushed his elbow hard against her back, and Mary fell down on the concrete floor. The bystanders looked on, everyone assuming that someone else would intervene.

Jan sprang into action. He rushed forward, determined to knock the man down, but stumbled over Mary and did a forward roll.

The man already had a head start on him by the time Jan was on his feet again. Waving his knife, he worked his way through the crowd. The people stepped back in fright.

"Stop him!" shouted Jan.

Right next to him was a stand that sold healing stones. He snatched a big black stone from a shelf and threw it at the fleeing man. The stone hit him right between the shoulder blades, but it didn't seem to have much effect.

"Hands off my things!" cried the owner of the stand.

"I hope that stone brings me luck!" responded Jan, and then put forth his strength to push his way through the crowd. Some in the crowd mistook him for the aggressor now and a couple of big men tried to stop him. They beat him on his upper arms and back as he pushed them aside.

At the end of the hall, there was more space between the different rows of stands and the wall. Here he was able to run faster. He passed a ticket inspector who pointed in the direction of a corridor and cried out, "Someone ran into there. Do you want me to call the police?"

"Yes, right away!" Jan shouted back as he sprinted past him.

The man in the tracksuit had enlarged his lead. Jan could see him running up a broad staircase leading to the second story of the building. Jan regretted that he hadn't snatched away the second stone. All he could do now was try to run even faster. He reached the stairs and skipped a number of steps as he climbed them. When he reached the second story, he saw the man running through the corridor and he realized that he couldn't catch up with him.

He decided to bluff. "Stop! Or I'll shoot!"

His words seemed to loan wings to the man's feet.

At the end of the corridor was a big window. The men held the stolen purse out in front of him with both hands and leaped. The window shattered, and he flew out.

A few moments later Jan stood there, with his feet on shards of glass, looking out through the broken window, gasping for breath.

Other people joined him and started to ask questions.

"What happened?" "Who was that?"

The man had disappeared. A deep dent in the roof of a car that was parked right under the window proved that the black stone Jan had thrown had brought luck indeed— not for the man who had thrown it but for the man hit by it.

"He managed to escape from me," said Jan, more to himself than to the people around him, for he said it automatically in Dutch. "And it probably has left him only with some sore feet and ankles. He's got Mary's purse..."

Suddenly there was the sound of sirens. The headlights of a police car shone over the dark parking lot at the side of the building complex.

"They are here already?" asked Jan in surprise, this time in English.

A woman standing next to him responded, "They patrol almost constantly during events."

The car stopped and two policemen got out. Jan broke a sharp fragment of glass out of the groove in the window frame and leaned out. "A tall man in a black tracksuit and white sneakers has jumped down here and disappeared with a stolen purse," he shouted.

One of the policemen spoke into his walkie-talkie. A second police car appeared.

"You stay right there, I'll come up to you," the man with the walkie-talkie shouted to Jan.

Then he had a short conversation with the driver of the second car. The driver nodded, revved the engine, and drove away.

Jan waited, looking impatiently at his watch. He didn't want to stay here- he wanted to go back to Mary. Finally, the police officer showed up, in the company of another man.

"Good evening," said the policeman to Jan. "My name is John Ballantyne. And this is Mr. Duncan, who witnessed what happened. Someone attacked a woman, cut the strap of her purse with a big knife, and then ran away. You went after him..."

"That's right. My name is Jan Glas."

"Who's the woman that got attacked? Your wife? An acquaintance?"

"Mary. Mary Landock. Haven't you asked her yourself? Or is she too much in shock."

The policeman frowned. "I haven't talked to her yet."

"She left the moment you ran after that man," explained Duncan. "I supposed that she was intending to follow you."

"I have to look for her," said Jan. "Right now, if possible."

"My colleague is already searching for her. Let's find a place where we can sit down in quiet," suggested Ballantyne. "Then we can talk things over. I'll need to see some ID, and I'll take a statement on what you've seen."

"I can show you my passport and my driver's license. I'm Dutch." "All right. Please, walk along with me. Will you join us, Mr. Duncan?" It was already past ten o'clock when Jan said good-bye to the police officer and quickly left the little room they had used, to have their conversation. Mr. Duncan had left earlier. Jan went back to the building where he had attended the symposium and asked there if someone had seen Pamela Mitchell or Hellen Derringer. They both had gone to the bar where they'd had a coffee break earlier that day. He found them sitting together at a table.

"Am I happy to see you," said Pamela immediately. She pointed at two little cell phones on the tabletop. "As soon as they have found Mary, they'll give us a ring. I hear you were with her when her purse was snatched. We've heard it all, but if you'll be so kind to tell it yourself... This is horrible, such a brutal attack. With a knife! I mean—did he really use a knife?"

Jan waved her words aside and, as if he hadn't even heard them at all, he asked, "Isn't she in her hotel?"

"No. We checked that right away."

"Does she stay in my hotel?"

Pamela lowered her eyes and shook her head.

"We've lodged our most important guests in the prestigious Tower Hotel."

"I'm not complaining about my room. It's just fine. All I would like to know is—"

Hellen Derringer interrupted him. "Please, tell us exactly what happened."

He told his story. Pamela ordered drinks. Then they discussed different theories.

"No doubt the man was out for two things," surmised Hellen. "The little version of the Machine of Colton and that mysterious living substance that was produced with it."

"The question is if she carried both things with her, in her purse," wondered Pamela.

"He might have been a purse snatcher," suggested Jan, but actually he found that hard to believe himself.

"We strongly advised her against mixing with the public," said Hellen to Jan. "I've also told you about Pamela's plans—she wants to keep this big news exclusively for ParaPsycho."

"Mary complained to me about that. She said you wanted her to lie low and not talk to the press. But I cannot imagine that she was stupid enough to go walking around here with these irreplaceable things on her. Maybe she's rented a hotel safe."

"I hope so," sighed Pamela. "But, for now, it is of more importance that they find Mary. Why don't these damned little phones start ringing?"

"She's probably sitting somewhere, having a drink, just like we are," said Hellen. "She left here and dove to the nearest pub to recover with a couple glasses of wine."

The clock struck eleven and they were asked to leave the bar. It was closing time.

Jan left the congress center.

The first pub he saw was already closed. He only knew the way to his own hotel. He had no idea where to search for the Tower Hotel. The pubs along the quay and in the harbor section were undoubtedly still open, but he realized that it was useless to go there-there was little chance that he would find Mary there. After having walked about aimlessly for some time, he decided to go back to his hotel.

It was almost twelve o'clock when he entered the lobby.

Koos Verkaik

It was quiet there and the lights were dimmed.

He stepped into the elevator, which brought him to the seventh story. When he stepped out again and looked into the corridor, he noticed immediately that there was a trunk standing right in front of the door to his room.

His room was almost at the end of the corridor. Behind it was a niche with a window that gave a fine view of the city and in the distance, the North Sea. He approached cautiously. The soft carpet deadened the sound of his footsteps. When he stopped and looked down at the trunk, he discovered black initials on silver colored locks:

ML. Mary Landock

He looked up and saw her was standing in the niche, her back turned towards him, staring out the window absent-mindedly. Suddenly, she discovered him in the reflection of the pane, and she turned around quickly.

"Jan, there you are—at last! I was so afraid that the man, with the knife—"

She ran up to him, wrapped her arms around his neck, and pushed herself against him. Only after some time did she let go of him again. It was only after she had taken a step backward and was looking up at him that he could read the fear in her eyes.

"Someone's stalking me," she said. "You must help me."

Jan was confused. All the emotions of this long day paled in comparison to what had gone through him when she embraced him. He desperately searched for words. The only thing he finally could think up was "I could have stolen your trunk without you noticing it. Anyone else had been able to do that as well—"

"I guess you're right," said Mary. "Please, let's go to your room now."

"All right."

He opened the door and picked up the trunk. Mary sat down on the bed and heaved a big sigh.

"Finally I feel safe again," she said. "The attacker got hold of your purse. What was in it?" "Nothing valuable," she answered. "The little Machine of Colton and the life form are in my trunk. Listen, I know that many people are looking for me right now. And, I'm very sorry that I didn't wait for you to come back to the hall of the conference center. I left there immediately and looked for a cab. When I walked up to a cab rank, I was followed by two men. On the way to the Tower Hotel, it struck the cab driver that a dark Volvo was right behind us all the time. When he suddenly turned off into a side street, the Volvo did the same. After we arrived at the hotel, the driver came inside and saw me to my room to make sure I was safe. When he left, I bolted my door and packed my trunk."

"I called the desk and asked for a bell boy to bring my trunk to the lobby, that way I had a companion. He ordered a cab for me, and I drove to the station. Trains go straight to London from there, but the two men turned up again at the station.

Thankfully, I saw them first and managed to escape their attention and went somewhere for a drink and to think things over. When I went to leave again, I spotted the Volvo at the side of the road, so I left via the rear exit and started walking, dragging the heavy trunk along with me. Then I came past your hotel. The Third Eye Association had booked rooms for all the guests in two hotels, and you were not with me in the Tower, so..."

Jan nodded yes. "Go on... ."

"Well, there's not much more to say. I asked for your chamber number and stepped into the elevator. The lobby was still crowded, but I'm sure that no one saw me who could have recognized me. I stood in front of your door, I paced up and down, I looked out the window...And finally, you returned. You came from Holland by car, didn't you?"

"Yes. I put the car on the ferry."

"Jan, I still have no idea who is stalking me, but the reason is obvious. Of course, you know as well as I what it is they want."

"Yes," said Jan for the second time.

"Please, pack your things and come along with me. Bring me to London. It's late, I know that, but I hope you don't mind. It's about ninety miles from here, the lab. I have some rooms there. It's the perfect place to hide the machine and the life form. There I'll feel perfectly safe. Can you understand that?"

Jan was already busy packing his trunk. If she had asked him to drive to the end of the world, he would have.

"Are we going back to Harwich again tomorrow?"

"I don't know. Probably. I cannot think clearly at the moment. The attacker with his knife...the stalkers, the Volvo...the excitement about my scientific discoveries—it's all too much. I have to get out of here."

"I understand. Is there a place for me to sleep in that lab?"

Her answer surprised him and made his heart skip a beat.

"Sleep with me. Then I'll know for sure that I don't have to be afraid of anything."

They left the room, went through the corridor, took the elevator and walked outside via the lobby. Jan told her about his chase and how the man had managed to escape with his reckless jump through the window. He informed her about the questioning by the police and about how worried Hellen and Pamela were about her.

"I'll call them. Later. First I want to get out of here. Right now, I feel like I'm going to pass out any moment."

It was quiet outside. They didn't see a Volvo parked anywhere in the street. Jan's Volkswagen stood at the back of the hotel. He put the baggage in the trunk and locked it. They got in. He started the engine and drove away slowly. The barrier opened automatically, and he pulled out of the parking lot. Before he could turn onto the road, he had to stop for a car that passed by at low speed. Jan began to feel a little nervous. He had planned to drive to London, after the symposium, but all by himself and not late at night.

"Don't you have a driver's license?" he asked Mary.

"No," she said. "I can't drive, I simply haven't the talent for it."

"You have to show me the way. I'm not used to this."

"Driving in the dark?" she asked.

"Driving on the left side of the road," he sighed. "One drives on the right side in all European countries, except here."

3

Southend-on-Sea - Present Day

Jan had a strange experience. Slowly he became aware of himself, in a totally different way than when waking up from a normal sleep. It was as if he had spent all his mental energy, and new powers had to be drummed up to activate his brain again. Something heavy was hovering about in his mind, something very much like a ball, a dark, cast-iron casing, filled with things he didn't want to see. He knew that the effect would be horrible, it exploded in his head; an insane truth would completely knock him out!

And then there was a warning spinning around in his head. "First come to your senses- don't open your eyes yet!"

There was a voice. A woman said in English, "Look, his eyes are rolling up and down behind the eyelids. I think he's recovering consciousness. Don't you think so, doctor?"

"I hope so. He won't feel the pain in his body. The effect of the anesthetic hasn't worn off yet."

Doctor... Jan tried to think. He was searching in the darkness. He remembered Mary Landock. Yes. Of course, he remembered Mary Landock.

He'd never seen a more beautiful woman before.

They had gotten into his Volkswagen together. Had they been involved in an accident? The doctor had mentioned anesthesia. Carefully he tried to move his fingers. His left hand clenched, and he felt the nails pressing in his flesh. He did the same with his right hand.

"Doctor, look... ." He was able to move his toes. Or was he? He didn't feel a thing. Then, all of a sudden, he tried to open his eyes and sit up.

"My legs!" He shouted the words in Dutch.

Then he fell back again, and his head sunk away into a soft pillow. His eyes fell shut. He had seen a small room with white walls and bright lights. The man and the woman wore white clothes. She called him doctor, so she must be a nurse.

No. There had been no accident. He knew that for certain now. He had driven to London with sweat on his palms. But he could not remember what had happened afterward. That was hidden inside of the heavy, dark ball in his head.

"Mr. Glas? Can you hear me?" asked a male voice in English.

"I can't feel my feet. There's no feeling in my legs at all," whispered Jan, stretching his arms and moving his fingers over his thighs. "Don't tell me that you had to amputate my legs...."

"No, you don't have to worry where that's concerned," said the woman in a soothing voice. "You have some bruises. Nothing serious, thank goodness! But it was a cause for concern that we couldn't wake you up. Is there something you want to say?"

Jan kept his eyes firmly closed and shook his head.

"No. All I want is to sleep."

He needed more time. To think.

"Very well then, we'll leave you alone," said the man. "All I want to do for now is tell you that you are in a hospital bed and that you'll be quite well soon enough. There's absolutely nothing for you to worry about. By the way, I am Doctor Finch." "All right," said Jan. He turned his head exploratively to the left, heaved a deep sigh, and then started to breathe regularly.

"He's sleeping again," said the nurse.

Only after a couple of minutes did Jan dare to open his eyes again. The bed next to him was empty. All he could see through the window was a blue sky and some slow moving, big, gray clouds—he was too far away from it to be able to look down.

The dark ball in his head made him feel dizzy.

"Please, don't let it explode," he thought. *"Not yet..."*

In his thoughts, he went back to the moment that he had driven his car from the ferry. He drove through Harwich to his hotel, spasmodically keeping it on the left side of the road. Everything that happened after that stood out clearly in his memory.

The hotel, the conference center, his speech and Mary's speech, Wesley Dunn having a heart attack.

Then he was driving in his Volkswagen again, with Mary sitting next to him. There were dimly lit roads. And then, on one of these roads, it all ended. His memory failed at that point, no matter how hard he tried to remember.

He whispered his own name, date of birth, bank account number, telephone number, the names of twenty different people he knew and had met recently.

It had nothing to do with the loss of memory, he knew now.

His eyes grew heavy. Now he really fell asleep again.

A couple of hours later he was awakened by a sound. The nurse came in.

"Mr. Glas," she said, standing next to the bed, "how do you feel?"

"I'm not sure," he answered.

"You're on a drip now, temporarily. I hope you'll be able to drink and eat. The doctor will come to take a look at you in a while."

"Doctor Finch. And you are...?"

"Samantha Ellis. Welcome to the Southend Hospital."

"Where is that? In London?"

"No. Southend Hospital is in Southend-on-Sea. About forty miles east of London. Don't you know what happened to you?"

"I really have no idea."

"The doctor will examine you. You're probably in a shock, and besides, you've been unconscious for quite a long time."

"I remember my entire life! Until the moment I left Harwich. I've made a speech there on the first day of the symposium. I have to go back... "

"Do you also remember the date?"

"Of course. March the second."

"I guess the symposium will be over by now. Today is the tenth."

The dark ball rolled through his head and caused a splitting headache.

"So many days that I can't remember... "

"Everything will turn out all right, Mr. Glas," said Samantha. "I'm going to replace your infusion."

"For how long am I here?"

"They brought you in the day before yesterday."

"Where did I come from?"

"There was an explosion on a plot right outside Southend-on-Sea. A barrack, apparently a laboratory. A burst of flame was visible all around. The police found you in a field next to the barrack. You must have been thrown by the force of the explosion. It was easy enough to identify you from your driver's license and passport that were inside your pocket. But it seemed impossible to wake you up. Now you'll soon be your old self again."

"Southend-on-Sea," said Jan in a soft voice. "I never heard that name before... "

Not much later he knew a bit more; Doctor Finch had come to examine him, the infusion had been removed, and he had enjoyed a good meal and had drunk eagerly. His bruises weren't serious. His clothes showed different burns and the skin of his arms and legs were slightly scorched. Part of his hair was burned away, and his face was red.

"There is no reason why you should stay any longer here in the hospital. Your health insurance is all right, but I think it's important that you see your doctors as soon as you're back in Amsterdam. You're missing a part of your memory, but that's probably not serious. Perhaps something scared you so much that you became emotionally confused. Or, you've protected yourself from an all too shocking experience. Still, you'll likely remember sooner or later. I think you'll know soon enough what exactly happened. Your car is in the parking lot at the police station. They also have your driver's license and passport. We turned them and your keys over to the police. I'll tell you how to reach the station. They're expecting you there, by the way. Ask for inspector Jack Parker. He's been here; he stood right here by your bed, but of course, he couldn't ask any questions."

"Jack Parker," repeated Jan. "Yes, I understand that they'll want to talk with me there and I have to go there any way to pick up my car and papers."

He left the Southend Hospital in his scorched clothes, with no other belongings than his leather billfold containing some folding money and coins, a credit card, and a card from his insurance company. Stubble stood out on his red chin and cheeks. Never before he had felt so strange. He walked the route Doctor Finch had mapped out for him, through streets he didn't know. The people he passed stared at him and probably thought that he was a hobo, an alcoholic, or a very ill man. Shivers ran down his spine when he realized that he really had no idea how he had ended up here.

He became more and more fearful with every step he took. A strange idea crossed his mind: he knew that it was the tenth of March, but what would people answer him if he asked them about the year? He stopped at a kiosk to check the dates of the newspapers. He heaved a sigh of relief and had to grin at himself—he had almost believed that it was possible to be flung back into the past or pushed forward into the future. Then he read a big headline on the front page of a local paper.

> High Jet of Flame Reduces Building to Ashes!
> Bystanders in a panic! Explosion still a mystery!

A photo showed blackened ruins. In the background, he could make out the edge of a wood.

He took the paper and produced some small change that he showed to the kiosk owner on the flat of his hand. The man looked at him with eyes full of disgust and astonishment and then he shook his head.

"I don't accept euros."

Jan realized that he had no English coins and started searching for a banknote. The man shook his head again. "I can't change that much." Jan put the paper back and turned around.

How come he still had all his English folding money? He began to wonder what he had lived on if he should find out later that he also hadn't used his credit card. All he could do was shrug his shoulders.

He started walking again, and all of a sudden he caught himself whistling a tune. He was discharged from the hospital, and as long as he was walking here he had no immediate problems, although he would be confronted with new problems after he had stepped inside the police station and had asked for inspector Jack Parker.

Jan stopped whistling.

Did the police know more about what had happened to him than he did? Was he under suspicion of anything?

Then there was something that set his mind at ease immediately. Only a moment ago Doctor Finch had told him that the police were expecting him to drop by and pick up his things. If the police suspected foul play, they would have come to the Southend Hospital to arrest him.

He put his hands in the pockets of his jacket and quickened his pace. He felt something in the left pocket and took it out. It was a calling card of thick paper, and he remembered immediately who had given it to him.

He read,

> Wesley Dunn, Raso Preacher
>
> Center of the Heavenly Vision
>
> Franks Knight, Florida, USA

Under this were listed different ways to reach him. But before he had read them, a shock went right through Jan. He had to stop. He staggered. With one hand he leaned against a lamppost. The dark ball inside of his head didn't explode or burst, but it broke open, and the contents slowly flowed out and filled his mind. His stomach contracted, and he bent forward as if he had to throw up. Passersby turned their faces away.

"The catastrophe!" he heard himself say, and right that moment it seemed as if something inside his skull came to an explosion after all. "There is a big chance that the end of the world is near... "

All he had eaten earlier in the hospital he now vomited on the paving stones. He looked around nervously with tear-filled, bloodshot eyes. Then he straightened his back, wiped his mouth on the scorched sleeve of his jacket, and put the card back into his pocket.

He still didn't know what exactly had happened during the last several days, but he did know that something malignant lay in wait in a well-hidden place somewhere in this world.

Something would store energy until it had reached its saturation point, and then it would become unstoppable and would cause total destruction.

Carefully he took a few steps. He felt so dizzy that he was afraid that he might fall down at any moment.

"You dirty drunk!" shouted someone.

He spits on the ground and mumbled a curse.

The police station was on the other side of the road. He would rather have gone back to the Southend Hospital, to be put in bed there and to sleep again for a long, long time, but he realized that he couldn't get there under his own steam. Maybe the best thing to do was to stretch his length on the sidewalk and wait for someone to ring for an ambulance.

He closed his eyes and swayed a little, actually intending to do so, when he heard someone call his name:

"Jan! Jan Glas!"

Someone slammed the door of a car. There was the sound of hurried footsteps. Someone took him by the arm and immediately let go of him again.

"Good heavens! What happened to you?"

He recognized the voice. It was Pamela.

Jan opened his eyes and glared at her. "Am I that repulsive that you don't dare to touch me?" he asked. Strangely enough, he drew strength from her reaction; it made him angry, and his heart pumped oxygenated blood to his brain with accelerated beats. Then he asked her in surprise, "How did you come to be here?"

"Everyone at ParaPsycho in London waited eagerly for a sign of life from you or from Mary. We'd already given up hope when we received a call from John Ballantyne at the Harwich police station; he said you were in a hospital here in Southend-on-Sea. So I called the hospital and I was advised to get in touch with the local police. I have an appointment with Inspector Parker, but he gave me to understand that he doesn't know exactly what has happened either."

"Jack Parker," said Jan. "I have an appointment with him as well."

"I'd just parked my car and wanted to cross the street to the police station when I saw you. Is everything all right with you?"

"No. I'll tell you all about it later. That's to say, all I know."

"How about Mary?"

"No idea. I wish I knew where she is."

She took him by the arm for the second time, and now she didn't let go of him.

"You must tell me everything right now. Parker can wait. Or is he expecting you at a certain time?"

"I've never talked to the man," Jan reacted peevishly.

"Then come with me. Let's find a pub and sit down together. How much time do you need to fill me in? A quarter of an hour?"

"I just told you—"

"Yes, you're very confused, I understand that. I've seen pictures of that burnt-down barrack. It was on television, the top story on several different stations. And of course, I've read the papers."

He leaned on her as they walked to her car. Pamela opened the door on the right side and helped him to sink down onto the seat. Not much later she was sitting next to him, at the wheel.

"Let's forget about the pub. We can have a quiet talk right here," she said, adding, with a smile, "with a fine view of the police station." Then her lips trembled and she hid her face in her hands and began to sob softly.

Suddenly Jan began to feel pain all over. The anesthetic Doctor Finch had given him had worn off. He looked at Pamela, with her short, dark hair and brown eyes; she was Mary's opposite, although she was very attractive in her own way. Pamela Mitchell was an intellectual beauty, and he admired her. Carefully he leaned over to her side, intending to put an arm around her shoulder, but then he changed his mind and sat up straight again.

Without looking at him, rubbing her eyes with her forefingers, she said, "Imagine our fear. First, someone has a heart attack, then two of our most important speakers vanish into thin air. Wesley Dunn will pull through thank goodness; you're sitting here right next to me in my car; but still not a trace of Mary... "

When she finally turned her face towards him, he could tell that the sight of his injuries frightened her.

"For heaven's sake—what happened to you? Did someone batter you?"

"I know I look terrible. Don't you worry, some clean clothes will do wonders for me. But that's of no importance now. I've received a message Pamela, a very clear message. How am I to make it clear to the police that I don't know exactly what happened to me, while I'm very sure about the fact that there is a big chance that the entire world will explode?"

Pamela gasped.

"It's obvious to me to which conclusions they will come to. They'll say that I'm just making things up to cover up the facts of the case. There's only one word applicable to someone who asserts that he can't remember what he did during the last few days, but does warn for a global disaster. liar!"

"Suppose that they find Mary," said Pamela. "Suppose that she's dead..."

"That—" began Jan, and then he stared at her with disbelief. "You think that I've killed Mary Landock, don't you?"

"No, no," Pamela hastened to say.

"In what kind of hell did I end up?" sighed Jan.

Then he started to talk, and after that, he listened to what she had to say.

A quarter of an hour later they entered the police station, where a counter clerk brought them to a small waiting room, where they sat and waited. After some time a middle-aged man with short, gray hair and little, round eyes arrived. He had taken off his uniform jacket. His fat belly kept the buttons of his shirt under pressure.

"Mrs. Mitchell and Mr. Glas," he said. He walked up to them and shook hands with the both of them. "I'm Inspector Parker. Which of you will come with me to my office first?"

Jan and Pamela had both risen to their feet.

"We're both very curious and have no secrets from each other," answered Pamela. "If possible, we'll both come with you."

Parker frowned and gave it a thought.

"Very well then," he said. "Walk along with me."

Once in his messy office, he searched for two wooden chairs and then shoved them up in front of his desk.

"Take a seat."

He sank down on the threadbare cushion of his own chair, and then he stared sadly at the disorder on the desktop. Then he looked at Jan searchingly.

"I can imagine that you would rather be at home in Amsterdam than here at the police station," he remarked. "Tell me, are you married?"

"No, I'm not," answered Jan. "Why do you ask?"

A smile cut through the pink face of the inspector as if a knife had sliced through a huge lump of marzipan.

"Doctor Finch told me that you can't remember what you have done during the last few days. Which seems the perfect excuse to me for a married man who had met a beautiful woman like Mary Landock in some foreign country. Now I'll have to reconsider my views."

"You can't just say something like that!" said Pamela indignantly. "Mary Landock is missing!"

Now the inspector burst out laughing. Then he said, "Why don't you ask Mr. Glas?"

"What am I supposed to ask him?"

"How Ms. Landock's doing, of course! When she was here yesterday, she told me that she would visit Mr. Glas in the hospital. To say goodbye to him."

He saw two surprised people in front of him. Suddenly the expression on his face changed to one of irritation. He spread the fingers of his left hand and touched them one by one with the forefinger of his right hand.

"There is a society which is engaged in a number of things that don't exist—the Third Eye Association. There is a magazine which restricts itself to the same absurd subjects—your ParaPsycho, Mrs. Mitchell. Two people vanished into thin air, but later we find out that they never disappeared at all. There is an explosion in an old barrack right outside of Southend-on-See." He had started with his thumb and now he tapped on his little finger. "And that last event brings all problems from Harwich and London to me, which—of course—makes me extremely happy. Now, please, let's stop this playacting right now. I think that the Third Eye Association and ParaPsycho have got more than enough publicity by now."

He leaned back heavily as if the things he just had said had made him dead tired.

"You've seen Mary!" Pamela called out. "Thank God, she's found again!"

"Maybe she's been in the hospital, maybe she stood at my bed," said Jan. "I've been unconscious most of the time."

"She came to the station here in Southend-on-Sea to report herself, because she had read that you were here in the Southend Hospital, Mr. Glas. At least, that's what she wanted me to believe. I was deeply impressed by the beauty of Ms. Landock, I can't deny that. I made a copy of her passport, but didn't verify it immediately. I only did so after she'd been gone for quite some time. It appears to be faked. She told me that she worked in a lab in London... "

"The Maximum Axion Laboratory Ltd. In East End," said Pamela. "I found out that no one knows her there. Our editorial office has its seat in London, and I live there as well, as you may know. I went to East End and visited the Max Ax. Mary had been introduced to me as one of the lab's most important scientists, but her name is unknown to everyone there. I myself think that she needed a front for secret projects. That her passport is faked, is news to me. Maybe she worked in the barrack that burnt down."

Inspector Parker smiled disdainfully.

"I can show you something about that. But first this—Ms. Landock lived in the East End as well. She had rented a furnished apartment there. Now I hear from the London police that she terminated the tenancy. It wouldn't surprise me if we never see her face again. Very possible that she's already left the country. Using her real passport. But her motives still remain a complete mystery to me."

He didn't give them time to process what he had said. He turned a monitor on his desk in their direction, and his thick fingers moved over a keyboard.

"Look here. This is the barrack. The interior. There was a remote-transmission security system, and the camera that was installed worked perfectly."

On the monitor appeared an untidy still life in hundreds of shades of gray. The barrack had no inner walls, and the total area was displayed. Along both long sides stood several wooden tables full of big and little glass beakers, connected by glass tubes. Here and there were cylinders of different length. There were pieces of appliances looking very much like control units, and under the tables stood various containers. It looked altogether very much like the workshop of a modern alchemist. Suddenly there was a bright light in the back of the barrack.

"A hatch is forced open, a window gets broken," explained Parker. "There was no burglar alarm. Outside, above the door, was a camera as well, but it obviously was put out of action.

Look, someone removes the sharp fragments from the window frame and climbs inside."

A broad-shouldered figure in dark clothes jumped to the floor and walked between the tables. He was wearing a balaclava and had a suitcase in his hand, which he put on one of the tables now. He shoved a number of the glass retorts aside, which fell to the floor and broke into pieces. A puddle formed on the floor. The man opened the suitcase. The contents became partly visible.

"Some kind of a machine," whispered Pamela. "Buttons and meters..."

The man walked on through the barrack, to a spot right under the camera. There he looked up.

"He has discovered the camera. No idea who he is, Mr. Glas," said the inspector, "but it's obvious to me that it isn't you. He is too broad, and you're too tall."

For a moment the man seemed to hesitate as if he might jump to break the camera from the wall, but then he turned on his heels and walked away. Long, straight hair became visible under the balaclava. He stopped at the suitcase and pushed some buttons, and then pulled a couple of wires out and placed the ends on two cylinders on the table. He produced a roll of Scotch tape and used pieces of it to stick the wires onto the cylinders. It caused a rain of sparks. The man pushed another button, and then he ran back to the hatch and climbed outside.

A few seconds later a flash became visible, followed by something looking like a fast-growing cloud of smoke—and that was the last thing the camera could register before it was destroyed.

"The explosion was so tremendous that we couldn't recover anything from the suitcase or its contents," said Parker. "We arrived a bit earlier than the fire brigade, Mr. Glas, and we found you at one hundred feet's distance from the smoldering barrack. Your car was parked at the side of the road, more than three hundred feet away. It is very well possible that you had such a fright that your memory fails when you try to remember what happened. There is no reason at all to suspect you of anything. I really would appreciate it if you would give me a call as soon as everything has become clear to you again. Honestly speaking, I'm very curious about what has happened to you."

Jan nodded yes and stared at the empty monitor as if he expected that it would show him everything he had done during the last days.

Pamela said, "All right, Inspector, but something happened here in Southend-on-Sea which we can easily call both spectacular and frightening. Who owned that lab?"

"I'll tell you. It was owned by the Maximum Axion Laboratory. Where Ms. Landock never worked."

"Striking, isn't it? And how did Max Ax react?"

"People from the lab are presently helping us search the heap of ruins for clues. A Max Ax spokesman says that the barrack once was used as a depot and that it had been completely empty. But we know better, for we have seen what the camera registered, haven't we? I wonder how the Max Ax people will react when they sit in your place and are allowed to watch the same movie?"

Jan and Pamela stayed for over an hour in Jack Parker's office. Pamela was glad that she had come here. She, just like Hellen, had felt responsible for Jan Glas and Mary Landock and had been extremely happy when she heard from the police that Jan had been found. Besides that, it had been her journalistic interest which had brought her to Southend-on-Sea.

Halfway through the conversation she stood up and walked to the window, took her cell phone and called Hellen Derringer of the Third Eye Association to inform her about the recent developments:

"Jan Glas is right here with me at the police station. Mary Landock has been here. We're in the office of Inspector Parker right now, and he says he doesn't expect we will see Mary back again. I've seen pictures of the barrack right before everything exploded. Cylinders, which made me immediately think of the Machine of Colton. I wonder if Mary was working there in secret. I'll keep you posted and come to visit you as soon as I'm back in London and can find some time."

After she hung up, Parker said to her, "Ms. Landock might have worked there. That's interesting. I can imagine that Mr. Glas would like to see where we found him... " He looked at Jan and saw him nod yes. "Well, drive along with me, we can have a look there and talk to some of our investigators and the people of Max Ax. We'll come back here again and then you'll get your papers, Mr. Glas, and your car of course. Are you coming?"

"I'd love to," said Pamela. "Fortunately I always have a camera with me. I want to shoot some pictures for ParaPsycho."

They left the police station, and Parker opened the doors of a big car for them. Pamela sat down in front and Jan in the back seat. They drove away. Jan realized that he hadn't told Parker about his vision yet.

He kept silent about it during the ride. But not much later, outside Southend-on-Sea, when he stood looking at the smoldering ruins of what apparently once had been a barrack, he said, "The world will go down. A scorching heat. All energy will be set free."

Inspector Parker, who had just stooped to slip under the plastic ribbon that marked out the disaster area, straightened himself again.

"I beg your pardon?"

Jan felt the sweat begin to drip down his forehead and temples.

"I feel it even stronger than a while ago," he sighed. "Although I don't remember that I'd been here before. But here I must have had my vision. About the end of the world."

"A vision?" Parker looked at him searchingly. "How strange that you didn't tell me about that earlier."

"He did explain it to me," said Pamela, who was standing next to Jan. "The recollection came as a shock to him, and all the details, undoubtedly horrible, still remain hidden in a dark corner of his mind—until he finds himself strong enough to cope with those as well. That's the way it goes with many people who have a shocking experience."

Jan nodded, but the inspector raised his hands in despair.

"What am I supposed to do with information like that? How on earth will I describe that in a report?"

"Reality doesn't reckon with police officers who have to draw up a report," responded Pamela sharply. She took Jan by the arm to make it clear that she stood at his side.

Police cars stood next to the vans of the Maximum Axion Laboratory. Men in uniform and men dressed in white examined side by side the blackened ground.

Parker muttered discontentedly and stepped under the ribbon.

Pamela, still holding Jan by the arm, remained silent now to give him time to think. After a long pause, Jan said, "I think you're right."

"About what?"

"There are things that hide in dark corners of my mind. And I fear the moment that I start to remember... "

Parker came back. He had put his hands in his pockets, and there was a surly expression on his face.

"We're not making much progress," he said. "The heat of the explosion was so intense that everything's reduced to ashes. The Max Ax people are surprised about such little discovery. They were convinced that the barrack was completely empty—and thus, I've invited them to come to my office and take a look at the movie from the security camera—but all of a sudden they found gold. It had melted and then congealed again, so they have no idea about the original form."

He raised his eyebrows when he saw how Jan and Pamela looked at each other in surprise.

"Do you know more about it?"

"The Machine of Colton," said Jan. "Golden wiring..."

Pamela explained to the inspector about the Machine of Colton.

"It is very possible that Mary worked on a thing like that in this lab," she concluded.

Parker heaved a deep sigh.

"I would gladly give you tenfold of that gold to have that barrack standing somewhere else than right here in Southend-on-Sea," he said. "I'd hoped that Mr. Glas could tell more after I had brought him here. But he hasn't made me the wiser, my own men have found nothing of importance, and a Max Ax spokesman tells me that his company is glad to be rid of that barrack now. The plot will get sold, and I expect someone will build houses on it as soon as possible. Max Ax is so wealthy, that they won't even bother the insurance with the loss of a wooden barrack. Besides, the plot will fetch a good price. I would prefer to forget about the entire affair, for no serious accidents have happened. On the other hand, there's still that movie which proves that the barrack wasn't empty at all and that there's has been a burglar who most likely is responsible for the explosion that woke up all of Southend-on-Sea."

He rubbed his chin and looked at Jan and Pamela.

"We're going back to the station. After that, I wish you a pleasant trip back to London, Mrs. Mitchell, and I wish you a pleasant time in England, Mr. Glas, although I'm pretty sure that you'll return to Amsterdam as soon as you can."

Jan drove his Volkswagen from the parking lot onto the road and stopped behind Pamela's car. She stood there waiting for him, and he stepped out.

"And now?" asked Pamela. "What are your plans?"

"I'll find a good hotel," said Jan. "First thing I'll do is take a bath, after which I'll go to a restaurant for a proper meal. Then I'll go to sleep. Parker is right, I want to go back home. I have much to arrange there."

"I hope you'll come back soon. We've got to sift out the matter thoroughly. Let's be honest, we have something here that's exceptionally interesting for ParaPsycho. We're always looking for articles that will astonish the readers. It is important for us to come up with sensational themes that provoke long discussions. It's obvious that we'll have to do without Mary Landock from now on, and that makes you our most interesting contributor now. I need articles that are so good that they shock the world. You know, I am allowed to offer you a job. You can become an editor or a special journalist—no matter what we call it, the salary remains the same."

"You are allowed to offer me a job. Who suggested that?"

"Being the editor-in-chief, I can make a decision like that all by myself, but it is our publishing company, Arnold McKay Publishing, that is pressing for action and asking me to come up with more interesting news about this affair."

"Didn't AMP sponsor the symposium as well? They must have lots of money."

"That's right, lots of money," repeated Pamela. "The owner became rich in the computer business. You must have heard about him. Arnold McKay. An American businessman with a great interest in the occult, in mystery..."

Jan began to smile.

"I'm not rich at all. So, if there really is a basis for cooperation..."

The smile disappeared again when he realized that sooner or later he would be confronted with the horrors of his visions. Where had Mary Landock gone to and had she really used the barrack as a laboratory?

"First a good rest, then to Amsterdam, then back to London. I promise you that I will come and see you soon."

Pamela reached out her hand, but then she suddenly changed her mind.

"You know what? Follow me. I know a very good hotel here. There's a restaurant as well. While you take a bath, I'll make some phone calls. We can have a nice talk together during dinner. After that, I'll return to London, and you can get some sleep. Hotel room and dinner at the expense of ParaPsycho. How about that?"

"Sounds fine to me," said Jan and walked back to his car.

4

Kentucky, Tennessee, Alabama, Florida
1885–1895

Even in his own time, there was nobody who could tell where Manuel Raso—who was called the Mad Visionary—originally came from. Fact is, that he once lived in Mexico and traveled to North America. Although he was a striking personality, he was only mentioned for the first time when he turned up in Kentucky in the year 1885, where he entered a barbershop in Lexington to have a shave.

The barber, Klaus Schmitz, an immigrant from Germany, could remember his customer very well, and his story was noted by one of the many historians who tried to follow Raso's track.

"The first thing that struck me was his coat. It was a long coat of gold-colored silk, with big black stars! Was he a magician or a clown? Under the coat he wore a threadbare suit and round his neck hung different amulets, among these were little sculptures of jade, as well as leather pouches with unknown contents. He kept his hat on when he sat down on my adjustable chair," Schmitz told the historian, "and at first he didn't react to my request to take it off. When I strongly insisted that he took it off, because I couldn't comb his long, greasy hair this way, he got angry. Everyone knows that I'm not intimidated, and my straight razor was ready at hand, but I shrunk back when he jumped to his feet. The chair shoved backward and creaked, the wooden footrest got kicked aside. He stooped and rushed forward, and I was afraid that he was going to use his head—hat and all—as a battering ram to hit me in the stomach. Suddenly, he stopped, and.took off his hat, I heard him growl:

"Then take a look at it, you town rat, and enjoy it!"

His long hair fell down in thick locks on his face. The upper side of his skull was bald, but don't you think of a monk's tonsure now! What I saw was a horseshoe-arched dent in the head. The sides were callused skin on which hair growth was impossible. Inside it was a chaos of bone splinters, dark skin, and crusts, covered by a transparent substance that made me sick—it must have been a mixture of moisture and pus. I covered my mouth with my hand and talked to him from between my fingers. 'Please, put on your hat again.' He did, turned around, and put the footrest up. Then he sat down again on the chair."

Schmitz shaved the face of his customer, holding his arms stretched out in order to keep as far away from the man as possible.

But this was not the end of the story.

Schmitz felt pity for the man and asked him what had happened to him. The answer was short:

"A horse kicked me."

"I know a good doctor here in Lexington. It would be wise of you to visit him. I'll give you the address in a moment. He lives not far away from here."

Raso's reaction was strange. He put his hands on his knees and began to move his upper body slowly forward and backward, making the movable upper part of the chair sway tremendously. At the same time, he started to whisper unintelligible words. No matter what Schmitz tried, he couldn't make the man sit still again, and it was only because of his professional skill that he didn't hurt Raso with his straight razor—he managed to shave him without spilling a drop of blood. Meanwhile, another customer had entered the shop and Schmitz wanted to get rid of Raso as soon as possible.

"And ready we are! That's fifteen cents then."

Raso looked up as if the words of the barber had brought him out of the trance.

"There's a little problem, I've no money."

The second customer, a broad-shouldered man in a worn-out suit, came and stood in front of the door and crossed his arms demonstratively. Schmitz waved his razor to and fro and said, "You knew that before you decided to step inside."

"I cannot deny that," said Raso in a calm voice, as he leaned over the edge of the chair and opened a big leather bag he had put down on the floor next to him.

He's going to fetch a revolver, thought the barber and looked in panic at the man at the door.

When Raso sat straight again, he was holding a sketchbook and a pencil in his hands. Despite the fact that Schmitz protested immediately—"No, no, thank you, there's enough rubbish hanging here on the walls!"—Raso opened to a clean sheet and began to work with great concentration. Again he moved forward and backward, and the pencil slid so fast over the sheet that it was as if he was just scribbling. A string of unintelligible words escaped from his lips. The most strange, however, was the fact that he didn't look down on the paper but stared up along the brim of his hat.

"What am I supposed to do with someone like that, Enos?" Schmitz asked the other customer.

"You just leave it up to me," growled Enos. "I'll kick him out. That leather bag's worth more than fifteen cents. I myself will give him a dollar for it. And who knows what we'll find inside of it?"

"All right. I'll take his bag... "

As Schmitz stooped to grab the bag, Raso tore out the sheet of paper and showed it to him.

"Here you are." The voice sounded strange, as if from far away. "It's for you."

Schmitz put down his razor and took hold of the sheet. He glanced at it in a careless manner, and then, suddenly, his look grew fixed. Tears began to roll down his face, and he trembled so much that the sheet between his fingers made a rustling sound. His voice cracked when he said, "Gisela!"

Then he broke out in sobs.

It took some time before the man managed to get control of his emotions again. Then he asked a short question.

"Did you know her?"

The answer of Raso was even shorter.

"No."

The barber wiped his tears with a big handkerchief.

"Gisela! It was because of her that I left Germany, it is because of her that I'm here!"

Enos walked up to Schmitz and plucked the sheet from his fingers. He saw a detailed drawing of a young, beautiful woman who had wrapped her long hair in a braid around her head. She stood in a richly decorated room. Four towers were visible through a big window.

The barber pointed at the towers.

"The cathedral of Bamberg in Bavaria," he sobbed. "Exactly as you can see it from the house of Gisela's parents. This is how she was standing there when I came to bid her farewell. I intended to marry her, but she chose someone else."

"How is it, that man knows that? " wondered Enos, while he nodded in the direction of Raso. They both looked at Raso now, who was working on another drawing.

"Even if he'd know her," muttered Schmitz, "how is it possible then that he is able to draw her, the room, and the towers that strikingly? No one has a perfect memory like that. It was twenty-five years ago!"

Raso produced strange sounds. He had put the sketchbook on his thighs and drew with his right hand, while his left hand played with his amulets. The pencil moved up and down rapidly. Again, he stared up at the ceiling. After some time, he tore out the sheet and gave it to the barber.

"This is how she's looking now."

Schmitz was moved for the second time. The memory of Gisela, which had been in his mind for all these years and that had been reproduced so perfectly in Raso's first drawing, was replaced in a flash now by the portrait on the second sheet of paper. He had never been able to visualize her at a more advanced age. Now he knew. There she was— still a beauty! He saw her face only, with big eyes that looked at him questioningly. There was no background.

"Is she happy?" asked Schmitz.

His question already implied that he believed in the talents of his customer.

"She has three children, two girls, and a boy. The name of the boy is Klaus."

"Klaus. My first name. She named him after me. But that's no answer to my question."

Raso shrugged his shoulders and stood up from the chair. He picked up his bag and hung it over his shoulder.

"Happiness is just a word, barber. She's doing fine. She wants for nothing. She cherishes good memories, just like you, and they help her through hard days. So long."

But the barber wouldn't let him go.

"I'll frame the drawings and put them up right here. They're so much more worth to me than the fifteen cents I asked you for. How about a nice, hot bath, mister, and after that a good meal and a drink in the Mad Dog Saloon? Hot water for your bath is no problem at all, and the saloon is nearby in the street. Please, give me a chance to do something for you."

"I'll come along with you," said Enos to Raso and Schmitz. "You can give me a shave while he takes his bath, Klaus. And I'll pay for his meal if he makes a drawing for me as well."

Both men looked at the stranger.

And the stranger nodded yes.

The Mad Dog saloon was big and square, with tables and chairs along three walls and a mahogany bar that took up almost the entire side. It was already crowded when the three men came in. Schmitz found Raso a vacant chair at a table in a corner and then walked up to the bar where Enos, tall and broad as he was, had made space for two. Waving a finger in the air, Schmitz drew the attention of one of the barkeepers and ordered whiskey for Enos and himself and beer and a hot meal for Raso. He took the drawings that, as he had said, he would hang on the wall in his barbershop, from under his white jacket and looked at them again.

Then he nudged someone who was standing next to him and started to tell about his strange experience. Soon more than ten men were standing around him and listening attentively to him and handing around the drawings.

"Be careful with it!" warned the barber. "Don't fold them."

After he had got the drawings back again, Schmitz put them back under his jacket. He ordered two more whiskeys and another glass of beer. He walked to the table where Raso was sitting, eating his meal. A couple of men followed him.

Others passed on the barber's story, and already everyone was standing near the table in the corner. Schmitz explained one more time what exactly was going on.

"This is Emanuel Raso, a magician," he said in loud voice. "He drew a woman the way she was when I left her twenty-five years ago, and he also drew her the way she is looking now. It is a fact that he never met her—not then and not now. It is simply incredible, inexplicable, but true. Now it's Enos's turn. He'll ask a question, and then Raso will get cracking! Pay attention! Step forward, Enos!"

The tall man pushed his way through the crowd. In the meantime, Raso imperturbably bolted down his red kidney beans with bread and meat and drank his beer. Although he was neatly shaved now and had taken a bath, he still looked bizarre in his silk coat with stars, under which he still wore his threadbare, dirty clothes.

"Is he an actor?" someone asked hopefully. "Is there a theater company in town—or a real circus?"

Big Enos looked a little embarrassed with the situation.

You know..." he started in a soft voice, "when I was still a kid, from six to seventeen, we had this dog. No, that's all I'm going to tell about it. I won't mention its color, and I won't say if it was big or small. It was a faithful dog, and I cried like a child—well, I was still a boy then, wasn't I?—when he drowned in the Ohio River before my very eyes. Oh, if you were able to draw him..."

Raso shoved his plate to one side and took the sketchbook and pencils from his bag. The men who were sitting at the table with him shoved back their chairs and took up their glasses.

It became quiet in the Mad Dog.

The pencil scratched over the paper, while Raso seized his glass of beer with his left hand and drank slowly. His eyes were closed. On the paper came into being the image of a shaggy, big, black dog with strong paws, a long tail, and erect ears.

"And now I'm beginning to get very scared... ." stammered Enos. "My God! That's him. It's really him! First, we just called him Black, but he liked beer as much as our magical artist here, and thus we named him Bacchus."

Raso tore out the sheet and gave it to Enos. Now everyone started to shout at the same time.

"Make a drawing for me!" "I beg you, listen to my request... "
"I've lost a dear relative and—"

A loud voice was heard above everything:

"It's just a swindle! He came in together with Enos, I saw that myself."

It became quiet again, and the one who had made the charge, even bigger than Enos, pushed everyone aside and came to stand in front of the table. He put his hands on the tabletop and leaned forward. A sheriff star gleamed on his waistcoat.

"Patrick McLaren was my best friend. He found gold, got robbed, and was brutally murdered. Show me his portrait."

Raso placed the point of his pencil in the center of a new sheet of paper. Nothing happened. "Patrick McLaren never existed," said Raso. "I mean—no Patrick McLaren who was your friend found gold, and was murdered."

The man grinned.

"Right you are. Okay, go on with the show, but don't you forget that I'm keeping an eye on you!"

He straightened his back, turned on his heels, and walked away.

"Very well then," said Raso. "I'll try to help as many people as possible in a short time. Paper isn't cheap, but today I happen to be a very thirsty man. All I ask is a glass of beer per drawing, plus the small change you can spare. Who's first?"

A tumult broke out. Everyone pushed forward. The tables slid over the floor, and

Raso was wedged so tightly between his chair and the table that he couldn't move.

The sheriff asked Enos to help keep order. Together they managed to silence the crowd, and then they picked one candidate at the time, who got the chance to ask Raso for a drawing of a person, animal, town, village, or landscape. A barkeeper walked constantly up and down with glasses of beer, and the pile of small change on the table grew steadily.

Grown-up men burst out in tears when they set eyes upon the drawing that was specially made for them. Raso had to take a second and a third sketchbook from his big leather bag. On one occasion the sheriff pushed an attractive, defiant woman forward.

"Raso. This is Lucille. No, I'm not going to ask you to make a guess at her profession, for that would be all too easy... "

The bystanders burst out laughing at his remark, and Lucille laughed heartily along with them.

"It's her turn now," said the sheriff. "Ask your question, Lucille."

"Well," she said, "honestly speaking I've more than one request—I would like to have a couple of drawings. I'm not paying with beer or coins, but I've much more to offer... "

She reached out her hand and lifted up Raso's hat. Then, seized with fear, she let the hat fall and gave a cry. The barber hastened to pick up the hat and put it back on Raso's head.

The atmosphere had changed. The people took some steps back—they looked at Raso from a distance, as if they all had become afraid of him.

Raso, who had drunk a huge amount of beer, stared out in front of him with bloodshot eyes and started to murmur. His fingers played with the amulets around his neck. Then he rose to his feet and jumped onto the tabletop. He spread his arms, and only now one could see that the sleeves of his coat were very wide. He looked like a giant bird that had spread its wings to fly away.

There, standing on a table in the Mad Dog Saloon in Lexington, Raso made the first of

a long, long series of speeches, which would give him the nickname 'the Preacher.' Between 1885 and 1895 he warned everyone who would listen, in Kentucky, Tennessee, Alabama, and Florida, against a big catastrophe that would cause the end of the world.

"Live your lives full of passion and devotion! You all belong to the last generations who are allowed to enjoy the hospitality of mother earth. Your children will lead a carefree life, just like their children. We still have about two hundred years to go. After that, it's all over. A huge catastrophe will wipe out all life on earth. There's no getting away from it! Unless we find the center in time. But that, my friends, is so well hidden that we should have no illusions about it. Give me another glass of beer.

Let's drink to our luck. For we won't have to witness the end of times."

The visitors of the Mad Dog reacted in different ways.

"He told me that he was kicked by a horse," said Schmitz in a soft voice to the sheriff.

And the sheriff muttered, "I heard of ordinary people, like you and me, who suddenly had special talents after a serious brain injury."

Lucille was scared, and she cried. Someone who tried to comfort her burst out in tears himself and whispered, "Oh no...the crack of doom!"

Some men brought Raso beer. Raso stooped, picked up a glass, and emptied it in a long gulp. He put it back on the table, picked up the next glass, and held it high above his head.

"I had a vision!" he cried out loud. His eyes clouded as he appeared to look inwardly. "You might call it a heavenly vision. I found myself in Mexico. I ate a large number of mushrooms that can make a man dream, and I drank something with it that had the same effect. And there I sat, on top of a hill, far away from civilization. Sweating in the blazing sun. I closed my eyes, and still, I was able to see.

"There were people around me. They called themselves Xi. They took me along with them to a town. In the center, between four pyramid-shaped temples, which they themselves called coiled-up snakes, was a large, square plot. There they'd built a complex labyrinth—narrow paths marked by posts that stood upright in the ground. These poles were of different material. Wood, encrusted with little jade images of jaguars, monkeys, and spiders. Different sorts of stone. Hollow poles of fired clay, filled with earth and powder. Along the poles was a system of stone channels. They were narrow channels, and the water that ran through them connected all the vibrations and energy of the poles. The channels flowed into a square pond in which they had built a stone island. Along the other side of the poles was a double row of tubes. The tubes were made of fired clay, and the seams were sealed with a thick layer of rubber. They formed a closed circuit and were filled with water in which different materials were dissolved.

"A Xi opened a sluice. The water rose in the channels and began to stream faster. There was a bubbling in the tubes. Whirlpools came into being around the little island. It was as if the water began to boil there. Yes—it was boiling from energy, that's what it was doing! The island disappeared behind a wall of hot steam... "

Raso stooped to put down an empty glass and pick up a full one.

It was deadly quiet in the generally noisy saloon.

"The Xi sang a song," continued Raso. "They clapped their hands, faster and faster, and it seemed as if they forced up the speed of the water that way. Shamans waded calmly to the island as if they didn't feel the heat of the water. They waved the fog away with their hands. At that moment, my friends, a black spot appeared high in the blue sky. It came down and grew bigger and bigger. Something fell down on the stone island, causing a sickening sound. I began to feel dizzy. The next moment I saw the Xi much clearer than before. Many of them had deformed heads. The shape was different from that of yours or mine. Anyway, something had come down on the island. The wall of steam had lifted, waved away by the shamans, and what I saw was a huge pile of wet clay."

Raso stooped again and picked up a glass of beer. Still, he seemed to stand firmly on his feet. His look had become clear again and everyone in the saloon had a feeling as if he were being addressed personally.

"Imagine how the shamans, with their grotesque, deformed heads; their feathers; their multicolored clothes, set foot on the island and started to work the clay with their hands!"

He made wild, clawing movements with his free hand.

"They formed the clay. It became a giant creature with a big head, thick lips, broad shoulders, long arms, and legs, and it was standing on immense feet. They concentrated on the energy of the universe, focusing on the inside of this creature and brought it to life! The eyes flamed up, the lips began to move. The Xi knelt down. They had brought something to earth which wouldn't let itself be chased away again. The shamans hoped that it would be a good god, but the contrary was true. They had conjured up an evil spirit."

His listeners shivered.

"They gave him different names, unpronounceable for me. Freely translated he was called the God Who Came from Heaven, the Many-Sided One, the Vexation. I myself call him Tacendo, which is an Italian music term for 'silent.' For he never spoke a word! His form was not permanent—he slid away from the island like a snake, and the Xi fled in panic when he changed into a giant jaguar. It took a long, long time for them to get used to Tacendo's presence. The god was able to transmit his thoughts to them and set them to work. Then the Xi found out that he also had another name: the God of Revenge. Yes, the Xi was helping him to construct a devilish machine. Altogether it was a strange cooperation. The Xi had used all their special knowledge to take energy from the universe, and this energy had manifested itself to them in the many forms of Tacendo. And Tacendo, in his turn, taught the Xi how to improve their lives. He gave the Xi a special script of dots and dashes and taught them about the computation of time. He appointed the day when the world would explode. The Xi was under his spell and considered themselves fortunate that the end of times still was far away from them.

"A group of shamans followed him on a long journey. Under the leadership of the mighty creature, they collected a great number of different materials. Jade, volcanic stone, clay, dried plants, rubber, and even gold."

Raso's words had a hypnotic effect, and it remained quiet in the Mad Dog.

Raso stooped again to put down an empty glass and pick up a filled one.

"The group returned home," he continued. "They made long wires from the gold and covered them with a thick layer of rubber. They made big cylinders. Massive cylinders, hollow cylinders, filled cylinders. And groups of three cylinders together, connected by the golden wires. On the stone island, they built a fifth pyramid with a flattened top. They placed the cylinders on the top. Then they covered the big square with earth, making the pyramids invisible. The upper side of the upright cylinders was right under a thin layer of dirt.

"Slowly, very slowly, the cylinders fed themselves with energy from the universe. Only two hundred years to go, and then the cylinders will be full, and their energy will culminate in an explosion. Tacendo figured out the time. For three thousand years the cylinders have remained undiscovered, and I don't think they'll be found in time. The earth will shake and tear open, a chain reaction will make volcanoes rise up everywhere— on all continents and at the bottom of all oceans. Everything that lives will burn. The earth's crust will become one big, red-hot mass, the seas will evaporate in a short time! No one can stop this process. For the thin layer of earth, I was talking about that hides the cylinders from view is the divine Tacendo himself! He'll destroy anyone who dares to pick up a spade!"

Raso clambered from the table, sat down again, leaned forward, let his head sink, and fell asleep instantly. His hat was shoved back but still covered the head wound. A barkeeper took away the empty beer glasses.

The crowd discussed what Raso had said. Fear forced up the consumption of alcohol. The profits had seldom been that high in the Mad Dog on a normal day.

The next day Klaus Schmitz put up two framed pictures of Gisela in his barbershop.

A month later an intriguing picture of Lucille was hanging up next to the mirror behind the mahogany bar in the Mad Dog. The owner asserted that Raso had made it after he had woken up the next morning in the saloon.

Raso himself had moved on and never come back to Lexington to confirm that.

He earned a good wage by drawing what the people wanted to see, and he made frightening speeches.

In Jackson, Tennessee, he was treated by a doctor, who worked on him for over an hour. The doctor had to cut away a lot of hair that had grown together with the head wound. Then he cleaned the wound carefully and disinfected it. After Raso had left, the doctor hung up a drawing next to his certificate—it showed his parents whom he had never known; he was an abandoned child who had come a long way.

In Brownsville, Tennessee, Raso made such an imposing speech that a number of people decided to join him on his journey. For inexplicable reasons he did not land in Arkansas next, which would have been closer, but went on to Savannah at the Tennessee River. Later he turned up in different villages and towns of Alabama. His group of followers grew and grew. It was not only the poor, prospectless, and meek who went along with him and accepted him as their source of inspiration. Among them were scientists and adventurers, vaudeville artists, medicine men, men and women in deep debt who left in the dark of night: all kinds of people who wanted to start a new life for all kinds of reasons.

The crack of doom was still far away, and therefore the people who traveled with Raso weren't downhearted at all. On the contrary! They celebrated every day and night.

This was made possible by two generous members of the group. Jonathan Knight was the only heir to a considerable fortune. His father had done good business in England, and his mother had belonged to the English nobility and had possessed an extensive estate and countless houses. Jonathan had come to America for no other reason than to look about and have a pleasant time, and he felt very comfortable among his fellow travelers. The other benefactor was a certain Phil Franks, a gold digger who had been lucky and had become fabulously rich. Having that much money, however, had made him scared, and he clung to Raso; he felt safe in the shadow of this strong personality.

Everything Raso wanted was paid by Phil.

Raso's fame preceded him, and everywhere he went he was surrounded by people who asked him to draw their forgotten, abandoned, or lost dear ones for them; and they paid him well for it.

Thus, the company traveled in comfortable coaches or on strong horses, and their possessions were loaded on big carts. Raso led his people to Florida. He settled on the west coast, at a little river that flowed into the Gulf of Mexico. There they started to build houses. A little town arose, and they gave it an odd name: Franks Knight, in honor of their two benefactors.

Raso remained the undisputed leader until his death in 1895 from a fever.

He had requested his followers not to mourn for him, but to organize a huge party.

They complied with his wishes and the party lasted for fourteen days. After that, the atmosphere in Franks Knight changed. It was Raso himself who was responsible for this change. When the partiers finally had sobered up, they remembered the last days of Raso's life. Sweating all over from his fever, the eyes big and bewildered in his emaciated face, he had stepped out of his bed several times and gone outside.

"Wait and see! Just wait and see! The world will be punished! It doesn't matter whether you live in sin or lead a decent life. The immense universe is a provoked monster, ready to spit out a little, insignificant ball; mother earth! You had better believe— no one will manage to escape. The little and the big animals, all the people, they will explode and nothing will remain of them. The Xi only acted by order, although they never realized that.

And Tacendo was nothing other than a power created by the universe itself, descended to earth to help the Xi finish the great work. Death is on your doorstep—don't you hear him knocking?"

At night he ran through the dark streets, waving a burning torch. Wet with sweat he looked like a frightening marsh monster. His bald, mutilated skull glistened in the glow of the torch. The people stayed inside, kept their doors and shutters closed, and listened, shivering with fear, to his roaring voice.

"I'm going to die, you hear? I'll lead the way, as always... I tell you that you're all ready to follow. All of you. It's useless to hide. No one will search for you. Nothing will be left of you or anyone else. You'll explode, no matter where you are. Mother earth will become a huge cloud of dust that will blow away in the endless universe! That's what the Xi has brought about, that is what was ordered by Tacendo. Go on with the party, for everything will become less horrible when you see it through drunken eyes. But listen, there's a chance to get off scot-free. Don't beget children! You hear me, you cowards? Don't beget children! For your children will have children as well, and they will witness the end of times! Is that what you want? I wouldn't think so! Don't beget children, and you will be saved. You—and no one else but you—will survive. Someone will turn up to lead the way."

Manuel Raso didn't die in bed. One night he had gone outside again. Waving his torch he went through the streets, stumbling, crying out that the world would explode soon.

"There's no one who can stop Tacendo!" were his last words.

Then silence fell.

Next morning someone found him in Frank Knight's main street—made up of only twenty houses and four shops—spread-eagled in the mud. The rain pelted down on him. His long coat, with big red stars, was soaked.

Once he had painted himself exactly the way he was lying there...

It was as if the dark clouds would never blow over again.

Florida flourished, but Franks Knight remained an out-of-the-way place, seldom visited by tourists, without progress, and with a constant melancholic atmosphere.

The old generation died out. Jonathan Knight and Phil Franks left a lot of money behind, but it was spent quickly. The inhabitants of the little place supported themselves by growing their own vegetables and fishing in the river and the sea.

A stranger who, for any reason whatsoever, drove through Franks Knight found out soon enough that he was the only one who had a car—the hamlet hadn't a gas station, and the inhabitants made use of horse and cart. The people had a striking preference for clothes decorated with big stars in all possible colors. In the four shops of Franks Knight, one could only get food, clothes, and tools, and the shopkeepers preferred to trade in lieu of money. They didn't sell books, magazines, or newspapers. No one had a television or a computer. There was one community telephone at the grocer's store. There was no hotel in Franks Knight, and strangers seldom stayed longer than a couple of minutes.

Another thing the stranger might have noticed was the absence of children in the town. There was no one there under the age of fifteen. Fifteen years ago, when Wesley Dunn had become Raso Preacher, he had reminded the townspeople of the words of Manual Raso, and they had not begotten another child since then.

Behind the main street was a park in which sat a stone mausoleum with the body of Manuel Raso in the center. Every citizen went there once a day to meditate and bow to the great visionary.

Whenever two people crossed on the street, they greeted each other politely, followed by a depressed "The end of time is near."

But there was also hope:

"Only a small group of people will be saved." That's what the great Manuel Raso had said, just before he passed away. "The inhabitants of Franks Knight will survive the disaster. Only them. Wait for the stranger who will come to save you!"

The end of time was almost there.

They remembered the words of Manuel Raso very well.

☽☽☽

Jan Glas sat upright in his favorite chair in his small apartment in the center of Amsterdam. He grabbed at the leather armrests with both hands. His mouth had contracted into a little strip, his eyes were big and round. He breathed quickly in and out. The sweat ran down his face.

Opposite to him sat his old friend, the historian Robbert Goudriaan, who looked down through his thick glasses at the papers he had put on his lap. The papers contained, in big black letters, the most important events in the life of Manuel Raso. On Jan's request, he had collected all possible facts about Raso—he had gone to several libraries and had consulted a great number of colleagues. Robbert had read Manuel Raso's story to him, without looking up from his papers, and now he directed his attention to Jan again.

He gave a visible start.

"Jan! What's the matter with you?"

Jan shook his head; Robbert gathered that he wouldn't speak and preferred that he didn't bother him.

"Shall I continue?"

Jan nodded yes.

"Very well then. That was the history of Manuel Raso. I have a lot of background information for you."

Looking again at his younger friend, he couldn't help suggesting, "Jan, why don't you get up? Walk around the room for a while. Get yourself something to drink. Is there anything I can do for you?"

There was no answer. Now Robbert himself rose to his feet and walked around the room—the papers still in his hand.

Standing with his back turned to Jan, Robbert tried not to think of the bad shape Jan was in; from the moment he had returned from England he had become more melancholic by the day, and now his state of mind seemed to have come to a breaking point. Time after time Robbert had asked if he could help him, but Jan had always refused his request.

"It's better to concentrate on Manuel Raso," Jan now said. "I want to know everything about him."

Robbert looked down through the window. The street still breathed the atmosphere of far-off days, despite all the modern adaptations.

Then he concentrated on the papers again.

"The Xi," he said. "We call them Olmecs, which means Rubber People. Manuel Raso had visions of Olmecs. They formed the oldest civilization of Central America, and therefore some also called them the Mother People. Raso found himself in Mexico, where he ate hallucinating mushrooms and drank a psychedelic liquid. His mind bridged the ages. The Olmecs lived in the south of Mexico from about 1500 to 100 or possibly 200 BC. If we only knew as much about them as we know about the Aztecs and the Mayans! Of course, no one has ever heard of Tacendo, for Raso made up that name himself. Further, he said that he wasn't able to pronounce his true names. The God Who Came from Heaven, the Many-Sided One, the Vexation, and the God of Revenge doesn't mean a thing to us either. The Olmecs made gigantic human heads, often deformed and helmeted, from basalt blocks. Some of them weigh more than fifty tons. It is often suggested that the first Olmecs came from another part of the world. From Africa? That's what several scientists consider. They knew all about arithmetic, and their calendars were very precise. They knew the written word, played a game with a rubber ball. Raso wore amulets, among which was a little sculpture of jade. It might have been an original work of art from the Olmecs, for they loved to work with blue-green jade. Maybe it was the image of a divine being—Tacendo!"

He held the papers behind his back now and looked up over the houses to the blue sky.

"They built temples, they worshipped many gods, of which somewhere therianthropic, which means half-human and half-animal. In this case often half-human, half-jaguar. It is interesting to note that Raso, said at least once that Tacendo transformed into a jaguar! Where did he get that information from, in his time? Remarkable, Jan, remarkable. Imagine that these mysterious people traveled all over the world searching for miracles and that they, after having settled down in Mexico, had been able to take terrifying powers from the immense universe! A divine entity that doesn't belong in this world, that will grow stronger and stronger through these powers of the universe, and then will cause a catastrophic explosion...That's not a merry thought Jan, and then there's more. I've read in books and articles from different researchers that the Olmecs predicted the end of the world! Which would explain their fascination for figures and data. They figured out when the disaster would take place, and it ended up in our time! Isn't that scary?"

He waited for a reaction. When it didn't come, he turned around again.

Jan looked different. He had calmed down and seemed more relaxed. His far-away look had disappeared but he had the look of a mystic. His irises had the shine of polished jade, and the pupils seemed unfathomable, deep as the universe.

"Jan," said Robbert.

Jan stared at the newest copy of ParaPsycho that lay on the coffee table in front of him. The cover showed a splendid picture of Mary Landock, and the headline said, 'Scientist Mary Landock Disappears.' The lead article started at page six and was all about the speech she had made during the symposium of the Third Eye Association. It was illustrated with pictures of her and Jan.

Next to the magazine were some letters and picture postcards, which all had the same sender:

Wesley Dunn, Raso Preacher, Center of the Heavenly Vision, Franks Knight, Florida, USA

Mr. Dunn had tried to get in contact in all possible ways, but Jan hadn't responded. Countless letters had been sent from Franks Knight. Short pleas could be heard on his answering machine:

"Please, Mr. Glas, call me back. I repeat my number once again,...Mr. Glas, I beg of you..."

Now Jan looked up at Robbert.

"Do you know how I've felt from the moment I woke up in the hospital in Southend-on-Sea? As if I've been looking at myself through a thick pane of glass."

He heaved a deep sigh and leaned backward.

"It's still not clear to me what has happened to me. But finally, I'm resigned to the fact that the world will come to an end soon."

"Jan! Have you gone mad? Do you really mean this?"

"But of course! It has nothing to do with the facts. It's a feeling I have. A feeling of certainty. And I also know what to do. First I go back to England to have a talk with Pamela Mitchell. You know, Robbert, I see you standing here in front of me, full of disbelief. You're bewildered. Bewildered—yes, that's the right word! Every member of the Mexican government will react in the same way, when I warn them about a disaster which will destroy the world. I'll ask Pamela to talk to the publisher of ParaPsycho. Arnold McKay is filthy rich. Pamela told me so herself. He must organize an expedition to Mexico. We will have to search with helicopters, with a lot of people, with—"

"Jan! Control yourself!" The voice of Robbert sounded loud and compelling. "I know as well as you that strange things have happened and that something special happened to you as well. But now you're going too far. The world will keep on turning for a long, long time, take that from me."

"Quite possible. But then we're talking of a world without any form of life! I go back to England, and after that, I go to America."

Robbert raised his hands in despair and stared up at the ceiling.

"Why America?"

"Franks Knight. I can help the people there."

"Help them? How?"

"They can survive the disaster. No one else but them!"

"How could such a thing be possible?"

"I'll show them the way."

Robbert sat down opposite to Jan.

"When will you go?"

"Tomorrow morning."

"Fine. Then I have enough time to talk you out of this. All I can hope is that you're not suffering from brain damage or something."

"Don't talk nonsense, Robbert."

Robbert burst out laughing. "Which one of us is talking nonsense all the time? Please consider this: you know for sure that the world will come to an end soon. Billions of people will die. Yet you don't seem worried about that. All you want to do is save a small group of people."

"I am only able to save a small group of people. That's quite a difference."

"Of course. Want or can. But shouldn't you be very scared or even panicked, when you know for sure that everything will end? I don't see any emotion, Jan. I'm beginning to think that someone gave you a brainwashing!"

"I react differently from what you would expect in a situation like this? Is that what you mean?"

"Exactly. You came home, and you were totally confused. You contacted me. I came searching for you several times. Every time I stepped into your living room, I noticed that you had caused more havoc than the time before."

Jan looked around. The floor was covered with empty bottles, clothes, newspapers, and all kinds of other mess. The dinner table was full of plates and dishes covered with leftovers. Jan shrugged his shoulders.

"Everything looks quite normal to me." "Do you really think so? I know no other who's as clean and proper as you. Until a few moments ago, your face was red all the time as if you suffered from high blood pressure, and you were always perspiring. After you had fetched it from the letterbox, the only thing you've done is stare at the cover of ParaPsycho. And now, all of a sudden, you look much better, but you're also raving. Once again, when someone knows for sure that the world will come to an end soon, he'd never react as casually as you are. Look at me, Jan, look at me!"

Jan's green gaze pierced through Robbert's thick glasses "We've known each other for many years now. We met in the editorial office of the newspaper for which we both wrote articles. From that day on you bombarded me with questions. You made me check everything that had to do with history first before you published it. We became close friends. You had no place of your own for a long time, and you slept in our living room on the couch. You sympathized with me when I divorced my wife. You cheered me up. You pulled me through a nasty period. I—"

"I know that very well!" Jan cried out. "Why do you bring all that up again?"

"Isn't that clear to you? Soon I'll be dead! That's what you'll have to realize if you really believe that all life will get wiped out. It's obvious to me that you simply don't give a damn about my death. You don't bother about me and all the other victims of the nearing catastrophe."

"Robbert, I'm very sorry, but I don't follow you. How I wish that I could understand you. You don't seem to understand me either. I have important things to do."

Robbert nodded.

"Then I've important things to do, too. I'll follow you, everywhere you go. Although I would prefer to take you with me to a friendly psychiatrist."

"You want to come with me? To America?"

"In my opinion, you're mentally ill, and I see it as my duty to come along with you since I cannot convince you that it's much better for you to stay right here."

"How are you going to pay for these journeys?"

Robbert asked him the same question:

"Where will you get the money from?" "From ParaPsycho. I'll travel as a journalist of ParaPsycho, and they'll agree to my plans. No doubt about that."

Robbert rubbed his chin with his thumb and forefinger.

"Maybe it's better to abandon my plan. I'm over sixty, but I still have to work hard to make a living here in Amsterdam. I cannot permit myself to be away for too long. Damn, Jan! If I was younger, I would stop you. I'd knock you out if need be so that you would regain consciousness in the waiting room of my friend the psychiatrist!"

"Right. You can't stop me. No one can stop me."

"Still, I won't give up, Jan. Listen to me."

Jan looked out in front of him and nodded. "All right, all right, I'm listening."

5

Florida - Five Years Ago

There were six men sitting on the wooden quay at the back of Restaurant Hernando in Nacre Cove, a little port town on the Gulf of Mexico. Elmore, Doug, Pedro, Francis, Otis, and Raphael, business friends from Tallahassee, had driven to the coast to go out fishing for a couple of days and to negotiate together. They had spent the whole day on a fishing boat, but the catch had been disappointing. Only Francis had almost succeeded in fetching in a big marlin. After a violent fight, he was ready to get him on board when the hook came loose, and the fish fell back into the water. It had been the only sensation of the day. There was not a breath of wind. The sun had turned the steel deck into a huge baking tray, and the ocean didn't seem to hide any other adventures under her smooth surface.

The ship's owner had distracted their attention with tall stories and a constant flow of cold beer.

Now the men sat down at a table on the planks, eating oysters and drinking large amounts of white wine. It was evening; the sun would go down in half an hour. From the sea came a cool breeze. There wasn't much talking. The waitress exchanged the empty bottles for full ones once again and then went back into the restaurant, knowing that the gentlemen didn't need her anymore for the time being. After a couple from New York had paid their bill and left, the six men were the only customers left inside.

Suddenly someone appeared at the side of the quay.

Elmore nudged Pedro.

"Look over there! To the left."

He said it loud enough for the others to hear it as well.

They saw someone, as careful as a feral cat, sneaking up the stairs to the wooden quay. He was a broad-shouldered man about six feet tall, dressed in rags. When he finally stood on the quay, they could see that he was wearing dirty, down-at-the-heel shoes. Long, almost felted hair hung down in thick twists to his shoulders, and his beard consisted of wisps of different lengths as if he had cut it recently with a blunt knife. Light brown eyes rolled up and down.

The waitress had cleared the tables, but at one table stood a single glass containing a drop of wine. The man jumped across the planks, fetched the glass, and emptied it as fast as he could. With one hand he wiped crumbs on the table into the other hand, which he held palm up against the tabletop. He brought the crumbs to his mouth, chewed a few times, and swallowed. Then he straightened his back and looked at the six men.

"Gentlemen, please...if there are any leftovers..."

The men burst out laughing.

"There's still plenty of everything," said Raphael. "Bread, mashed potatoes, lots of oysters, and full bottles of wine. But you can't sit down at the table like that, my friend. You'll have to wash first. Jump down from the quay. We'll watch you get a ducking."

This remark was well received by the others. They decided immediately that a dive into the sea was no guarantee for a free meal. The man should have to do more for that.

"He has to stay in the water," said Doug, a giant of a man whose chair creaked with every move he made. "Then we can feed him. If he swims around right in front of the quay, he can try and catch everything we throw to him."

"Right. Catch it like a pelican," said Elmore, "or dive like an otter. Get a move on, friend, jump!"

The man didn't hesitate. He ran over the planks and dove into the harbor. The six friends stood up and took their full plates and a bottle of wine with them. Staggering on their feet, bumping up against each other every now and then, they went to the waterside. There they sat down, their legs dangling over the edge. Right beneath was the man, who, in his wet clothes and swamped shoes, desperately tried to keep his head above the water.

"Now start washing!" commanded fat, Doug. "Always wash your hands and face before you have dinner."

The man began to tread water, while he used his hands to wash his face and beard.

"Your feet! Wash your feet!" said Otis, and the men were overjoyed to see how the poor beggar's head disappeared under the surface and how his feet popped up and how he tried to touch his shoes with his hands. His head came above the surface again, and the man coughed. Now he swam back to the quay and tried to cling to it. Two of the men pushed him back with the hard soles of their expensive shoes.

"Catch!" said Doug and threw out an oyster.

The swimmer tried to catch the oyster but missed. The man laughed at him, and all together they started to throw food at him. Every now and then the man managed to catch something, and then he swallowed it without chewing. Pedro stood up and started to empty out a bottle of wine. The man came nearer, but before he was able to reach the spot where the trickles hit the water, Pedro raised the bottle to his lips. Pedro took a swig and then flung the bottle into the water. He was the first to go back to the table.

The others followed.

"Let's all have one glass of whiskey and then go back to the hotel," suggested Raphael.

"A good idea," grinned Francis. "The bar will be open till late there. We can have a couple drinks there as well. The last one who's still able to stand puts all the others to bed."

None of them bothered about the man in the water. They simply forgot about him.

The waitress brought them their whiskey.

The sun went down.

)))

The man who was so tiny and thin that others had named him Shrimp, drove an outstandingly big car. Shrimp was thirty-five years of age but had the looks of a teenager. His sharp suit had cost a fortune, and his Mercedes was one from the highest price bracket. On his way home he passed Nacre Cove and decided to stop there and have a drink and a bite to eat in Restaurant Hernando.

It was already dark. He parked the car and stopped the motor. In the beams of the headlights, he saw a strange figure sitting on a bench in front of the restaurant. An unkempt man, a hobo perhaps, with long, felted hair and a disheveled beard. His torn clothes stuck against his body.

It looks as if he's all wet, thought Shrimp.

Yes, the man looked like a big, wet dog who had been chased away by someone with a garden hose.

Shrimp switched off his lights. Just as he started to get out, he saw the door of the Hernando swing open. Six men stepped outside, and he could tell immediately that they all were drunk.

It seemed wise to him to remain sitting in the car until they had passed him by.

The men stumbled down the wooden stairs, reaching for each other to prevent themselves from falling down. All of a sudden they got sight of the man on the bench, and they became visibly excited. They stumbled up to him. The man stood up laboriously, but he was pushed back onto the bench.

The scene was lit by a lamppost and the light that shone through the windows of the restaurant—Shrimp had a good view of what was happening. It was six against one, and the soaked man had no chance of escape. He was pushed around, and Shrimp heard angry voices. One of the drunks lifted him up, and another gave him a punch to the jaw. The man fell on the ground and rolled next to the bench. There he curled over on his knees, crawled backward, and evaded kicking feet. And then all of a sudden the provoked man jumped to his feet, and Shrimp saw that he held a big stick—probably a broken branch—in his hand. The six attackers shrank back. Two of them stumbled and landed with their backs against the bench. The soaked man was holding the stick in both hands now and lashed out. He hit the head of fat Doug. The sound of it could be heard inside the Mercedes.

The big, fat man remained standing motionless for a moment and stared in disbelief. Then he fell backward and was caught by one of his friends, who lowered him softly until he lay full length on the bench.

"Doug!" shouted somebody. "He's dead! He beat Doug to death!"

Then Shrimp performed an instinctive act, which determined the fate of the murderer; he opened the door to step out, but a second later he changed his mind and closed it again. The five friends stood in bewilderment over the dead body of Doug. The killer, who had thrown the stick far away from him, looked around in panic. It was quiet now in Nacre Cove. No one had reacted to the loud voices that had sounded just a moment ago. The soaked man had seen the courtesy light of the Mercedes go on and out when had Shrimp opened and closed the door. Fast, on the toes of his worn shoes, he ran up to the car. Shrimp realized too late that he hadn't pushed in the button of the central locking system. Again the courtesy light went on and off, and then the man was already sitting next to him. None of the five friends had noticed; only when they straightened themselves again and looked around did they realize that Doug's murderer was no longer there. They talked among themselves nervously. Two of the men knelt down with Doug, while the third took a cell phone out of his pocket, and the fourth and the fifth ran back to the restaurant.

Shrimp started the car. Never before had the soft humming of the engine sounded so improbably loud to his ears. He backed up carefully. He hadn't switched on the lights yet. Behind a parked van he ventured to turn around, and then he drove away slowly and turned left onto King Street, where he switched on his lights. He turned left again and followed St. George Street and then he reached the dark highway.

The stranger was the first one to speak.

"You're helping a murderer."

The voice sounded strangled, and the words were followed by a short sob. "My God!" he cried out. "I've actually killed someone!"

Shrimp concentrated on the road. He turned into a crossroad that led back to the coast again.

"If you really want to help me, then put a bullet through my head. Do you have a gun with you? Put me out of this misery. I've become my own enemy. I simply don't want to live any longer. Please, help me—kill me… "

Shrimp reached out his right hand.

"What's the name of the man whom I can please with a bullet?"

The stranger shook hands with him.

"Don. Don Adler…"

"Shrimp. That's what everyone calls me behind my back. I'm not in possession of any firearms, so, for the time being, you'll just have to go on breathing."

After this, it remained quiet in the car. Shrimp stopped in front of a high metal gate and used a remote control to open it. He went up the drive. The gate closed behind him. The headlights shone on a big, two-storied, white villa, built Victorian style with high pillars on all sides. In front of the house was a square bordered by high oaks. As Shrimp crossed the square in the direction of the garages, he could hear Don Adler swearing to himself. He stepped on the brakes, and when the car came to a complete stop, Shrimp looked to his right. He saw that Don had buried his face in his hands. Now he could hear him crying plaintively.

"Listen—" began Shrimp.

Don reacted immediately.

"Who are you? The devil himself? This is what it was all about... And it has made a murderer out of me!"

"I don't understand. What was it all about?"

Shrimp opened his side window. The man next to him smelled awful. It was a miracle that he hadn't opened the window earlier. He drove up slowly to the garages and used the same remote control he had used for the gate to open one of the doors.

"Oak trees!" sighed Don. "And a house like this. Oh, not out of stone. I would never have got the money together for that, no matter how hard I worked. You're showing me what I had in mind all the time. What I wanted was a wooden house between the oak trees. For Angelica. Do you hear? For Angelica!"

The garage door closed again behind them. A light was burning in the garage. Shrimp had placed the Mercedes between a Jaguar and an Oldsmobile. On the other side of the Oldsmobile stood a sports car, an ink black Porsche. Shrimp stepped out.

"Are you going to sit there forever?"

Don gave no answer. Again he buried his face in his hands. He cried, heartrendingly loud.

Shrimp walked on. He left the door that gave entry to the house open. In the big living room, he poured himself a glass of whiskey.

Half an hour later he heard footsteps and then a voice.

"Shrimp! Where are you?"

"Walk up to the door at the end of the corridor."

Don Adler made a hopeless impression. He looked like someone who didn't expect anything more from life. After he had sat down and had heaved a deep sigh, he asked, "And what are you going to do now? Call the police?"

Shrimp had to laugh.

"You step into my car uninvited. You ask me if I will be so good as to put a bullet through your head. Then you call me a devil because I live in a house between the oaks, and now you want to know if I'm planning to hand you over to the police. How about a glass of whiskey? Wouldn't that be a much better idea?"

Don nodded yes. "Please, oh yes, please. And if you only knew how long it has been since I have had a proper meal... " "We'll take care of that as well.'

Shrimp stood up and poured him a glass of whiskey. Then he waved a hand through the air and said, "You'll have noticed that it's a mess around here. I just don't take the time to clear it away. The biggest part of the week I'm doing business, visiting my companies—and there I have all my offices tidy and representative. Here I prefer to be alone."

"But now you're saddled with me."

Don took a sip. His face twisted. But soon he took a second swig, and not much later he put the empty glass in front of him on a coffee table. Shrimp refilled his glass.

"I'll probably get drunk very soon, Shrimp. I'm not used to that stuff anymore."

"And that on an empty stomach," grinned Shrimp. "Come, let's go to the kitchen. Don't forget to take your glass with you."

The chaos in the kitchen was worse than in the living room. But the cupboards, the fridge, and the freezer were well filled, and Shrimp turned out to be a good cook.

"How about a nice, big steak? With mashed potatoes and different vegetables?"

Shrimp left Don in peace while he ate. He sat down at the table opposite to him and looked at him in silence.

Don ate in a strange way. First, he started to gobble. He cut the meat into big pieces and stuffed them into his mouth. Then he put down his fork and knife and sighed—after which he picked them up again and went on eating. Shrimp had opened a couple of bottles of beer and put them on the table. Don emptied them one by one. When he had emptied his plate, he looked up at Shrimp. Tears trickled down his cheeks into his beard.

"Do you want some more?"

"I'm still hungry, but I'm afraid that I'll have to throw up if I go on eating. Thanks very much. I could do with another beer."

Don leaned back heavily and stroked his stomach.

"For a moment I was thinking of absolutely nothing, while I concentrated on my food. It gave me a feeling of happiness. But now it's all coming back to me. Damn, I'm a murderer! But what was I supposed to do? All I did was defend myself."

"What do you want to do?" asked Shrimp in a businesslike voice. "Wash yourself, have a shave? Sleep? Or talk?"

"Talk. Now there's finally someone who will listen to me. I hope that will make me feel a bit relieved. Or perhaps I'll break down..."

He took a bottle of beer and started to turn it around nervously with all ten fingers.

"Believe me, I'm not a violent person at all. That is to say, as long as everyone lets me be. I won't deny that I was in many a fight when I was young. Everything changed after I met Angelica. I'd never realized that you can love someone that much. My schooling doesn't mean a thing."

He put the beer bottle on the table and held out his hands, palms up. The fingers trembled heavily.

"But these hands can work."

He took the bottle again with his left hand and tapped the forefinger of his right hand against his temple.

"And I have a good head on my shoulders. I worked hard and learned fast. At times I had two or three employers at the same time. Then I was delivering papers in the morning, worked in construction during the day, and was an odd-job man and went out moonlighting after that. On the weekends I was a bouncer. I also worked as a courier. For a couple of years, I drove a truck through Florida, Georgia, and Alabama. Soon we could buy ourselves a mobile home, and we were happy about it. We had a terrific spot in a mobile home park, not far from Jacksonville. Right next to us stood an old oak. Many a time we sat there in the shadow, under the branches of our oak, Angelica and I, talking about our future. I told her about my plans. I would buy us a piece of land. I would build us a house there. A wooden house with a huge front porch. And if there were no oaks around, I would plant them myself!" He took a swig and held the bottle so tight that it wouldn't have surprised Shrimp if he had pinched it into pieces.

"That's what I wanted to do for Angelica. Build a house with my very own hands. Work and save money, that's what it was all about then. I didn't know better and believed that Angelica felt the same way about it. So I didn't complain if she had spent too much money on clothes again. I just worked even harder...lots of hours."

"Did Angelica have a job as well?" Shrimp wanted to know.

Don didn't react. Maybe he hadn't even heard the question at all.

"One day I called on an old man who owned a lot of land. And what do you know? He was willing to sell me a piece of ground and for a very reasonable price. There were oaks there as tall as the ones here. Soon I understood why he wanted to do some business with me. He wanted to have someone around because he was lonely and wanted to assure himself of help if something should happen to him. We clinched the sale with a couple of drinks. I felt so good that day, I didn't feel like working. I wanted to go home. You know, Angelica didn't expect me home so early. She was lying in bed. She was not alone... ."

"You went berserk," guessed Shrimp.

"You might say so," said Don. "You know what blind rage is? I can tell you, you're really blind, and don't see what your fists do. Or you're not able to remember what happened after the event— that's another possibility. Men from other mobile homes came when they heard the noise and tried to calm me down. Angelica's friend was sent to the hospital in an ambulance, with serious injuries. I was sent to prison. Angelica never came to visit me. As soon as I was released, I went home. There was another mobile home standing on our spot. That hurt. It was a much bigger one, and they'd had to saw off branches from the oak tree. Our oak tree! That hurt even more. Someone stepped outside. A stranger looked at me, and there was that blind rage again. I was a free man for no longer than half a day. Why hadn't I been able to control myself? That man stood on the spot where I should have been. With Angelica. He had damaged our tree. I hit him hard on the chin. Several times. Back in jail, a warden said that he knew exactly how men like me were. 'They always come back.'

"After a long time, I was released again. I had precisely one single dollar in the bank. I went searching for Angelica. Before I knew it, I was roaming. Without her, life seemed meaningless; and it still is to me. I had no roof over my head and not a penny in my pocket. Every day I realized a bit more that searching for Angelica was useless. She would never come back to me. Why did she cheat on me? Who can tell? But it is a fact that a woman can make a hobo out of a man. She took my future with her, together with my joy of life. I'm sure you can't imagine how you feel when your daily activities are reduced to searching for something to eat."

"No, I can't" was Shrimp's short reaction.

"Finally I looked so bad—well, you can see that for yourself. Every day was the same for me. Except for today."

Then Don started telling what had happened from the moment he had stepped on the quay behind Restaurant Hernando, looking for food. Again the tears ran down his face.

"I'm not someone who will try to commit suicide," he ended his story. "Dissatisfied with life, deeply disappointed, I'm doomed to wait till death comes to take me away." He pushed his forefinger against his right temple. "I cannot press a button in my head which makes me see things in another perspective. I cannot simply shrug my shoulders over what happened in the past and not think of Angelica anymore. Why couldn't I control myself when those six men came up to me?"

"Blind rage. Once again..."

"It was not wrong to pick up that stick. But instead of using it myself, I should have given it to that big man. Then he could have killed me with it."

Don put his empty beer bottle on the table. Suddenly he rose to his feet and walked to the kitchen door.

"I'm tired, I feel dizzy," he said. He shuffled out the door.

When Shrimp entered his living room a few minutes later, he saw that Don lay on the couch, sleeping.

Shrimp turned off the lights.

Next morning, Don locked himself up for a long time in one of the bathrooms on the first story. Shrimp waited for him in the kitchen. He put breakfast on the table and made several business calls with his cell phone.

When Don came out he was wearing a white bathrobe that was too tight around the shoulders, he had cut his hair and shaved off his beard. He smelled of aftershave.

"You've become quite another person," laughed Shrimp, as he switched off his cell phone. "Good morning."

"Good morning," reacted Don. His voice sounded gloomy.

"Hungry?"

"If you should tell me that I had nothing to eat yesterday and only dreamed of food, I would believe you immediately. A horse could run around freely in my empty stomach!"

"Then we'll have eggs, bacon, and toast for starters," declared Shrimp. "Sit down. I have something to discuss with you."

"You must have thought about what you'll have to do now. Maybe you regret taking me along with you. Were you afraid of me? Didn't you dare to kick me out of your car?"

"I wouldn't have succeeded. You're much stronger than I. And then that blind rage..."

Shrimp started to laugh, but Don didn't laugh along with him.

"What is it you want to talk about?"

"Listen. I'm a businessman. I make agreements which bring profit to both parties. First, we must go back in thought to yesterday evening. As far as I know, there was no one in the neighborhood when those men came up to you. On the other hand—there are five witnesses of the murder."

"Right," said Don. He pushed back a chair and sat down at the table. "They'll give an accurate description of you. The police will find out soon that many people have seen the hobo with his felted hair and disheveled beard. There is even a big chance that someone remembers that the name of the hobo is Don Adler. The only man who can put in a good word for you after you get arrested is me. For I can tell them that I saw it all and that you acted in self-defense. It will not help you very much. It will be my word against that of those five men. You can bet on it that they'll all tell the same story. They've already talked that through together. Your warden will be proved right. Men like you always come back to jail, all their long lives. You're doomed to wait till death comes to take you away like you yourself said yesterday. Well, Don, I think you would prefer to spend your long days in freedom."

"That's true," said Don with a sigh.

"Very well then. I understand that you're a skillful man. Someone who can work with his hands. You even intended to build yourself a house."

"That's true as well."

"Have you ever worked with metal? Can you, for instance, weld, and can you work with an oxyacetylene torch?"

"I guess so. I worked for half a year for a metal trader. Everything had to get sorted. Big pieces of apparatus had to get pulled together. We had to use both welders and oxyacetylene torches to do it. What is it you want from me, Shrimp?"

"I can see to it that you go into hiding. You're going to work for me. In isolation for a few years on end. After the work is done, no one will be searching for you anymore. Or, in the worst case, we'll know who you should avoid. If the police are still interested in you I will see to it that you leave the country unseen., on a ship, via the Gulf of Mexico. I'll pay you generously for your work. Your money will be put in the bank. It will be a fair return for your time. And I hope that you will come to terms with yourself during all that time."

"Sounds interesting. What kind of work is it?" "I'll explain that to you later after you've had breakfast."

Shrimp had made eggs with bacon and put them on a plate. He shoved the plate over the tabletop towards Don. "The toast is also ready. Think it over while you eat."

"What should I think over?"

"What you would like to eat next."

Early that afternoon they left the house via a back door. Don was wearing working coveralls, that he had found in the big garage; none of the other clothes of the short Shrimp fit him. He wore clean socks and his own old, dirty, worn-out shoes. In his left hand, he held a bottle of cola, in his right hand a plastic bag with seven thick filled rolls.

At the end of the garden was a metal porch. Shrimp pushed a few buttons of the electronic lock to open it. A narrow path wound between high weeds and bushes. There was a sickly smell in the hot, windless atmosphere, which soon changed into the stench of decay.

"Where are you taking me to?" asked Don. "This ground is my property," answered Shrimp. "I have named it Lost Harbor. The air is very damp here. Once there were different lakes here and a little tributary river with a harbor. The harbor was not at the mouth of the river, but a few miles inland. No one had ever succeeded in making a profitable yacht basin out of it. Too few people were living here. The tourists had hardly discovered this region. As you might have noticed yesterday, Nacre Cove is the nearest village. It's still rather quiet there. Someone started a breakers' yard here, at the harbor. Whether the old ships came here under their own power or got towed, it was their final voyage. The breaker's yard wasn't profitable either. For two years there was not enough water to feed the tributary and the bed ran dry. Vegetation overgrew the bottom of the river, and the little lakes changed into marshes. The branch of the river got blocked by a dam, a hundred miles further up. Now it's partly marsh and partly forest here. There's no water anymore in the harbor, as you will see for yourself in a little while. At the seaside, everything has run wild, too. It's a nature reserve there now, and it's really beautiful.

"Between that terrain and my ground is a spring, which has been running for thousands of years. It has formed a little lake and the superfluous water streams to the bay where once the river flowed into the Gulf of Mexico. From that spring we will pump water into the harbor. There are tubes and there are pumps and engines. There is more than enough oil in the tanks in the storage depots to keep the engines running. That way we will be able to fill the harbor again."

"Why should we do that?"

"I'll explain that to you later. You know, Don, you're absolutely safe here. The terrain is set off with fences and barbed wire. This is the perfect place to go into hiding. And that's what you want, isn't it? Or do you think differently about it now?"

The two men stopped. The sweat was running down their faces. Don held the cola bottle under his armpit and tapped a finger on his forehead.

"Hell is right here in my head, Shrimp. Outside here is a cool paradise compared to what is burning in my brain. I'll work for you. It doesn't matter what I have to do. You can count on me. I want to work and forget and hope that the outside world will forget about me, and the things I did as well."

"Then we agree. And we'll agree even more after I've told you how much you're going to earn."

Shrimp started walking again.

Don followed him and started to eat the rolls.

The winding path led to a road paved in big cobblestones and overgrown with weeds. At the end of the road stood a clump of high trees. They stood there in the shadow under the thick foliage and looked down on a square terrain that once had been the breaker's yard, with an old quay and the dried-up harbor behind it. There were sheds and barracks. Parts of ships and components of engines lay around everywhere. Rusty ships lay higgledy-piggledy about the bed of the harbor.

"The harbor isn't very deep, as you can see," said Shrimp. "It had never been suitable for big oceangoing vessels. For the breaker's yard it was widened and deepened, and they braced the quay. Then it was possible to tow in coasters of more than two hundred feet long and break them up here. Look: the coasters in the harbor there have survived—they're all old and rusty, but they're still able to float."

Don looked at him in surprise.

"Is that your intention? Do you want to sail these old ships? Is that the reason why you want to fill the harbor with water? And do you want to make the river navigable again? You don't have the right to do that in a nature reserve..."

"No, no. Of course not. I've been talking about floating, not about sailing. Besides, the engines have already been taken out. The river will never come back. You're absolutely right, I am not allowed to change a thing in the nature reserve. All I need is water, and we will pump it from the spring, which is as good as mine as a part of the reserve—and no one will notice it."

They sat down, with their backs against the trunk of a huge tree.

"Six ships are still in good shape, where the hull is concerned. The others are worthless. The first thing you'll have to do is make the outside of the six ships rustproof, paint them and tar them. And then you must pump enough water into the harbor to let the ships float again. We must put the ships in a row, next to each other. As deep as possible in the marshy ground." "How would I do a thing like that? That seems impossible to me."

Don took a bite from his roll and shook his head.

"I hope you have enough talent to improvise; and persevere, just like me. This is one of the things I'm going to help you with. In one of the docks over there, I'm keeping a little tugboat, which was originally owned by the breaker. I've been assured that it still works very well. Together we'll get that engine running again. Have you ever steered a ship yourself, a yacht perhaps?"

"Yes." Don fell abruptly silent. Only after half a minute had gone by did he continue. "Together with Angelica. When her father was still alive, he had a boat and he often went out fishing. He taught me how to steer it. It came easily to me. Sometimes Angelica and I went out sailing together. We moored in nice, little harbors. What a beautiful time that was."

A silence followed, which Shrimp didn't dare to break. Finally, it was Don again who started to talk.

"Six ships in a row. What's that supposed to be? Do you want to make something special with it?"

A smile passed over Shrimp's face.

"You've said it very well. Something special."

He jumped to his feet.

"Come, let's go and take a look in the different buildings. Then you'll see that there's a lot of useful tools present. Once the ships lie next to each other, the real work will start for you. But you'll have a good bed to sleep in. There's a canteen with a kitchen, fridge, and freezer. Everything is a bit old, but it all still works fine."

"Just like that tug."

"Exactly, just like the tug."

They walked along the quay and through the sheds for half an hour. Then they entered a wooden office, where they stayed for more than three hours. When they finally stepped outside again, there was a satisfied smile on Shrimp's face, while Don looked ahead, with a determined look on his face. Walking side by side they made their way back.

"I just can't wait to get cracking," said Don. "That's the spirit," said Shrimp. "You're the man I've been looking for all this time. And just when I thought I'd never find you, you stepped inside my car... " * Filling the harbor with water was a time-consuming affair.

"Like filling a swimming pool with a trickling faucet," thought Shrimp impatiently, after he had come to take another look.

Don shrugged his shoulders indifferently and continued to work from the early morning until the late evening. First, he had reconditioned the hulls of the coasters and made them rustproof, painted, and tarred them exactly as Shrimp had instructed him. Then he had gone to see how he could close the mouth of the harbor. There were wooden lock doors, which could slide out from double concrete walls on the outer quay. It cost him many days of effort to set the old mechanism in motion. He didn't believe that the old lock doors could withstand the pressure of the water, as there was no river water on the other side to give sufficient counterpressure. Therefore, he made use of supporting beams and made a huge mountain of stones and soil.

Next, he built a system of tubes from the spring up to the harbor, which he connected to the electric pumps, which in turn were driven by thumping, smoking engines.

The water spurted inside. First, it all disappeared into the thirsty earth. After the ground had saturated, pools began to form. Don got up several times a night to keep the engines running.

In the meantime, the supply of materials and tools were delivered as agreed upon, at the big house whenever Shrimp was at home. He put everything at the gate at the back of the garden; when he went to look there the next day, he could see that Don had been there to take it all away. Don made use of a little tractor with a trailer, with which he could maneuver easily over the narrow, winding path.

Countless trucks found their way to the white house. They came from all parts of Florida, Mississippi, Alabama, and Georgia. Making use of as many suppliers as possible, Shrimp tried to ensure that no one started to ask what he was going to do with all that stuff.

Don Adler slept in a good bed and had more than enough food in store. During the day he only drank coffee and mineral water, and at night he had two or three bottles of beer. He had no television and only listened to the radio. The news didn't interest him, he only listened to music, that often lulled him asleep in his easy chair. The radio was built into a little red helmet, and the speakers slid over his ears when he put it on. It became his favorite way to relax.

The water level in the harbor was gradually rising. The old coasters began to lift up. Soon, stripped of their upper structure and contents, they floated on the clear water from the spring. Other wrecks were so broken that they remained lying on the bottom or came up a bit and then sank again.

Shrimp and Don managed to get the engine of the tug going. Dirty black clouds of smoke came from the funnel and went up in the windless heat. Shrimp could only hope that it wouldn't draw attention. "Let's get cracking!" said Shrimp.

After they had towed the first two coasters to the center of the harbor and tied them together with thick ropes, they managed to bring the other four ships there. The tug was brought back to the dock, and after the engine was stopped, the funnel let its final cloud of smoke escape with a short gasp.

Shrimp went back home.

When he came back a week later to take a look, there were only a few pools left on the bottom of the harbor, and the six coasters had sunk deep down into the mud. The tug hung down from steel cables in the dock. Shrimp had spectacular plans for it.

"Good work, Don."

"I used a crane to take away a few metal partitions," said Don. "The water streamed away quickly. The ships lie perfectly there. They will not move an inch."

"Then the most important work is done. From now on I'll come to visit you less frequently. You know what you have to do next."

"I don't need help any longer."

"Every time I come I'll bring foods and drinks with me, especially fresh vegetables, fruits, and meat. Thanks for everything, Don."

They went to the canteen together and drank a couple of beers. Shrimp never asked personal questions, and Don always acted detached. When they talked, they never used many words, and more than often they were silent. Finally, Shrimp left again, and Don got to work.

Lost Harbor had become his home. He sweated out his sorrow in the daily heat, and at night he fell fast asleep. He began to like working with oxyacetylene torches and welders more and more. He thought that Shrimp had given him a perfect job, and he did his utmost to bring it to a good end. Often he thought of Angelica, but he didn't believe that he still loved her.

I'll be a rich man when the work is done, he often said to himself. I'll ask Shrimp to sell me a little piece of ground. He has enough. Then I'll build myself the house I always wanted to have. One day, when Shrimp had come to visit, and they sat down on the quay together watching the coasters, he brought it up. Shrimp's reaction came promptly. "I don't sell any ground. But I do give it away. To good friends like you. I know a perfect place where old oaks grow. When you finally live there, Don, in your own house, you'll find out how easy it is to find you a woman who'll make you forget about Angelica. Shall we drink to that?"

"We'll drink to that," said Don. "If you only knew how grateful I am!"

They drank and fell silent. Don never asked questions about what Shrimp did in everyday life, how he had gathered his capital. He knew by instinct that he shouldn't discuss personal affairs with Shrimp. And Shrimp, in his turn, thought that he already knew more than enough about Don and never bothered him with questions about his past; mentioning Angelica this time had been an exception.

Time passed by.

No one on the outside world seemed to miss Don Adler.

6

Florida, Forty Years Ago

Susanne Martens took off her white apron with black stars and hung it on a hook in a corner of her office. She washed her hands with green soap and looked at herself in the mirror above the washbasin.

"Where did your smile go?" she asked in a soft voice.

The corners of her mouth sank, and she answered her own question. "I lost it. Somewhere on my way through this life, and now it is untraceable."

After she had dried her hands, she sat down on the chair where her last patient had sat a little while ago.

Susanne was no real doctor. Outside Franks Knight, she had no authority at all, and one would undoubtedly call her a quack.

But here she was respected and especially reliable. Nothing could be worse for a patient than when Susanne knew no remedy, for then there was a big chance that they had to ask for an ambulance to bring the sick person to a strange town somewhere far away.

She was aware of the fact that the inhabitants of Franks Knight were unworldly people.

She herself always stared her eyes out when she had a chance to leave the town. A few times she had been able to take a short trip with her husband Patrick, and they both had felt like astronauts visiting another planet. Everything seemed strange to them, everything was so different—and at the same time it all was exciting, interesting, and inviting.

For her and Patrick the laws and rules of Franks Knight were less hard and strict than for most of the other inhabitants. She was indispensable and could count herself among the notables. Patrick was one of the few who was also known outside the little town. Being a man of genius, he took care of an important source of income. Patrick was a clockmaker. He built clocks of metal and wood. They were all impressive works of art, which sold to outsiders for a lot of money.

Susanne shook her head slowly. She leaned with a hand on the armrest of the chair when she stood up again. She pressed her other hand on her side, and for a moment her face twitched with pain when she straightened her back. The pinched expression on her face made her look older than she actually was. She had put on weight during the last months.

She went down a narrow corridor and stepped into Patrick's workshop.

It was full there—every bit of space got used—but there was no chaos. His tools hung on the wall behind him, all kinds of components were stored in wooden boxes on shelves at the opposite wall. Patrick sat down on a chair that was provided with four little wheels so that he was able to move easily around a big table on which all kinds of equipment was set up—big and little vices, drills, a milling, a saw, a grinding machine. There were clocks in different stages of completion and beautiful decorated oak panels.

Susanne had obtained all of her knowledge from former generations, and Patrick had been taught by elder clockmakers.

Susanne sat down on a wooden stool opposite him.

"How was your day?" he asked, without looking up from his work. He stared with one eye through a magnifying glass, behind which he finished off a little cogwheel with a file.

"Believe me, it was worse for me than yesterday," she said. "What about yesterday? You didn't tell me about that." "No. I didn't find that necessary. Because it's always the same. A body of curious tourists had parked their cars on Main Street. They stepped out and asked the first passerby they met where they could find a bar. It was Joe Pendelton from the grocery, and he answered, of course, that we don't have a bar here in Franks Knight. Then they said that we were all stark raving mad and that they had been so wise to bring along their own drinks. They got bottles of liquor from their car and passed them out to each other while they walked through the street. They went through the park behind Main Street and reached the mausoleum of Manuel Raso. They sneered at it, but we're used to that."

Patrick nodded yes. "We're used to that," he repeated. "That's right."

"Someone stepped over the cast-iron fence and opened his trousers. He was intending to make water against the mausoleum. Joe Pendelton hadn't trusted them from the moment they addressed him and had followed them, together with some others. Words passed between them. Soon the first blows were struck. I had to stitch a wound on Joe's left cheek. Someone had waved a knife around. Someone else got a front tooth kicked out of his mouth—Carlos Manzanera the horse breeder. Three of the tourists had scratches and bruises. I helped them, too. All three of them were drunk. I just did my job, no more, no less. But today...Patrick, I feel so guilty. I'm fed up with having to examine over and over again if one of the women is pregnant or not."

Patrick looked at her from above the magnifying glass now.

"We all know the law, don't we?" "No kids." "Everyone has to obey." "Yes." "Is someone pregnant?" "No, fortunately not." The doorbell rang. Patrick's workshop was in the front of the house. He stood up and opened the door. Wesley Dunn the Raso Preacher stepped inside. He was a young man of only thirty-five years of age, but he was the undisputed leader in Franks Knight, and his will was law. He had returned his people to the strict observance of Raso's commands, and his bunch of heavies was notorious. No one dared to leave Franks Knight without his permission.

The exit routes were watched day and night. Cowardly fugitives were heavily punished.

"We'll wait for the end of times together," Wesley Dunn always said. "And then we'll survive together. We only— inhabitants of Franks Knight."

Patrick greeted him and then walked back to his place at the table again, where he picked up the little file and the cogwheel again.

Wesley came down to business right away.

"The community needs money, Patrick. And you're rather late with your new clocks. Customers are waiting, and they are eager to pay."

Patrick nodded and said nothing. Wesley turned to Susanne.

"He hasn't been ill, has he?"

"Of course not. You know that as well as I, for you come to visit us a couple of times each week. He does his utmost, he works hard. The clocks will soon be ready."

Wesley took off his gold-colored coat with the big black stars. He was making it clear that he wasn't planning to leave soon.

"I do understand, Patrick," he said. "You're going to surpass yourself. This will become one of your masterpieces."

He made a gesture at the beautiful mechanism of the new clock, next to which the oak panels that would form the case lay ready. The clockwork was intricate. On the face stood a magician of inlaid copper, wearing a long coat covered with stars, making invoking gestures; it was Raso. Golden stars danced all around him. The clock could show the minutes, hours, days, and the position of the moon. The wood carving on the panels showed a fleeing crowd. Men, women, and children climbing up along the edges. On top of the front panel—in which a round hole had been cut for the face—stood another image of Raso. This time it was a small silver statue with golden stars on its jacket. The tiny figure held a sharp scythe in its hands with which it threatened to hurt any fugitive who came too close. Driven by an ingenious mechanism, the silver Raso would turn around every hour, and his scythe would sway closely over the heads of the climbing figures below.

"This is the last one," said Patrick now. "The others are ready. I will deliver the clocks personally to the customers so that I will be able to place them and adjust them myself. I don't have to travel far for that-all the customers live in the neighborhood. As soon as I'm back again, you'll get the money."

"Of course," said Raso "a bodyguard will come along with you, and we'll send for a van with a driver from the outside."

"No bodyguard," said Patrick. "He would only get bored stiff. I'll arrange the van myself. By the way, Susanne will join me."

Wesley raised his eyebrows.

"Why's that?" "She needs different herbs and all kinds of other things only she knows about."

Wesley looked at Susanne and noticed that her face had become red. She was perspiring and it looked as if she was in pain.

"What's the matter, Susanne?" he asked.

"I'm tired," she said. "Patrick is right, I have to stock up on a few things. I'm running short of different medicines. There have been quite some fights with outsiders lately. I'm running low on sedatives, I need bandages, antiseptics—you name it. My supplies of potions and pills dwindle by the day."

"I understand," said Wesley. "It's a pity that I'm not allowed to bring in my men against curious strangers. As soon as we start to defend ourselves with a well-aimed shotgun, the police cars enter Franks Knight with wailing sirens. Very well then, Patrick, arrange it all yourself—and take good care of your money."

"Don't worry about a thing," muttered Patrick. "I know how to take care of my own business."

Wesley folded his hands on the tabletop and asked Susanne and Patrick to do the same. All three of them closed their eyes.

"Manuel Raso," said Wesley, "we're thinking about you all the time, and we are grateful to you. For you have shown us the way. Now we prepare for the worst. Soon we'll be the only survivors in a destroyed world. We'll wait for the stranger who'll show up to save us, as you have predicted. We have fulfilled all the conditions. We're the last ones, there are no children. Give us the strength, later, to rebuild the world with our bare hands."

Susanne moaned, and Wesley looked up, annoyed. Then he closed his eyes again and continued:

"I'm in charge here, Raso, out of my own free will. I keep the people of Franks Knight together. We'll welcome the stranger and allow him to lead us. In the meantime we'll make our daily bow in front of your mausoleum, to greet you and to thank you. Manuel Raso, we'll never forget you. We'll live, thanks to your heavenly vision." "We'll live, thanks to your heavenly vision," repeated Susanne and Patrick.

Wesley stood up and put on his long coat again.

"You're good citizens. Finish your work, Patrick. And you, Susanne, should try to take it easy. I wish you a pleasant trip. Come back safe to Franks Knight."

Patrick saw him to the door. Wesley stepped outside. Patrick closed the door again and turned around. He saw Susanne standing at the table, her face twisted with pain. Tears were running down her cheeks.

"Susanne! What's the matter?" "I'm so sorry!" she moaned. "What's the matter?" he repeated. "The baby's coming too soon," she said. "Too soon? When?" "Now. Right now. You've got to help me... "

☽☽☽

Patrick had gone to the mausoleum in the park to make a bow. After that, he had walked to Joe Pendelton's grocery on Main Street. Joe stood behind the counter. The stitched wound on his left cheek formed a long, red stripe that went up a bit when he smiled.

"Patrick. The end of times is near. Did Susanne tell you wild stories about me, and are you come to see for yourself how bad it is with my injuries?"

"The end of times is near," said Patrick. "The more scars, the more important the hero. No, no, I come to make use of the telephone."

Joe gestured at the telephone, which stood on a corner of the counter.

"Go ahead."

Patrick produced a piece of paper, unfolded it, and read the phone number he had written on it as he pushed the buttons. He called Hamlett's Garage and asked for Nicholas Rhodes.

"I'll see if the old man's here somewhere," was the reaction at the other side of the line. The next moment the same voice sounded, muffled, probably because a hand covered the microphone. "Nick! Here's one of these crazy friends without a driver's license for you on the phone!"

Patrick made an appointment with Nicholas.

"No problem. I can be with you within half an hour."

Twenty-five minutes later Patrick was back home again, and Nicholas stopped a little black van in front of the door. Two of Wesley's bunch of heavies, armed with clubs, passed by and remained standing curiously near the van.

"Better help us instead of standing there looking on," said Patrick.

With combined efforts, the four men put the new clocks into the van. In the meantime Susanne had stepped outside, holding a reed basket in her hands. The basket was covered with a little blanket. She got into the van quickly and sat down on the back seat. She rocked the basket softly to and fro and hoped in silence that the baby wouldn't start crying. Nicholas slid behind the wheel. Patrick got in. The doors closed, the engine started.

Nicholas had worked for many hours as the first mechanic in Hamlett's Garage, and now, at seventy, he still went there every day. When the weather was good he preferred to be outside, on the lot where the secondhand cars stood. Anyone who wanted to buy an old car for a couple hundred dollars and drive away with it immediately could count on his help. He saw to it that the battery was charged and did whatever was needed to get the engine going. He was one of the few outsiders who had managed to make friends with the inhabitants of Franks Knight. He enjoyed driving the unworldly people around and having a talk with them. He did not condemn their peculiar way of living. He was curious about their habits and the food they gave him on the way—special pies, tasty cookies, and spicy tidbits.

Thinking he knew all about the people from Franks Knight by now, he looked with surprise into the rear-view mirror when he heard a baby cry.

"What's this?" he asked. "I really was convinced that you were not allowed to have children—I mean, how?"

"Nicholas," said Patrick, "we've known each other for a long time now. We're in trouble. Please help us!"

))))

It was early the next morning, a Saturday, and Nicholas Rhodes found himself alone on the lot for secondhand cars next to the buildings of Hamlett's Garage. The garage itself was still closed. Nicholas had just put a heavy battery into an old Ford and wiped the sweat from his brow with the back of his hand. All of a sudden he was caught by strong hands. The left back door of the Ford opened, and he was pushed onto the back seat. While he sat up straight in fright, someone shoved in next to him.

"Nicholas. You know who I am, don't you?"

Nicholas had never seen him dressed otherwise than in a long coat with big stars, but he immediately recognized the man who was now wearing black trousers and a black sweater.

"Wesley Dunn, the Raso Preacher."

"Exactly. And I'm not alone. If you look outside for a moment, you'll see two men standing there. You know us so well that I'm sure you've heard of Wesley Dunn's bunch of heavies. These two are my best-trained men. They'll go through hell for me. One word from me, and they'll kill you."

"Please," begged the old man, "don't hurt me."

"That depends on you. I'm going to ask you a couple of questions, and I expect honest answers. It's as simple as that. Do you understand?"

"Please—"

Wesley gestured at one of the men. The side window on Nicholas's side was smashed to pieces with a club. The splintered glass sprayed Nicholas in the face and fell onto his lap.

"The next blow will land exactly here," said Wesley. He placed a finger on the bald forehead of the old man. "Listen to me. You've been back for quite some time already now. We saw the black van. You parked it here and got out. You were alone, and you stepped into your own old Buick to drive home. Patrick Martens delivered some expensive clocks. He took his wife Susanne with him. Why haven't they come back with you?"

The old man was scared to death. He knew he would pay with his life if he lied. Therefore he spoke the truth.

"Maybe they'll come back to Franks Knight soon. They just don't know what to do, they have their doubts."

"Don't speak in riddles. They have their doubts about what? Is it about the money?"

"Partly. They can use it, of course."

"My patience is at an end."

"Patrick and Susanne have broken an important Franks Knight law."

Wesley beckoned the man who stood on the other side of the broken window. The man raised his club.

"No!" the old man cried out. "No! I'll tell you. Susanne has given birth to a son."

Wesley Dunn's mouth fell open.

"O, Raso. Great Raso!" he muttered. "A child! This is a disaster. This should never have happened. Are you sure?"

"Yes."

"Have you seen the child yourself?"

"Yes."

Wesley tried to think.

"Susanne examined all the women. But who examined Susanne?" he asked himself aloud. He punched his left fist into the palm of his right hand. "She's never been thin, how were we supposed to know?... She was in pain. I've seen that myself. O, mighty Tacendo, god of the Xi, what can we do?" He addressed Nicholas. "Tell me exactly what happened from the moment you left Franks Knight in the black van."

Nicholas started to describe the ride; they had dined in a restaurant and slept in a motel that night. The next day they had delivered the last clocks. Then it was time to go back home, but Patrick and Susanne had other plans.

"They wanted to have time to think."

"All you have to tell me now is where I can find them."

Nicholas heaved a sigh. Then he said, "The Spring Tide Motel, not far away from here—five minutes by car."

"I know where to find it. We'll walk. Don't you tell anyone that I have come. Is that clear?"

"Yes, yes, of course. That's clear."

"What's the room number?"

"Thirty-eight."

Wesley opened the door and stepped out.

"If you keep your mouth shut, you'll live longer. Sorry about that broken window. See you, Nicholas Rhodes."

Nicholas realized that he had betrayed Patrick and Susanne. He turned his head and looked through the rear window.

Wesley and his men left the lot. Once outside the gate, they started to run.

Nicholas immediately went into action. He got out of the car and hurried to Hamlett's Garage. A moment later he was standing in front of a side door, shivering with emotion, searching his pockets for his bunch of keys. He always had the keys to the garage with him. Once inside he went straight up to the little office he had used in former days as a mechanic to note down the hours he had worked on repairs and which components he had used.

He could probably do something for Patrick and Susanne to make up for his betrayal. Wesley Dunn lived in another world. He knew of only one telephone in Franks Knight—on the counter of Joe Pendelton's grocery—and he had never seen anyone using it when he was in the store. It probably hadn't occurred to Wesley that Nicholas might call the motel. Nicholas knew the owner of the Spring Tide Motel very well. Almost every week he had a drink together with Sammy Corbetta. He knew the number by heart and pushed the buttons nervously.

"The Spring Tide Motel. How can I help you?" "Sammy, it's me, Nicholas. Now listen carefully. You've to do something for me, and you have to do it fast! Tell Patrick and Susanne Martens to get out of there right now.

Someone's on his way to them, and I know they don't want to meet him at all. This is important, you hear? Did you understand what I said?"

Sammy Corbetta reacted calmly.

"Understood, my friend. It's all right. Tell me later why I had to do this—when you buy me a drink!"

"Thanks," muttered Nicholas.

He sat down. His heart bounced inside his chest like a rubber ball. Although it was still early in the morning, he longed for that drink together with Sammy.

☽☽☽

Patrick and Susanne were aware of the fact that they attracted attention in their peculiar clothes. Patrick wore a flannel suit whose black jacket was covered with big white stars, while the white trousers showed black stars. Susanne wore a long, wide dress—vivid green with orange stars. Everyone who saw them would know immediately they were from Franks Knight.

Koos Verkaik

When they left the Spring Tide Motel, they started out walking on the shadow side of the road, and soon they found a path that led to an oak wood. Patrick carried the reed basket with the baby.

"Where are we going to?" asked Susanne.

"I don't know. As far as possible from the motel. I know the way here no more than you."

"Are you sorry?"

"About what?"

"The child."

"I don't regret a thing."

"Me either, but does our son have a chance? I mean, when the world comes to an end...We've never really discussed it—simply accepted things as they seemed to be. Do you really believe in the crack of doom?" "If I only knew," said Patrick. "If I only knew..."

☽☽☽

Wesley Dunn and his two helpers realized that they had arrived too late. Sammy Corbetta told them, with a stony-faced that Patrick and Susanne Martens had left early that morning for an unknown destination.

"People come, and people go. Do you really think that I know where everyone comes from or where he's going to?" Wesley left Corbetta's office.

Outside, he saw a car parked in front of one of the motel rooms. A man, presumably a traveling salesman who had done business on Friday and was leaving today, lifted two heavy bags into the trunk.

"Good morning," said Wesley. "Can I ask you something?"

"Of course," said the man. He straightened his back and produced a professional smile.

"Have you seen a man and a woman leave a while ago? They were probably showily dressed."

"Did they look like clowns? Clowns, without their makeup?"

"That's one way to put it."

"I stood here staring at them for quite some time. I've spent the night in a hundred different motels, but I never saw guests before who left without luggage and didn't even have a car. They went walking. I think the man carried a child. A baby..."

"Where did they go?"

"First they walked along the road here, at the right side. Look, do you see the edge of the wood there? They turned to the right there. Not far from that electricity pole. Two clowns disappearing into the wood. And you? Are you a circus director forcing your runaway artists to come back?"

He had to laugh about his own remark, until he noticed the two men who accompanied Wesley, both holding a club in their hands. He was a traveling salesman indeed, and he had learned to mind his own business. He wished Wesley luck and hastily got into his car.

Wesley and his men walked down the road in the direction of the electricity pole. In the little wood, Patrick and Susanne

Martens didn't know where they were. Soon Wesley Dunn and his men didn't know where they were.

Everything outside Franks Knight was strange.

They turned into different paths, and it was a downright miracle that Patrick, looking back at a certain moment, saw three darkly dressed men approaching at walking pace.

"It's Wesley Dunn," he warned Susanne. "We've got to hurry up!"

Fleeing in a strange neighborhood came down to changing directions at random. They started to run until Susanne gasped that she was willing to give up.

"I'm too tired. Our son is hungry. Besides, he needs rest."

"Keep going," Patrick urged. He put a hand on her shoulder and pushed her forward. "There must be a way to escape from them."

Dunn kept on chasing them. The distance between them grew smaller and smaller.

"You go along by yourself," panted Susanne. "Take the child with you. I'm exhausted. Such a short time after the delivery I'm just not able to exert myself this much."

Patrick wouldn't hear of it. He assessed his chances. Wesley Dunn and his men were closing in on him. If it should come to a confrontation, he could never win.

"Come!" he said.

Putting down the reed basket and taking the baby out of it, he stepped off the path and slipped between the trees. Susanne followed puffing and stumbling. After a while, he told her that they could slow down now because he didn't suspect Wesley would follow them here.

"He'll probably stay on the roads and paths. He'll get lost, just like we did. We all find ourselves in the unknown."

Unexpectedly they reached a road again, and after they had followed it down for a couple of minutes, they saw houses. To his great surprise, Patrick recognized one of them.

"Look! I delivered my most beautiful clock here, remember?"

He touched the gate. It was not locked. They followed the broad drive and walked up to the big house. Patrick pulled the bell. Behind the door, far away, he could hear it ring.

Susanne looked back in fright.

"Please, let Wesley stay away. What are you up to?" "I have no idea. Maybe they'll allow us to hide here and..."

The door opened.

"Mr. Martens. What a surprise. Miss your clock?"

A thick-set man smiled at him in a friendly fashion and then looked at the baby that Patrick held in his arms and the woman who was standing next to him—Susanne and the baby had stayed in the van with Nicholas Rhodes when Patrick had delivered the clock earlier.

"You're all sweaty. Come inside, please, come inside."

He pushed the door open wide and made an inviting gesture. Patrick and Susanne came in and heaved a sigh of relief when the man closed the door behind them.

Not much later they sat down in the big living room, where the clock stood on a walnut sideboard. The silver Raso with the golden stars on his coat stood ready to swing around his scythe as soon as another hour had passed by.

"Is your wife home?" asked Patrick. "I have something on my chest, and I would appreciate it if she were here as well. I have just made an important decision."

He looked at Susanne.

"I can only hope that you'll agree," he said.

Susanne, who had taken the baby from him and rocked it in her arms, looked at him questioningly.

The next morning a big gray Cadillac stopped in front of the house of Patrick and Susanne in Franks Knight. Patrick and Susanne stepped out and waved as the Cadillac drove away again.

They didn't have the baby with them. Patrick took a key from his pocket and opened the door. He stepped into his workshop, and then he stopped abruptly.

Wesley Dunn was sitting on a chair, with his feet on the tabletop, between tools and cogwheels.

"What're you doing in our house?" Patrick cried out after he had pulled himself together.

Susanne bumped up against him, grabbed his arm, and then came standing next to him. The door slammed shut. Other men were around the workshop. Patrick recognized them. They were members of the council committee, identifiable by their golden clothes with black stars. Wesley wore red with purple stars. His long coat gave him a stately, almost royal appearance. He looked grim; his mouth was a little, horizontal line. No one spoke a word. Patrick took a leather case from his inside pocket, opened it, and took out a wad of banknotes.

"Look what the clocks brought in. We only bought ourselves something to eat, paid

Nicholas Rhodes, and spent the night in the Spring Tide Motel." As if he had drawn courage by hearing his own voice in his own workshop, he repeated his earlier remark. "What're you doing in our house, Wesley? I cannot tolerate this. Susanne and I are tired, all we want now is to take a rest."

Wesley raised his eyebrows slowly.

"Your house? That remains to be seen. I think that you've lost all your rights, but I'm not allowed to judge that all by myself. The entire population of Franks Knight will decide on your fate in a meeting."

"But—" uttered Susanne.

Wesley sat up and banged the table with both fists.

"I don't want to hear your voice at all, Susanne Martens!" he shouted. "You've broken the laws, you haven't thought about our lot, you have denied Raso, the great Raso! Now sit down, the both of you!"

As soon as they had taken a seat opposite to him he looked at Susanne and said, "We've been sitting together here for quite some time, and yesterday we were here as well. Grace Walker joined us there."

Susanne bit on her lower lip. Grace Walker had been educated by her and would succeed her, just as all wisdom where medical affairs were concerned had been passed on to herself.

"You cleaned your doctor's office thoroughly, but not good enough for the eyes of Grace. You've given birth to a child there. Only your husband was with you. You acted against all the rules, and maybe you've put a curse on us that will ruin us all. Maybe we're no longer Manuel Raso's chosen ones now! You could claim that Grace is wrong, but then there's another witness, someone who actually saw the child. Nicholas Rhodes."

Susanne decided to keep silent. Wesley banged the table again.

"Where's the child now? Tell me. I want to know!"

"Stop it!" said Patrick. "No one talks to my wife this way, and you must realize that you're still sitting here in my workshop! Now pick up the money and leave, and take the men on the council committee with you. There's nothing the matter. I want to have a rest, and then I want to go on doing what I can do the best—make new clocks."

"You liar!" said Wesley. "Do you think that you stand above the law? I would climb down if I were you. You've violated the trust of all others. Susanne was a woman of distinction, and she lived according to the rules of Raso. She examined all women.

And now she's the one to give birth to a child! You have kept the pregnancy a secret. Will Franks Knight be destroyed as well now, when the final day has come?"

Patrick bowed his head.

Susanne started to sob softly.

Wesley said, "Guards will be placed at the front door and at the back door. You are not allowed to leave this house. Even a short walk to bring a salute to the mausoleum is forbidden."

"Please—" moaned Susanne.

"Your tears come too late. We're leaving you now—I'll hold a conclave with the council committee. Then we'll have to inform the people. Arrange a meeting. Pass judgment. I'll come and knock on your door personally when the time has come for you to appear in front of the full population of Franks Knight. Together we'll assess the upcoming disasters and determine an appropriate punishment for the offenders of Raso's laws."

Wesley pushed his chair backward and stood up. Without speaking another word he walked to the door. The council committee, of whom no one had spoken a word, followed him.

Patrick and Susanne stayed behind in the workshop, prisoners in their own house.

"Was it a good idea to come back, Patrick?" she asked.

His shoulders went up, the corners of his mouth went down.

"I don't know. We have nothing to do in the big world outside Franks Knight. We simply couldn't settle down there, but for the child it's different. Our way of thinking is totally influenced by Raso. A newborn has no load to carry and can develop on all possible sides."

"Develop," said Susanne, after which she burst into tears. And then, "Development needs time. And there is no time. For nobody, not even for our son. What have we done? He has no chance, the entire world population has no chance. If he had stayed here with us if we had decided to keep him..."

Patrick waited until she had managed to control herself again.

"Now listen to me," he said. "We both wanted the child to be born. That has been our most important goal. We never had any further plans. We tried to flee, knowing full well that the big world could never become our home. Someone like Dunn would keep on looking for us, forever. When we stood there in front of the house of the man who bought the clock, I finally made a decision. Our boy would stay there if he was welcome. And we would go back to the little town where we were born, to our home, to the place where we belong. Now our destiny is in the hands of all the people we know so well. I hope for their understanding. Just as I hope that the end of times is not nearby and that our son will grow up and become a man who has adapted himself to the miraculous life in the big world." He took her hand, kissed her on the cheek, and continued. "Yes, try to imagine—imagine that they will not judge us too harshly and that there will be no world disaster. Sooner or later no one will even remember that we have a son. If I go out then, to sell my new clocks, I'll visit our son. I will do that more often, of course, until I'm too old to leave Franks Knight... "

"Will you take me with you?"

"But of course!" he cried out, glad that she seemed to feel a bit relieved now. "Just wait and see. I'll take you with me as often as possible. Listen, together we're strong. We'll wait here bravely until we hear that knock on our door, and we will follow Wesley Dunn to the big meeting with our heads held high."

He tried to look her in the eyes, but she turned her head away.

In the silence that followed Susanne started to worry again. During her pregnancy, she had thought, lived, and worked like a follower of Raso, as the human being she had become within the city limits of Franks Knight. Now her motherly love fought for a wide space in her mind. She shouldn't have left her child behind. She wanted to have her son with her, cherish, protect, love, and raise him. Now she was on the verge of panic, especially when she imagined how she would run outside and push Wesley Dunn's guards away. In her mind, she ran out of Franks Knight and straight up to Hamlett's Garage where she asked for Nicholas Rhodes. She would ask him to bring her to the house of the man who had bought Patrick's most beautiful clock. Nick would remember where to find the man. She actually panicked when she rose to her feet to walk up to the door and realized that it was forbidden to leave the house. Someone would stop her immediately—hard-handed, if necessary. Patrick jumped up and managed to catch her when she fell.

"Bring me to my doctor's office," she whispered. "I need some medicine. Preferably as much as possible, so that I'll fall asleep forever! Patrick! What have I done? I have left my son behind in the big world!"

"Don't you worry," responded Patrick. "Everything will turn out all right. I promise you, everything will turn out all right."

The waiting took a long time. They stayed in the workshop all the time, even at night, to be able to hear the knock on the door. They had hardly any sleep. The shutters were up so that no one was able to look inside. People passed by, hurling abuse at them.

"Traitors!" they shouted. But they didn't dare to knock on the door. "Your child's already damned! It will go down with the rest of the big world!"

Susanne was taking sedatives again and again. Patrick tried to concentrate on finishing off little cogwheels with his files.

They were surprised by the feeling of relief that arose when finally someone used the knuckles of his fist to bang on the wooden door. They rose to their feet immediately.

"Give me your hand," said Susanne, "and don't let go... "

It was early in the afternoon. The sun stood high in the sky. For quite some time they hadn't heard anyone walk past the house and hurl abuse, but now they saw, to their surprise, that the full population of Franks Knight had gathered in the street.

Everyone was wearing black clothes with orange stars, including Wesley Dunn and the men of the council committee.

Not a word was spoken. Wesley pointed to the end of the street and Patrick and Susanne started walking. A silent man came and walked in front of Patrick and Susanne, to show them the way. He went into a side street. The shutters were down everywhere. When they had passed through the park behind Main Street and neared the mausoleum of Raso, Patrick and Susanne stopped and stared out in front of them in fright. Palm trees had stood around the mausoleum for many years. They had all been cut down, except for one, and were piled up on a grass field. They couldn't tell why this shocked them so deeply. They couldn't guess the reason for it, but it scared them tremendously. Wesley pushed both of them forward, and they walked on again. They made a bow in front of the mausoleum. Everyone else did, too, and then the parade went on. When Patrick and Susanne passed the cut-down palm trees, they could see that countless nails had been hammered deep into the trunks. They looked back to the one tree that was still standing near the mausoleum. The trunk was undamaged.

Via a side street, they reached the main street, and everyone stopped in front of the city hall. Wesley walked up to the high doors, opened them, and disappeared into the hall. Not much later he appeared on the balcony on the first story, above the doors. He leaned over the stone balustrade and started to say something, but then changed his mind and pointed over the heads of the people.

Everyone looked back.

A car had stopped and a family—father, mother, and two children—had stepped out. The woman started taking pictures. Someone from city security went to tell them that they should leave. They got into the car again. The engine started, and the car went slowly backward, turned around in front of Joe Pendelton's grocery, and drove away.

Wesley Dunn let his gaze travel over the silent crowd, and then he looked at Patrick and Susanne Martens.

"We have held a meeting without you," he said, loud enough for everyone to hear. "That was easier. If you had been present as well, I would have had too few people to protect you. Even though I managed to calm everyone down, there's a slight chance that someone is willing to lynch you after all. Take a few steps forward, Patrick and Susanne Martens, so that everyone can see you."

After they had done so, he continued:

"Bow your heads, sinners! No one can tell with certainty if you have caused a disaster or not. And if so, no one can tell either if the disaster can still be averted. You have heard your fellow citizens. They shouted at you that your son will not escape from his punishment, because all that lives in the big world will die at the crack of doom. During the long meeting, I have listened to the good people of Franks Knight. Everyone had an opinion about what should be done with the both of you. I noted down different sorts of punishment. Some of them I combined, others I rejected—something I am allowed to do in the capacity of Raso Preacher. Then I gave a color to each different punishment. I gave the order to tie a ribbon of each color to each palm tree at the mausoleum. There were nine trees. Everyone got eight nails. Each one should hammer their nails—during the day, but also during the night if they preferred—into the trunk of eight trees. The trunk with the fewest nails would determine your punishment. For the nails were to be used for the punishments which, according to the ones who used them, were not considered to be the right ones for you. Allow me to explain to you why I chose this particular method. For I could also have decided that everyone should receive one nail only and hammer it into the tree of his choice—"

"Sinners!" someone cried out.

A stone was thrown from the crowd. It hit Patrick right between the shoulder blades.

"Sinners!" repeated many others.

A second stone flew through the air, came down, rolled past Susanne, and disappeared through the open door into the city hall.

"The next one who throws a stone receives a proper beating from the city security, is that clear?" shouted Wesley. "Further, I demand absolute silence!" As soon as it had become quiet again, he continued. "I wanted everyone to think well about what he wanted. A nail for every punishment which wasn't good enough. It turned out to be the perfect method. Eight trees got covered with nails. The ninth had no nail at all. I ordered the eight trees cut down. The roots of the old palms reach under the mausoleum. Raso has given us his permission, and now I want to have this horrible affair behind me as soon as possible. New times will come, and new trees will grow around the mausoleum. That's all I have to say. Your fate is fixed. No, I'm not going to inform you about the eight punishments, and I will see to it that the ninth will be executed. Patrick and Susanne Martens, turn round and make a bow to your fellow citizens who have passed judgment over you. Then follow the council committee to the city hall. This is an order."

Patrick and Susanne let go of each other's hands to turn round, but they were holding hands again already when they made their deep bow to the townspeople. Patrick's face was twisted with pain when he straightened his back. The stone had hit him hard. Then they turned and together, hand in hand, they walked up to the open doors. They stepped into the hall, followed by the council committee and some members of the city security. A rain of stones clashed against the doors right after they closed.

Inside, one could hear the voices of the angry crowd through the high windows:

"Sinners! Sinners!"

Patrick and Susanne had been in the city hall so often that they were almost able to remember every visible stone. Patrick always went there to discuss the amount of money he would need to buy material for his clocks, and Susanne, being a respected and notable citizen, had attended many a meeting there and reported on the state of public health. They expected that they would go upstairs now, to the first story, to Wesley's offices, headquarters of the Center of the Heavenly Vision and different meeting rooms.

But they went down a marble staircase instead, to the cellars of the city hall. To their surprise, they noticed that great numbers of cardboard boxes were piled up along the sides of the broad corridor. The city archives were stored in these boxes.

The steel door to the records cellar opened. Wesley made an impatient gesture with his hand. Patrick and Susanne walked inside. A cold draft made them shiver when the door closed behind them. A key turned in the lock and someone drew the bolts.

Patrick and Susanne looked around.

The filing racks, which had contained the boxes, had been taken away. All the ceiling lights were burning. The concrete floor was covered with thick carpets. There was furniture arranged throughout a couch, two easy chairs, a dining table with two chairs, cupboards, and a bed. They knew there was a bathroom as well, which normally was used by the archivist.

"Look there!" Susanne cried out. "An oven. A fridge, a freezer..."

She began to walk around and opened different cupboards.

"There's plenty of food and drinks," she said. "The fridge and the freezer are filled. What's the meaning of all this, Patrick?"

Patrick sat down in one of the easy chairs and discovered a row of books on a shelf and a painting with the portrait of Raso.

"That's not easy to say," he sighed. "Franks Knight never had a prison. You can't escape from this cellar. So they made a prison out of it. The first one. For us."

"But all these luxuries. The food, the furniture..."

Patrick pondered on it for a while.

"We're the first prisoners in the history of the town. We're shut off from the outside world. That's obviously our punishment. We don't know how long we'll have to stay here. That makes the punishment even harder. They've given us all this luxury to make our seclusion, not into a hell." He nodded. "That must be it, Susan. This room is very nice, but still, there are four concrete walls and a steel door. This is our punishment. We must have patience, a lot of patience... "

Susanne sat down as well.

"A heavy punishment it is. Every second I'll have to stay here, I'll have to think of our son—who'll remain inaccessible to us."

Wesley Dunn had appeared on the balcony again.

"Everyone who threw stones at the city hall will be punished," he said. "The city security will take care of that. Now

I ask everyone to kneel down. We'll think of Manuel Raso in absolute silence for the next ten minutes. After that, we will invoke the god Tacendo and beg him to forget about the incident with Patrick and Susanne Martens. I will end with reading the holy laws of Raso to you once again. Listen to me carefully and follow my instructions. Together we will manage to strengthen the close ties with Tacendo. There's still a lot to be done. I confidently believe that we're still the chosen people!"

The inhabitants of Franks Knight knelt down. A loud cawing crow flew from the roof of the city hall to the top of a tree. After that, it was silent in the city. Deadly quiet.

Ten minutes later Wesley raised his hands up to the sky and cried out, "Tacendo, mighty Tacendo. I know that you hear me, I know that you look down on all of us…" The people rose to their feet and listened, hands folded, heads bowed.

7

Mexico - Present Day

Arnold McKay, that immensely rich and multitalented man, sat in the shadow on the porch of an enormous hacienda in Tabasco on the south coast of the Gulf of Mexico—not far from La Venta, which had been an important center of the Olmecs in the faraway past.

He wore a white suit with a white hat and held a big glass of ice water in his hand. He sat at the edge of the porch, just out of the scorching sun, where he had been filmed and interviewed by people from a Mexican television station. While the reporter, the cameraman, and the sound engineer were leaving, two people from a radio station walked up to him. He made an inviting gesture to the empty chairs at his little table.

Behind him sat a group of men who had come with him from the ASA.

Opposite to the hacienda, on a large grass field, stood a huge helicopter and an airplane.

The radio reporter was a woman in her early thirties, who wore her long black hair in a ponytail. She started to talk about common things. After her colleague had placed a microphone on the table and had adjusted his recording equipment, she asked him for permission to start her interview.

He nodded yes.

She explained briefly where she found herself and who was sitting opposite her. Then she asked her first question.

"Mr. McKay, it is not easy to give a short description of you. When I say that you are a businessman, I do no honor to Arnold McKay the technician, when I tell that you are a scientist who respects the laws of nature, it's difficult to reconcile this with the fact that you—being the publisher of countless magazines in the scientific field as well—are sitting here face to face with me, as the owner of ParaPsycho, a magazine giving quite another, alternative insight into lots of affairs—"

Arnold burst out laughing and the sound engineer quickly adjusted his equipment.

"Well done!" Arnold cried out. "It is very clever, to sum up so much information without a pause and without a hitch. My sincere compliments!"

He took a sip of water and then said, in a much softer voice, "It might seem as if I'm a man full of contradictions. But that isn't so. A man of science doesn't preferably occupy himself with hocus-pocus, but on the other hand, we know many laws of nature, but surely not all of them! Life itself, our earth and the immense universe still have countless secrets. ParaPsycho was born from my own need to counterbalance the exact sciences."

He laughed again.

"I knew from the start that I would lose on it. No problem. I know how to combine things. I brought valuable equipment from the USA with me and had a team of expensive scientists accompany me, but there are also a group of business friends traveling along with me with whom I hope to sign some interesting contracts. Besides, I'm sitting right here at the hacienda of my good friend engineer Sebastian Estanol, with whom I have worked for years on end, at methods to make a future without buttons—in the future, we'll do everything with the power of our minds. Well, there we already have a subject which is suitable for both a purely scientific magazine and a magazine like ParaPsycho. Sebastian has loaned me his house, and it's great that he owns a chopper and a plane—and a piece of ground big enough to use as a runway!"

"There's a lot going on with ParaPsycho. Can you tell the listeners, briefly what has happened and why you are here?"

"Let's see if I can summarize the facts as concisely as you did. A Dutchman by the name of Jan Glas chanced upon a very special document from the year 1745, written by a certain Adriaen Kalf, who called at the port of the Cape of Good Hope with his ship the Starfish. Kalf had to transport something which we started to call the Machine of Colton. The machine was supposed to withdraw energy from the universe and build up horrible powers. That's one.

"An English woman, Mary Landock, showed at the symposium financed by me, with a modern Machine of Colton! She even showed her baffled audience a bizarre form of life which should not be terrestrial. Mary Landock disappeared in a mysterious way. Someone slated to make a speech the next day was a certain Mr. Wesley Dunn, who calls himself a Raso Priest. He had a heart attack. ParaPsycho reported about the symposium and also printed an article about the Heavenly Vision of Manuel Raso. This Raso claimed, at the end of the nineteenth century, that the Olmecs here in Mexico had made the god Tacendo appear. They built an appliance, according to the principles duplicated later by the Machine of Colton, which absorbs energy from the universe. It is supposed to be so big that it will destroy the world as soon as it builds up too much energy and explodes. The Raso Priest, Wesley Dunn from the Center of the Heavenly Vision, figures that we all will witness the crack of doom. It can happen any time now. A lot of journalists have been searching for Wesley Dunn since that article was published."

"He lives in Franks Knight in Florida," the reporter interrupted him. "He and his people live under special circumstances and according to odd laws."

"That's right. You're well informed. Of course, someone from ParaPsycho went there as well—Jan Glas, the man who showed the world the interesting document from Captain Adriaen Kalf. But we're sitting right here—"

"Yes. What are you going to do? What do you want from our listeners?"

Arnold nodded at her. She asked the right questions.

"Where there's smoke, there's fire. So, I am here to search for that ancient version of the Machine of Colton."

He burst out laughing again.

"Don't think that I'm so naïve as to think that I can search every square mile of the valleys of Tabasco and Veracruz with a chopper and a plane, not to mention that I would be able to find out what's hidden underground in the tract of land from Yucatán to Chihuahua—and who knows if there's even something to discover in the Sierra Madre as well, for the Olmecs never seemed to be too lazy where traveling was concerned."

"They came from very far originally, although there's still no one who can tell us anything about their origin. Very well, then, you need our listeners to provide tips."

"It's my intention to stay here for a long time. Anyone who has a tip or an important information, anyone who knows anything about a huge, hidden Machine of Colton, can report this to us via the media. Don't misunderstand me, I have no permission to dig wherever I want. We need to obtain permission for that. Thanks to the influence of my friend

Sebastian I can come and go as I please and can do my research undisturbed, along with my team of specialized people."

"I understand. Later in this show, I'll give the listeners different ways to contact us or you."

"Fine. Thank you very much. We'll listen to everyone who has information about a life-threatening, destroying machine. Has anyone one searched thoroughly enough under the Aztec temples? We have the best and most modern equipment at our disposal. We can see straight through anything. We will check out interesting tips, and then we'll go for it. If there really is something, we'll find it!"

"You sound very confident."

"As confident as a group of Olmecs who were able to transport a piece of stone of more than fifty tons over a distance of seventy miles or more..."

The conversation went on, and they discussed the civilization of the old Olmecs. Arnold turned out to be an expert. After the interview, when the sound engineer had switched off his equipment, the reporter asked, "A machine which is that old, which fills itself with energy from the cosmos and can come to an explosion any moment now—that has to be nonsense, hasn't it?"

Arnold said, "You would be very surprised at the answer to your question if it was given by someone of the Center of the Heavenly Vision!"

The reporter stood up and reached out her hand to him. Arnold McKay rose to his feet as well. She shook hands with him. Only now did it strike her that he was short—it was his imposing personality which made him big.

The tips streamed in. Sebastian Estanol's hacienda had become a busy headquarters, where all clues were verified and from where Arnold and his team swung into action; the chopper and the plane got frequent use.

Different television and radio stations gave their assistance, as did newspapers and magazines. The Machine of Colton became a household word in a short period of time.

Still, most of the clues related to other subjects—many took the opportunity to draw attention to other inexplicable affairs for which they wanted to hear an explanation.

An editor of ParaPsycho was present at the hacienda and noted down all these different things; many of them were interesting enough to write an article about.

There were hidden runways for unidentified flying objects along the coast of the Yucatán. The Machine of Colton could be found there as well. Some claimed that they had been kidnapped by extraterrestrial creatures. Different kinds of monsters were walking around all over South America, killing cattle and drinking their blood. Could Arnold catch one and show it to the world? People presented complicated theories about the Olmecs; they had come from Africa or they were of extraterrestrial origin.

Many were incensed when Arnold didn't pay further attention to their indications.

Arnold himself was realistic and blunt:

"I didn't come here for that. What I need is pure information about the Machine of Colton."

The research was an almost daily subject in the news bulletins in Mexico and the USA. Television reporters went along with Arnold, and the stations sold their reports to a great number of countries—the Machine of Colton became world news.

The Mother Culture of Central America, as the Olmec civilization was called, had prepared the way for the mighty empire of the Maya and had inspired many other nations. Television stations made use of scenes from old documentaries about Olmecs, Mayans, and Aztecs; showed the remains of their impressive buildings; and gave historians, futurologists, technicians, and philosophers, ample opportunity to comment upon the existence of a thing like the Machine of Colton.

It didn't take long before the Machine of Colton had a reputation to rival the Holy Grail.

The quest went on.

A farmer from Tabasco, Pedro Pereira—he kept cows and pigs—related that his family had lived for generations on the same land and that a story was told from father to son about a secret hidden underground.

"My grandfather told me that it has to do with the Olmec civilization," he said. "It's about a hill at the back of the land where my cows are grazing. Once Grandfather dug away a part of it. He found some shards and an undamaged pot. He didn't dare to dig any further. He literally said he was afraid to lay bare something which was too horrible to see."

This information was taken seriously. The farmer lived not too far away from Sebastian Estanol's hacienda, and the team visited it by helicopter.

Sebastian himself was the pilot, and there was room for a dozen men and a lot of equipment. A film crew from Villahermosa, who worked for different television stations, followed in a van. A curious delegation of civil servants who were authorized to give permission to dig up the hill made their way in a car.

"It doesn't matter who owns the ground," Sebastian explained to Arnold in the chopper. "We cherish our treasures from the past. If something interesting is found, the government wants to have a guarantee that nothing gets damaged and that everything is done by the rules. Therefore, I'm only too glad that I know so many people from the government very well. They are just as enthusiastic about this as we are! You know, Arnold, that mysterious Machine of Colton is gaining more and more fans every day!"

Arnold had to laugh when he heard this through his headphones.

"That story about skipper Adriaen Kalf and his encounter with Samuel Colton in Africa really touched me," he responded. "And now my magazine ParaPsycho gets scoop after scoop where the machine is concerned. I had secretly hoped for success and for interesting articles for a big audience—and now we've almost the entire world in our grasp!"

They had flown over cities and villages and extensive oil fields with refineries, over cacao and banana plantations, forests, and marshland, and now they had reached a small cattle-breeding area. Right before they landed they looked down on the land of the farmer Pedro Pereira. It was a large terrain full of rubbish and ruins.

"The only valuable thing is the ground itself," remarked Arnold. "I wouldn't pay many dollars for what's on it. Even his house is about to collapse, and there are holes in the roof."

"But who can tell what you're going to find there," said Sebastian, as he let the chopper swing around and descend. "I don't think anyone has been here before, to dig. Look, that must be the hill. Someone's standing there waving at us. That must be Pedro Pereira. How about my aviation skills? I found my way easily, didn't I?"

Now they both had to laugh.

Sebastian landed the chopper in a meadow where he had seen no animals-he didn't feel like sending a herd of cows or a number of pigs into stampeding panic. The man they had seen came up to them slowly, as if he didn't feel like leaving his hill.

He wore a broad straw hat, a faded shirt, and wide trousers. Sebastian was the first to shake hands with him.

"Senor Pereira?"

"Si."

When Arnold joined them, Sebastian made clear that the first phase of negotiation had already been touched on.

"He wants to see the money. American dollars. Cash. But I know you've taken that into account."

"Sure," reacted Arnold. "I've reckoned with that."

Arnold enjoyed his stay on the Pereira farm. He felt relaxed all the time. During the day he led his team. Every evening there was a barbecue for his team; the civil servants; and the people from the newspapers, radio, and television. Pedro Pereira always came up with huge amounts of meat. At night everyone slept in an old, ramshackle stable.

Making use of advanced equipment, they concluded that there was something lying under the hill. Something big, probably a stone building. If the Machine of Colton was there, they should have discovered metal, even gold, but there were no indications of that.

"Maybe we'll find a cellar covered with a thick layer of stone," suggested someone. "Anything could lie underneath, even things we're not able to see with our equipment."

Arnold made the decision right away:

"Dig!"

Pedro agreed for it brought in dollars. The civil servants agreed, for this called attention to the rich past of Mexico. The television people did their job; the cameras registered everything from the first spade that went into the ground. A Mexican archaeologist, who had come with the civil servants, took the lead now.

Half a day later it was the archeologist who was the happiest of all people present. They had found a building under the hill that looked very much like a little pyramid.

"Every explorer in Mexico still dreams of making a discovery which can compete with our Chichén Itzá, the Mayan town which belongs to the seven wonders of the world. No one seriously believes they will ever lay bare something like the Temple of Kukulcan at Chichén Itzá, but here we have found something special. We have to find out if it was built by the Olmecs or the Mayans. There's a difference of many hundreds of years between the two, but still, it isn't easy to tell immediately who the builders were. I'm going to invite some colleagues. Everyone must stop digging right now. Mexican specialists will take over."

Arnold was disappointed. He hadn't discovered the Machine of Colton here. But on the other hand, he was proud that his expedition had come up with something of incalculable value. The special equipment registered even more constructions outside the hill, and there even was a rumor of metal hidden underground. The Mexican specialists arrived, and walls were dug out. The presence of metal gave hope. But it turned out to be a zinc pig trough, buried under the half-decayed planks of a barn.

Arnold went to take a look at the walls. Some of them were already ten feet high, and they hadn't even reached the bottom yet. He stepped across an excavation ditch and climbed along the rough stones and looked around. His attention was drawn to Pedro Pereira, who was making gestures at Sebastian Estanol.

He probably wants more money, he thought.

Then Arnold took a step to the left. Although he was standing on a wall, he was level with the unexcavated grassy land, and perhaps that was the reason why he was unaware of any danger. He stepped into the air, fell down, and landed at the foot of the wall. He had given a cry as he lost his balance, and now he was screaming with pain.

Not much later two men climbed down into the hole and tied a rope under his armpits. He was hoisted up carefully.

The chopper brought him as close as possible to a hospital.

Arnold sat down on the porch of Sebastian's hacienda that evening, watching the sun go down, with his left foot in a cast. For the time being, this would be his permanent seat. He was drinking mineral water again, but this time he had added a lot of whiskey to it.

He listened to a radio station from Tabasco. The news about his unlucky fall had spread fast. He recognized the voice of the woman who had interviewed him here at the porch not long ago.

"We've all heard about the curse of the pharaoh," she said, "about the accidents which happened after Howard Carter had discovered the tomb of Tutankhamen in 1922. How do we interpret the accident of Arnold McKay? Is it still too early to speak of the curse of Colton? Of the curse of Manuel Raso?"

Arnold shook his head slowly. Sebastian sat down next to him at the little table.

"Put your glass down, Arnold," he said, "and I'll pour you some more whiskey. It will lessen the pain."

"You've always been a good friend," said Arnold. "Thanks. As long as I sit here, taking advantage of your hospitality, you're in charge of all projects."

"Deal. I'll inform you every day accurately about the state of affairs."

"You know where to find me," grinned Arnold. "I won't walk away."

Sebastian poured himself a whiskey as well.

He had worked together with Arnold for many years and respected him. Arnold was always thinking ahead and saw new possibilities where others thought they had reached the end. Arnold knew how to integrate different branches of science. Their most important project had concentrated on the working of the human mind and the adaptation of computer technology to thinking. They had come far with that. Technology had become an annex to the brain, and the possibilities were legion.

Now they sat there together on the porch, drinking whiskey and reminiscing.

It had become dark. They looked up to the stars.

Sebastian sprawled in his chair. With no one else around, he used Arnold's nickname every now and then- he didn't mean it spitefully—he just did it to express his affection.

"What a beautiful night it is. How about another whiskey, Shrimp?"

"I told you a while ago," grinned Arnold, "I won't walk away."

Arnold was able to listen and talk and think about quite a number of things at the same time. Now that Sebastian had used his nickname, his thoughts started to float back automatically to the time his old friends had called him Shrimp for the first time. He was short and thin and lost every fight with boys of his own age, but he had strong friends who took up for him. Shrimp could look back on a beautiful youth.

He grew up in the lap of luxury, being the only child of Louis and Emmy McKay. As a child, Arnold had the talent to discover the truth behind things that appeared ordinary to others. It was the little things that struck him—the details. A certain look from his father, a slip of the tongue from his mother. He developed the strange idea that his life, his lot, had to do with the big clock that held such a prominent place on the mantelpiece in every house they lived in.

They moved regularly. From Florida to Georgia, from Georgia to Colorado, from Colorado to Texas, from Texas to Alabama.

Heavenly Vision

Shaking moving vans did no good to the complicated clockwork. When they lived in Birmingham, Alabama, the silver man with the golden stars on his jacket refused to swing his scythe, and the clock ran slow.

Arnold was sitting at the table in the living room reading a book when a clockmaker came in. His father talked to the man in a hushed voice. Arnold's intuition told him that he should pretend that he still was reading and wasn't paying attention to what happened near the mantelpiece or listening to what his father and the clockmaker were talking about.

"It's a unique clock," said the man. "Valuable, that's for sure. Not only because of the silver and the gold or the woodcarving. The clockwork itself is of sublime quality-I've seldom seen another piece of such outstanding craftsmanship. Where does it come from?"

Arnold turned a page and pricked up his ears.

"We've lived in Florida, not far from a little place called Franks Knight. A crazy sect has settled down there... "

Arnold knew that his father was looking at him now, and he heaved a deep sigh and shook his head, while he let his forefinger slide along a line.

He caught words he had never heard before.

"Center of the Heavenly Vision." "Manuel Raso, an insane visionary." "The silver man there, with his scythe, that's Raso."

Soon he understood that the clock had been made in Franks Knight and that his father had paid a large sum of money for it.

Arnold was eighteen years of age and went to college, but the clockmaker had come during the summer holidays.

Arnold had his suspicions about the clock and about himself, but he wouldn't ask his parents questions they probably wouldn't want to answer.

The next day he searched for information about Franks Knight.

A week later he told his parents that a friend of his, Micky Sharpe, had asked him to come along on a trip to Florida. Because Arnold had an excellent academic year behind him, he received permission to go, and his father gave him his first credit card and a nice amount of cash.

"Florida is preeminently the state to become a man in a short time," said his father. He gave Arnold a meaningful wink. His mother said that was exactly what she worried about.

"Please don't do anything foolish when you're so far away from home!" Micky had family in Perry, and they drove there in the car of Micky's mother. Arnold stayed there for a couple of days, and then he went on by bus. He traveled to the coast and then went southward till he reached Nacre Cove.

Franks Knight was nearby.

His father had told him that he was born in a house just outside Nacre Cove. "In the middle of the forest. You couldn't see the houses of the neighbors. We found it restful there, your mother and I, and it was such a pity that we had to move."

Arnold had thought of everything. He had read that the peculiar people of Franks Knight were teetotalers and that there was no alcohol for sale in that little city. When he walked through Main Street there, he had a bottle of whiskey in his inside pocket.

Arnold, sitting on the porch of the hacienda in Mexico, took a pull and listened with half an ear to what Sebastian had to tell. In the meantime, his thoughts were far away, in Florida's Franks Knight, where he walked through Main Street as a boy and opened the door to Joe Pendelton's grocery.

Joe was quite a bit older than Arnold. He was long and thin, and his face wore a suspicious expression. His skin was pale as if he never came outside. He screwed up his eyes when he saw Arnold standing there, crossed his arms, and leaned his back against the shelves behind the counter.

After Arnold had made sure that there were no other customers, he said, "I'm not here to buy anything, I just need some information. I've heard that special clocks are made here. My name is Arnold, and I'm a student. I'm working on a big article about exclusive clocks. Could you help me, please?"

Joe relaxed. His arms sank down, and he put his hands into his pocket.

"I'm Joe. Joe Pendelton. I'm sorry, boy, but you're a couple of years too late. The last person who made clocks here was—"

He abruptly fell silent, and his wary look returned.

"It's important to me," said Arnold. "I've seen a clock with a little silver man on it, wearing a coat with golden stars. Every hour he swings around a scythe. I know the silver man represents Raso, and I swear, sir, that I have much respect for your strong belief in this man. The vision, the crack of doom...I know that many people laugh about that, but I take it very seriously."

"Now, that's nice," said Joe, who, however, didn't look any less suspicious. "We don't hear that often. Many clocks have been made with the image of Raso on them. The knowledge of making clocks went from generation to generation. Patrick Martens was the last man who knew the job. I knew him well; he may have been the best of all the clockmakers."

"How can I prove to you that I have respect for Raso and all that has to do with him?"

"Well," said Joe. "You're a unique boy. Most young men come here in large groups to jeer at us... You could make a bow, a deep bow, in front of the mausoleum. You'll find it not far away from here."

Arnold had thought of everything. He had a photograph of the clock with him, and now he took it out of his pocket.

"Please, take a look at this. The one who owns a piece of art like this must be a very happy person. I know something about clocks. Enough to know that this is a unique exemplar. Who is able to make this, is entitled to call himself a great artist."

Joe had taken the picture and looked at it attentively.

"I'm not sure, but this could very well be the work of Patrick."

"With whom in Franks Knight could I have a talk about clocks and this outstanding artist?"

"With me as good as with anyone else. I told you already, the trade disappeared with Patrick, and I don't think you'll find someone who can tell more about it than I. I knew Patrick very well."

He closed one eye and looked hard at Arnold with the other. "Besides I'm one of the few who is willing to talk to strangers. That has everything to do with my grocery. Every now and then people from outside Franks Knight come here."

"All right," said Arnold. "Thanks. When do you have time?"

"Right now," answered Joe. "It's late in the afternoon, I'm not busy, and I don't expect any more customers. You know, I actually find it interesting to have a talk with a stranger."

"Strangers have strange customs," said Arnold, counting on it that Joe knew nothing about life outside of Franks Knight. He took the bottle of whiskey from his inside pocket.

"We like, for instance, to take a nice swig every now and then."

"Liquor?" asked Joe, pointing at the bottle. "That's forbidden here."

"Of course. To all the people of Franks Knight. But not to—"

He opened the bottle and took a sip.

"Not to the people from the big world," said Joe. He watched Arnold take a second sip and wipe his mouth with the back of his hand.

"What do you like to drink here? I mean, besides water, milk, coffee, or tea. Raso was someone who never said no to a good glass of beer, wasn't he? And he loved to visit saloons regularly."

"We like to drink green and red syrup," said Joe.

Arnold's unique intuition worked perfectly. He knew what he had to do. He remembered, after all these years, exactly what he had said to Joe.

He still was making spontaneous decisions—even this very day, on the land of Pedro Pereira, where he had let himself fall down from an old wall intentionally to hurt himself, so that he had to be carried to a hospital, after which he would have witnesses who could confirm that he had been sitting here, on the porch of the hacienda of his friend Sebastian Estanol, when all kinds of strange things happened in Florida... "Syrup!" he cried out in the grocery of Joe Pendelton. "Man, that's the best basis of the nicest mix. Pour yourself a glass, and then I'll put some whiskey in it. Don't you worry about a thing, it's no big deal, it's just nice. You know, Joe, syrup and whiskey, that's what I call—no, that's what we in the big world call...Heavenly Vision!"

Joe came from behind the counter and walked up to a shelf with tens of glasses on it.

"This is a grocery, but I sell all kinds of everything," he said. "Even glasses. Even syrup. That's because we don't have many shops here. I must have almost anything here that the people of Franks Knight need. You know, Arnold, if I wasn't here for them, they couldn't buy anything at all!"

Arnold grinned behind Joe's back and couldn't help thinking that it was as if the mere smell of whiskey had already been enough to make Joe talkative. Joe took a bottle of green syrup and poured the glass half full.

"Should I add water to it?" he asked.

"If it's sickly sweet, I would say yes. A bit of water. And then a bit of whiskey. After that, we're going to have a nice talk together, Joe..."

Arnold continued talking and knew that he sounded very mature. He was going to reach his goal, he was sure of that. He was about to hear the truth about himself. It was a strange sensation.

Maybe I'll buy myself a house in this neighborhood one day, he thought all of a sudden. Not far from this insane place. It's beautiful here. I have the idea I would really feel at home.

Joe closed the shop. They sat down at the side of the counter, where a little table and some chairs stood ready for customers who wanted to take a rest for a while or have a chat.

On the tabletop stood glasses, a bottle of syrup, a bottle of mineral water, and the bottle of whiskey. Joe shook his head slowly.

"Oh man, how can you drink that stuff straight?" Arnold poured himself just a little bit. Again and again, he filled up Joe's glass. And he told about the big world. About freedom, airplanes, holidays, politics, music, books, cars, and pretty girls. It didn't take long before Joe was tipsy, and not much later he was almost drunk. Then Arnold started asking about clockmaker Patrick Martens again, and it was Joe's turn to get talking. He had known Patrick and his wife Susanne very well. But after he had praised Patrick's craftsmanship at length and had told that Susanne had cured many of his ailments, he fell silent and stared out in front of him. He reached for his glass and almost turned it over with his fingertips. Arnold took the glass and poured water and syrup in it and a lot of whiskey.

"Here you are. Tell me what happened to Patrick."

"I don't know if I'm allowed to do that," said Joe.

A big, grown man like you is allowed to do anything he wants," remarked Arnold. "Sometimes you just shouldn't care about the rules. You know—it can be exciting to break them. No one will ever know about it, this is something between you and me. We're sitting here, drinking whiskey together like brothers, and brothers don't have secrets from each other. All right? Well, Patrick and Susanne. What happened to them?"

"We have rigid laws here in Franks Knight," sighed Joe. "Do you know which law has the most drastic consequences?"

Arnold looked up in surprise. Suddenly he knew. His suspicions began to take shape in his head and suppressed all other thoughts.

"I can see it in your streets. All you see is full-grown people. You have no children. I have read about it, but it never occurred to me that Patrick and Susanne..."

Joe nodded yes, and it seemed as if he couldn't stop nodding.

"Joe!" Arnold cried out.

"Yes. Having children is not allowed here. We are Manuel Raso's last followers. And of all the women, it was Susanne, who examined all others in her capacity as a doctor, who gave birth to a child. She was chubby, you know, she wore wide dresses. No one had noticed that she was pregnant. They decided to escape. Someone from outside Franks Knight took them with him. Patrick went out selling clocks, and Susanne had said that she had to fill up her stocks of medicine. Wesley Dunn, our undisputed leader, our Raso Preacher, soon found out the truth. Patrick and Susanne came back, without the child."

"Was it a son or a daughter, do you know?" asked Arnold. He tried to keep his voice as indifferent as possible.

"A son. I'm sure of that. No one ever took the trouble to find the child. It was there, the damage had already been done. Wesley drew up all the rituals that we had to follow during the next years to show the great god Tacendo that we were sincerely asking for forgiveness. Besides that, he expected all citizens to find a proper punishment for Patrick and Susanne. Wesley came up with different possibilities and let us make our choice. Finally, we all agreed."

Joe took a draft. Arnold made impatient gestures.

"Go on. What was this punishment?"

Joe stroked his chin with the thumb and forefinger of his left hand.

"The boy..." he said, brooding. "There was this rumor that Patrick and Susanne had left him behind with someone to whom he had sold a clock. But we didn't know the names of his customers. No one was interested in who the clients of the clockmaker were, as long as he sold his clocks."

Arnold heaved a deep sigh and poured himself some more whiskey, too.

"The archive cellar under the city hall was emptied. What remained was a big, bare cellar with a steel door. The room was furnished handsomely and a huge supply of food and drinks was carried inside. This way it became Patrick and Susanne's prison. A cellar without windows."

"In there they served their sentence..." muttered Arnold. "They couldn't get out, they couldn't visit their child. For how long did they have to stay in there?"

"Please, give me some more whiskey, will you?" asked Joe.

Arnold filled up his glass.

After taking a few drafts, Joe said, "No matter how much food you have, sooner or later it's all eaten. The same goes for drinks. I have no idea when Patrick and Susanne realized that they could only prolong their lives by eating less. No one knows that, because the door was never unlocked again."

Arnold shuddered with horror. Now he knew everything, even though Joe hadn't finished. He could have silenced him now and stood up and walked away, to save himself the pain of the next words, but he remained sitting there.

"At a certain moment, the water was cut off as well. Maybe they had been so smart as to fill the bath and all the empty bottles and pots and pans with water, who can tell? They starved from hunger and thirst in their luxury cellar. An offering to Tacendo. It was the only way to save ourselves. Only that way could we make sure that we, here in Franks Knight, will still be walking around after all life in the big world has been destroyed."

Arnold didn't know what to say for a long time. Only when the bottle was empty, did he asked, "Did no one ever open the cellar door again?"

Joe shrugged his shoulders. "Yes, of course. The files were returned to the cellar. Everything is again as it has always been."

"But without Patrick and Susanne."

"Without Patrick and Susanne," repeated Joe.

Arnold knew now that his real family name was Martens, but he would never know which first name his parent had chosen for him. He stood up and said good-bye. He unlocked the door of the grocery himself and stepped outside. He was drunk, even though he hadn't taken much of the whiskey. Being an eighteen-year-old boy, he had never tasted the stuff before—all he had were a couple of beers.

While Arnold reflected on all this and emotionally experienced it again, he also listened to his friend Sebastian, answered his questions shortly, and made a remark every now and then.

Still, his thoughts must have wandered off to the past too intensely, for all of a sudden he felt a hand on his shoulder, and he started when he heard Sebastian's voice.

"Arnold! I see tears in your eyes! Does your leg hurt that much?"

"Yes," was his immediate reaction. "It's that damned leg. But fortunately, you have the right anesthetic in that bottle there."

Sebastian burst out laughing.

"Right you are. We'll have a last glass, and after that, we'll turn in. Tomorrow I take over the lead from you, and I certainly don't want to be walking around with a hangover then!"

They drank their whiskey in silence, looking up at the stars. Then they rose to their feet. Arnold used crutches and limped behind Sebastian.

They went inside through the French doors and from there to the big hall. Arnold remained standing at the foot of the staircase and wondered how to climb up.

"Don't worry," said Sebastian. "My servants have prepared another room. You're sleeping here on the ground floor. All your things are already there. Come with me, I'll show you the way."

"I could always count on you," said Arnold. "Thanks. For everything."

8

Florida - Present Day

"Hell is right here in my head, Shrimp," Don Adler had said when he had come with Arnold to Lost Harbor for the first time.

He had no idea what more was going to happen there in his head during the five years he was going to work for Arnold.

He and Arnold stepped into a wooden office. There he received his instructions. The feeling of guilt concerning the murder was almost unbearable. Lost Harbor was an ideal hiding place. Here he could forget his anger, frustration, and grief about Angelica, and time would help him to understand that he had acted in self-defense in Nacre Cove and that it had never been his intention to beat someone to death. But the tasks he had to perform here seemed as good as impossible to him.

Arnold tried to convince him that it could be done.

"The right tools, a luxury shelter with a good bed, and the best food and plenty of drinks. And when you feel tired, you sit down for a while. Look, this will make you feel relaxed ."

Arnold produced a little red helmet and turned it upside down so that Don could see the inside.

"At first sight, it seems to be nothing more than a helmet. There are no buttons or slides. The built-in speakers will cover your ears when you put it on. All you have to do then, Don, is think. After some time you'll discover lots and lots of new possibilities. You'll have no more time to worry about Angelica, and what happened in Nacre Cove will get pushed away into a dark spot of your memory. I can tell, for I've developed this appliance myself. Here, just try it. Sit down and then put it on."

Don took a seat and placed the helmet on his head. He folded his hands in his lap, and his closed his eyes. Arnold studied his relaxed expression and smiled. Don looked odd—the red plastic sat tight around his head, and his short-cut hair spread wide out under it so that it looked as if the top of his skull had been removed.

Arnold McKay and Sebastian Estanol had parted after they had sold all their gathered information and discoveries to a big company who was willing to pay a fantastic amount of money for it. Sebastian didn't know that Arnold had found the buyer himself because Arnold had simply asked him to keep silent about it. "Otherwise the deal is off."

He had said to Sebastian, "We won't get much further with our research. It's time to concentrate on other things."

After that Arnold struck off on his own. Thanks to Sebastian, he had discovered how he could reach the brain, that complicated lump of protein, by electronic means—how he could understand it, instruct it, and influence it. The moment he understood that there were more possibilities than Sebastian suspected, he wanted to end the cooperation as soon as possible.

He knew very well that many people, especially the laity, would compare his methods—if they should ever hear about it—with a modern kind of hypnosis and conceive that he had found a way to manipulate the mind, to which the spirit was seen as a mysterious, immaterial power. He approached everything in a purely scientific way. He didn't start from hazy principles but followed the laws of nature. And the laws of nature told him about the birth of the universe, about the forming of galaxies, stars, and planets.

Life originated from dead matter and life produced thinking creatures, and their brains were nothing more or less than a product of nature—a wonder big enough to keep one surprised for a lifetime. Brains are still matter, and he knew how to handle matter.

Often he had said, "You can't see how the brain works by taking it out of the skull and cutting it into little slices, just as you can't see how a complicated machine works by taking away the case and pulling off all the little components one by one. Only in-depth research brings understanding and insight, no matter if it's about the human brain or advanced computer systems."

Sometimes he added in jest, "In both cases, you're beginning to know a bit about it when you manage to place everything back in its right place and get the thing working again." He never saw a brain surgeon or a computer expert in his mind's eye, but a faceless man—for he had had never known him—who was busy building the most complex clockwork.

Arnold McKay left much work to specialists. He gathered information, bought information, and more than once he even stole information. Thanks to his reputation the doors of the labs opened for him all over the USA and Europe. He worked for different companies, and every now and then he was appointed managing director. As soon as he knew enough, he moved on. He set up companies everywhere that made large profits and were sold again for big money.

In the meantime, he had devised his plans.

He needed someone who was willing to work for him in Lost Harbor. For some time, he had planned to kidnap someone and put the helmet on his head. But that was too risky, and besides he wasn't strong enough to knock someone down—his nickname wasn't Shrimp for nothing. Then Don Adler stepped into his car, and the problem was solved...

Don seemed to be indefatigable. He had always been strong, but during the years he worked in Lost Harbor his power had grown in a spectacular way. When he took a rest and put on the helmet, he automatically found the music he loved and the images he liked appeared in his mind's eye. Shrunk into himself, his fantasy fed by the equipment in the helmet, he was the leading character in wild dreams. He never felt alone and had no wish for human contact. In the meantime, his tasks were whispered to him. The equipment switched off automatically when he fell asleep so that he was able to have a natural rest.

Now, five years later, the work was done. Don remained in Lost Harbor and waited for instructions for his final order; he knew that it would come to him through the helmet.

Because he couldn't sit still after such a long period of working, he got up early every morning, drank two cups of strong coffee, and then went outside to see what he could do. The harbor had disappeared, and in its place now was a big square with palm trees along the borders. In the center, he had built a stone bar and in the right corner a covered stage that looked very much like an old-fashioned bandstand. All that remained of the harbor was the old tugboat. It stood, with its keel deep in the ground, in the left corner and formed a strange contrast to the bandstand. He had made the boat rustproof and had painted it. It had been an incredibly difficult job to tow the tug, which hung from the dock on steel cables, over a path of grease-covered wooden beams to its final position.

He scraped the weeds from between the stones, swept the big square, cleaned up the entire place, and burned all kinds of things that had become useless.

Shrimp had taken care of everything; Don would be able to prove that he had worked for Shrimp for five years and that he had been on the payroll. There was a big sum of money for him in a bank in Perry. The taxes were already paid.

Actually, Don hoped to be able to stay in Lost Harbor for a while longer. He felt at home here, and he had no concrete future plans.

But all of a sudden, one early morning—he had no idea that it was a Sunday—he received information through his helmet. As the information came to him, he was not aware of it at all; he was merely listening to some nice music. When he took off the helmet, he heaved a deep sigh and whispered, "So I'm leaving here after all, after all these years..."

First, he should go to Franks Knight, a little place not far from Lost Harbor.

He knew where to find it. He had often passed by it when he worked as a trucker.

Standing on the square he gave a good stretch and looked around. Pointing to the left, he said, "There's Nacre Cove." Then he made a quarter turn and pointed in front of him. "The nature reserve," and, pointing over his shoulder with his thumb, "Shrimp's house. All I have to do is follow the road from there to..." he made another quarter turn and pointed in front of him. "...end up in Franks Knight."

All new orders lay arranged by time of execution in his brain. Don went back to the wooden office that had been his home for five years. He put the helmet away in a steel safe and cleared the breakfast table. Then he stepped outside again and walked away without locking the door—the only one who would come here was Shrimp. He had seen no other person here during all these years.

"I'll come back here one more time," he thought, "so I don't have to say goodbye to this place yet..."

He crossed the square and then took the path that led to Shrimp's house.

Perhaps there was no other house in Florida more burglarproof than this one, but Don knew the codes and opened the gate without any problem by pushing a few buttons in the right sequence and then did the same to enter the house through the back door.

That very moment, on the porch of the hacienda in Mexico, a signal from a built-in feature of his cell phone told Arnold McKay that everything was proceeding on schedule.

Don Adler is in my house, he thought. This going well...

Don went through the scullery and the kitchen to the living room. He knew that he was alone here, but he started and stood rigid with fear when the big clock on the mantelpiece struck. A silver figure on top of it turned around, swinging a tiny scythe. Then he slipped into the hall. There he opened a cupboard, again using a code, and took out a black plastic bag containing a soft bundle. He went outside through the front door and then through the garden up to the gate at the end of the drive. Not much later he was walking down the road that led to Franks Knight.

It was a strange experience to be finally outside of Lost Harbor. It was still early in the morning, and this was no busy road. Every now and then a car passed by, and he had to keep himself from jumping to the side and disappearing into the forest. When he came across two walkers, he remained looking straight in front of him and felt how his heart began to beat faster. The man and the woman greeted him kindly, and he greeted them, too. He slowly breathed in and out through his nostrils while he walked on.

No one recognized the hobo of five years ago in this clean-shaven, muscular man. Besides, he knew that no one had connected the murder near Restaurant Hernando with him.

He was a free man. He was going to render Shrimp a few more services, and after that, he would go to Perry to the bank to take out some money and get himself a credit card.

He thought of Angelica, and then he shrugged his shoulders. A smile passed over his face.

"Even if I should come across her right now," he thought, "I wouldn't accost her. It's over and done with Angelica. I've become another person."

Just before he reached Franks Knight he turned a forest path. Three hundred feet farther up he stepped behind a tree. There he took off his tracksuit and took some other clothes from the plastic bag. When he turned up on the road later, he was wearing a wide coat and trousers of a shining material, bright red and covered with yellow stars. On his head was a brown cap with golden stars. Its long bill threw a shadow over his eyes and nose. The coat had a stiff standing collar, which hid his nose and mouth. Anyone would take him for an inhabitant of Franks Knight.

Franks Knight lay at the Gulf of Mexico and had its own little harbor. Old fishing boats, one even rustier than the other, blocked the broad entrance to the harbor. They were lying next to each other on a horizontal line, linked together with thick iron chains to prevent other vessels from entering. No one could reach Franks Knight from the sea.

Along the highway that led to the little place stood vans from different television stations. So many people from the press had gathered that they easily outnumbered the population of Franks Knight.

Publications in ParaPsycho had made Franks Knight famous overnight. The newspapers had taken over the news, and radio and television stations paid all possible attention to it.

The facts had been reiterated time and again, the same as the reporter in Tabasco had done when she interviewed Arnold McKay so that everyone understood exactly what it was all about: The document from 1745, wherein the Machine of Colton was described, and the same machine demonstrated by Mary Landock. Mary's presentation of the mysterious form of life. Her mysterious disappearance. The worship of Manuel Raso by the people of Franks Knight. Raso's prediction of the crack of doom. Only the people from Franks Knight would survive. Somewhere a giant Machine of Colton was hidden, which was sucking up the energy from the universe. One of these days the machine would explode. A team, under the leadership of businessman Arnold McKay and his former business partner Sebastian Estanol searched for the hellish machine in Mexico, where the Olmecs had built it together with the god Tacendo. Jan Glas, a Dutch publicist who had found the document of skipper Adriaen Kalf and had an experience in England that he himself described as a heavenly vision. Now Glas claimed to be able to save the people of Franks Knight from disaster. ParaPsycho had gotten the scoop again and was describing Jan as the new Manuel Raso.

And now rumors were buzzing where Jan was concerned. He should be on his way to Franks Knight. The end of the world was nearing, and he should give the chosen ones a chance to escape the catastrophe...

So it was understandable that the press had surrounded Franks Knight like guards around a castle. Even if Jan Glas arrived via the water, they would know about it, for there were yachts waiting near the fishing boats.

In the meantime, every reporter tried to find news and information in his own way. And so they went through the streets of the little place, searching for inhabitants who were willing to speak. But all doors remained closed, all shutters were down, and anyone who showed up on the street was always in a hurry and looked out straight in front of him.

The press looked curiously at the big mausoleum, which was surrounded by high, forty-year-old palm trees. They jostled each other in Joe Pendelton's grocery, where they had to grin when they looked at the old-fashioned, black, Bakelite telephone on the counter next to the till. Joe was friendly and gladly sold them his products, but refused to be drawn out.

Long ago he'd had a long conversation with someone from the big world, which had provided him with a nasty habit; under the counter, he always kept a bottle of whiskey, from which he took a sip regularly. It was not easy to get hold of a bottle of liquor. At night he had to try to avoid the city security and leave Franks Knight unseen, and then he had to walk all the way to the Spring Tide Motel, where Al Corbetta, who had taken over the motel from his father Sammy, sold him a bottle for a reasonable price. But everything Joe earned in his grocery was public money, so in fact, it was theft every time he made a grab from his own till to buy himself liquor. He mistrusted all people from the big world, and he didn't care that the press was making fun of the telephone and undoubtedly found him a freak or even a fool.

"Do you really believe that the world will be destroyed? Do you think this will happen pretty soon? Can you tell us some more about Manuel Raso? What exactly is the Center of the Heavenly Vision? Where can we find Mr. Wesley Dunn, and what exactly does a Raso Priest mean for Franks Knight?"

Joe remained silent and gazed at them with his most vacuous look. As soon as they had left again, he reached for the bottle, unscrewed it, and took a pull. The time that he mixed his whiskey with syrup and water was far behind him.

On a hot, cloudless Sunday morning a big, silver gray, Plymouth convertible left Perry for Franks Knight. It was a rented car with a chauffeur. In the broad leather back seat sat Jan Glas and Wesley Dunn.

Wesley wore a black suit with golden stars. He had asked Jan if he was willing to put on a long, green coat with purple stars, and Jan had done so. They hadn't left Perry yet when journalists who had spotted them had already called their colleagues in Franks Knight:

"The Dutch Raso is on his way. Now you know why you couldn't find Wesley Dunn anywhere; he was in Perry waiting for the arrival of the man who's going to save him and his people!"

Wesley, who had devoted his life to Raso, who terrorized his own town by forcing everyone to live according to the rules, who used strong-arm tactics and never showed mercy, seemed to be completely meek for the first time, now that he was sitting next to Jan Glas. Today he wanted to put all his cards on the table, and therefore he had chosen a convertible and had dared to ask Jan to put on the coat. Now he was desperately searching for words.

"Thanks one more time for being here, Jan," he finally said.

The wind blew the words away before the driver could catch them.

Jan nodded yes. "I see it as my duty."

"After all my requests, my telephone calls, my letters..." sighed Wesley. "Now you're here. At last."

"I've come to help you," said Jan. "Don't you worry about a thing, I know what I have to do. We'll have to wait for the right day, the right hour. And we don't have to wait too long anymore. It's no longer a matter of years and even not of months or weeks. Within a couple of days, the catastrophe will be a fact. You'll be saved."

Wesley sighed two, three times.

Suddenly, it was as if a heavy load had been taken from his shoulders. Or maybe it was closer to the truth to admit that he had put the load, which he had carried for so many years, on Jan's shoulders now. And immediately it was easier for him to talk.

"The symposium in England..."

"In Harwich?"

"Yes, yes, in Harwich. It all became too much for me. I was confronted with facts that completely swept me off of my feet. I am seventy-five years of age. Not that old, but still...That weak heart of mine! I heard you talk about the man in Africa who gave a machine to a Dutch captain. Then came that woman, the stunning, beautiful woman, Mary Landock, and she showed that little appliance—a very little version of what the Olmecs once made and hid! I was so scared, I started to sweat, and my poor heart—"

"'I cannot die this way, there's still so much to be done!' That's what you said. You begged for help."

"Yes. I'd already given you my card. I wanted to have a talk with you. I also wanted to talk with Mary Landock. You were so well informed, you came with news about what the Olmecs had created together with their god Tacendo..."

"To me, everything about that was new as well," said Jan.

Wesley raised up his hands and felt the counterpressure of the wind.

"You hadn't even had your vision by then!" he cried out. The driver looked into his mirror and raised his eyebrows. "Was it a presentiment? Did I know, deep down in my old, sick heart, that you were the man I had been looking for all the time? The second Raso, the man who would show us the way?"

He folded his hands now and closed his eyes.

"Thank you, Tacendo, thank you a thousand times, god of the Xi! I've obviously done everything the right way, for you haven't let us down!"

Then he talked about Raso for a quarter of an hour, while he leaned back and looked up at the blue sky. Jan listened, nodded, and said every now and then, "That's right. Tacendo is great. Raso was his most important servant!"

Next Wesley told what he had in mind after they had arrived in Franks Knight.

"I think it a good idea to talk to the press comprehensively. We should both come with explanations and answer all their questions patiently. We shouldn't conceal anything from them, we shouldn't beat about the bush. Maybe they will leave us in peace then. You won't believe your eyes when we arrive. They're standing everywhere with their cameras and microphones."

"All right. We'll make time for it. After that, I hope to be able to speak to the people of Franks Knight. If I have to do that somewhere outside, the press will be present as well."

"We have no hall big enough for everyone."

"I will set their minds at ease. It will happen soon now. The great turnabout, the big explosion—when the big hand of Tacendo crushes the earth and will only show mercy to us."

"Tacendo is great," said Wesley. "We human beings can only make a guess at his motives, and we must be glad that we are the ones who will be saved. Truly, Tacendo is great!"

Then he fell silent and listened to Jan, who told about his vision.

In the meantime much had changed in Franks Knight on this Sunday morning. The press people didn't have to stand there any longer with their arms crossed, staring out into the empty streets—everyone knew that Wesley Dunn was on his way from Perry, in the company of Jan Glas. If they hadn't received the information from their colleagues in Perry, they would have known it anyway by now, for all of a sudden all the people of Franks Knight had come out of their houses.

They wore their best clothes, wide trousers and long garments in vivid colors, full of sparkling stars. They all wore hats. Everyone went to Raso's mausoleum first to make a bow and then went up to the highway via Main Street. There they waited. They talked to each other nervously but ignored questions from the press.

There was more happening. Curious tourists and people from the neighborhood had found out as well that something was going on in Franks Knight. Maybe an early motorist had seen something and had warned others, after which the news had spread fast. Soon there was a long row of cars parked on the right side of the highway, and Main Street was full as well. The people stepped out of their cars and started walking through the streets. They laughed at the locals, jeered at their clothing, and took pictures of them.

"You idiots!" shouted someone. "Who do you think you are? Are you so much better than we, that you will survive a disaster while we're all bound to die?"

"Don't you feel pity for us?" someone else cried out. "Do you really think that we're going to die, and you not? Are you not going to help us at all?"

The ranting and raving were taken over by others. Soon members of the crowd were rattling the shutters and kicking the doors. The atmosphere grew grim. Police cars drove with wailing sirens past the parked cars on the highway and became stuck on Main Street. There were too few cops to prevent a row.

"This is getting out of hand," said a police officer, who saw men and women in vividly colored clothes full of stars, being pushed around by bystanders.

Then a loud voice sounded from the highway and was repeated and relayed by other voices in all the streets of Franks Knight.

"There they are! There they are! Wesley Dunn and Jan Glas!"

The people—locals, tourists, press, police, rubbernecks—pushed forward to the square at Main Street, counting on Wesley and Jan to go straight to the city hall.

And then the fat was in the fire. The main reason for the mass fight that followed was the words of a young man from Nacre Cove, who clenched his fists and cried out, "You're all old and gray, childless, useless fools! How do you dare to think that you will outlive the youth?"

It was as if he gave others a reason to start the fight—the people of Nacre Cove and Franks Knight had lived in peace for generations on end. The people of Nacre Cove had never thwarted the peculiar dissidents of Franks Knight in any way. Maybe there had been repressed feelings of hatred the whole time, which came to the surface now, on this day. And then, all of a sudden, there was talk of a generation conflict as well, in which a young man said in a loud voice that he had nothing to do with the opinions of a group of elderly people who claimed that they would be the only ones to survive a global disaster.

The young man's cry was caught by others in a number of variations. "Who do you think you are, gray clowns?" "Childless, toothless! You'll all die pretty soon anyway!" The police couldn't do much. There were too few men there to break up the crowd.

There were no big cities nearby, and assistance had to come all the way from Perry.

In the meantime, the silver-gray Plymouth was driving slowly past the parked cars along the highway. Wesley and Jan had no idea what they would find when the chauffeur turned on to Main Street.

The young men in the mob, who had thought there wouldn't be much resistance, soon ran into the opposition of the city security and Wesley's personal bunch of heavies. Wesley's men used clubs.

Someone kicked in the door of Joe's grocery. People pushed inside and started to destroy everything. The other three shops were broken open as well. But Wesley's gang of heavies went inside, too, and what happened inside remained unseen to the eyes of the police.

Finally, the driver had managed to turn the big, broad Plymouth on to Main Street. The people of Franks Knight stopped fighting and raised their hands into the air—for a moment it was as if they wanted to express their surrender with this gesture, but then it became clear to everyone that something special was going on. Everybody left the street and stepped up onto the sidewalk to clear the way for the car.

The solemnity of the moment was not only palpable to the people of Franks Knight—the outsiders also were caught up in the changing of the atmosphere.

Wesley and Jan had stood up between the front and back seats, holding the headrest with one hand and waving with the other. Jan's coat flapped to all sides like a star-spangled flag. Wesley saw that the windows of the shops were broken, he saw men with bloodstained faces and torn clothes. Somewhere, sounded a cry of distress. One of his gang of thugs waved a bat.

Cheering sounded from all sides.

"There they are! Wesley brings our savior to Franks Knight!"

"Welcome! Welcome!"

Four bold young men pushed their way through the crowd towards the open car. They reached for Jan and Wesley. One of them jumped up on the trunk. Other men came closer, threatening. The members of Wesley's gang were too far away to run to the rescue.

"You'll be dead before the world explodes!" the man on the trunk cried out. "We'll see to that, you fools!"

"All you do is sow fear and panic!" shouted another. "We'll cure you of that once and for all!"

The man on the trunk lashed out, and his fist hit Jan between the shoulder blades. Jan fell forward and clutched the head restraint with both hands. He gasped for breath and fought the feeling that he had to throw up. A second blow hit him in the neck. Next to him, Wesley had turned and kicked at someone who tried to get ahold of him. The chauffeur had stopped the car and made desperate gestures.

The situation seemed hopeless.

But then someone pushed the crowd aside with force and wildly worked his way up to the car. A man in red clothes with yellow stars and a brown cap with golden stars grabbed the hoodlum on the trunk by the ankles and flung him to one side. The man made a half-circle through the air and changed into a missile when his attacker released his ankles—three or four other men fell to the ground. Wesley was happy with this help, but he was astonished at the same time.

"Who are you?" he cried out. "I've never seen you before!"

The man gave no answer and concentrated on the fight. He used a power that verged upon the improbable.

Jan watched as the man knocked down all the attackers in a short time. Something happened in his head. It was as if a drop had formed at the edge of his subconsciousness and now fell into the pool of his memory.

"I know who he is," he heard himself say to Wesley. "He belongs to me. You might call him my guardian angel. We met in England, and he turns up everywhere I go."

The attackers scrambled to their feet, their faces twisted with pain, and ran away. The Plymouth drove on slowly and reached the square in front of the city hall. The crowd had arranged itself quickly as if the hand of a god had swept them together sort by sort. The people of Franks Knight in their colorful, star-studded clothes filled the square. Behind them stood the rubbernecks. The press had withdrawn and now went back to their vans, which they tried to drive up as close as possible to the square now.

The police, reinforced now, remained in the background, playing a waiting game. It seemed that the violence had stopped, for the time being, at least.

The Plymouth accelerated after Jan and Wesley had stepped out. The people moved out of the way, and the car disappeared.

The chauffeur was in a big hurry to get away from this madhouse.

In the meantime, Jan and Wesley, followed by Don, had entered the city hall, and not much later Wesley appeared on the balcony. It became quiet on the square.

"This is an important day!" he cried out. "For we welcome the man who will lead us from now on." He leaned with one hand on the stone balustrade and pointed with the forefinger of his other hand behind him. "Jan Glas is inside. The man of the heavenly vision, who sees it as his biggest task to save all the people of Franks Knight from disaster. He will make a speech later this day after most of the curious bystanders have left. I want to thank the press present here for their attention—you're all welcome in the council hall, where Jan Glas and I will be happy to answer all your questions. We will ask you for your identification at the door. The press conference will start in half an hour."

9

Nacre Cove, Franks Knight, Lost Harbor - Present Day

Jan Glas and Wesley Dunn sat next to each other at a huge walnut table in the council hall, like two captains who had stayed behind after the crew had left the sinking ship. Right in front of them was the rough sea of press people. Don had gone to another room in the big building. Two of Wesley's gang of heavies were standing in front of the door.

Wesley pointed out someone each time who was allowed to ask a question. Most of them turned to Jan Glas.

"Mr. Glas, you came all the way from Amsterdam to Franks Knight to help the people here. Everyone knows the history of this little place, which was founded by Manuel Raso.

Do you really believe that the end of the world will be a fact soon?"

When Jan put his elbows on the tabletop and hid his mouth and nose behind the stretched fingers of both hands and thoughtfully stared up at the ceiling, the reporter went on, "I mean, the crack of doom has been predicted many times before, but look here—we're all alive and kicking."

Someone burst out laughing. Others grinned along with him.

"In other cases, it was predicted natural disasters-the will of God-or a farfetched, cowardly action of extraterrestrials," said Jan, as he let his arms sink until his hands touched the tabletop and leaned forward to the dozens of microphones in front of him. "This is quite something different."

"Tacendo is a god as well, isn't he?" shouted someone else. "A god of the Olmecs."

"That's right," said Jan. "The difference, however, ladies and gentlemen, is that we have concrete facts this time and not with an arbitrary theory."

"You're aiming at something which we have started to call the Machine of Colton," reacted the reporter. "Others are making a thorough search for it right now in Mexico."

"While it might be hidden somewhere else as well," said Jan. "Somewhere else in South America, or maybe here in the USA, not far away. Who can tell?"

"All right, all right, Mr. Glas, but let's be honest about it. As long as that big Machine of Colton isn't found we have nothing else than a theory, haven't we?"

Wesley banged the table so hard that all the sound engineers—a fraction of a second too late—adjusted their equipment.

"As Raso Preacher from the Center of the Heavenly Vision, I have serious objections against remarks like that. What are questions to you, are facts to us. In that way, we are so much different from each other. I'm no man who'll ever pretend that we in Franks Knight are better people than other world citizens. Who never knew Raso, hadn't the chance to join him. And we're only the far descendants of those who actually have known him. However, the fact remains as they are: We will survive. All others are doomed to death."

A displeased muttering went up. Wesley rose to his feet. His high leather chair rolled away behind him on six little wheels.

"You all find yourselves in a holy house! This city hall is the center of Franks Knight, and here everything turns on the doctrine of Raso. I will not tolerate any form of contempt from your side. Who wants to laugh at us, should do so elsewhere, as far as possible from here. Is that clear? Very well, then we can go on now."

He turned around and drew up his chair.

The next question was asked by a journalist who had evidently studied the case.

"Mr. Glas," she said, "first you came up with the adventures of Captain Kalf, with his confessions from around 1745, and then, all of a sudden, you get sensational visions in England. Could it be that the text of Kalf made such a deep impression on you that you started to hallucinate in a spontaneous way?"

Wesley, who had sat down again, shook his head compassionately.

Jan answered, "I can imagine very well that you ask me this. I take into account that it all had a divine origin—that it was Tacendo himself who passed the writing of the captain on to me so that I should be able to explain my visions better in a later stadium. This all can be no coincidence, it is divine predestination. I feel absolutely confident about that."

"But isn't it absurd to really believe that the end of the world is near and that there will be only a handful survivors?"

"I totally agree with you," said Jan. "Yes, it is absurd. It is just as absurd as the entire history of our earth. A planet on which life came into being spontaneously, where photosynthesis filled the atmosphere with poisonous oxygen—indeed, poisonous oxygen, which gave adapted forms of life a chance and let them evolve into complex, breathing animal species like human beings. The world is a madhouse, and we are at the crack of doom. No one can change that anymore. We have to deal with the horrible legacy of the Olmecs, and I have been chosen to save a little part of mankind from doom. Long ago a time bomb was placed which only had to fill itself with heavenly energy to come to explode. We, you, I—no one who lives now has had any influence on that. I accept the facts and will do my utmost to save these people."

"Well spoken," Wesley backed him up. "This is the truth and nothing but the truth.

Through the great magician Manuel Raso, the god Tacendo has chosen a small group of people who will survive a disaster."

The press people became impatient, reacting indignantly and angrily. But Wesley and Jan didn't give in.

The press conference was televised all over the world.

Special programs were broadcast to inform about the latest developments with Arnold McKay in Mexico.

Arnold and his team had done countless interesting, important excavations, but the Machine of Colton remained untraceable.

In every country, people reacted to the news in different ways. In England many made bets on the point of time that the world would explode; in the USA people gathered who always had believed in the arrival of extraterrestrials with sinister designs; in different South American countries, the pious prayed for a solution that would prevent the approaching problem. The French preferred to remain noncommittal; maybe they still remembered their compatriot who at the end of the last century had claimed, in connection with the predictions of Nostradamus, that the Russian space station Mir, which had plutonium on board, would crash into Paris and that the city would be completely destroyed. In Japan, some wanted to know precisely which equipment Arnold McKay used in Mexico to search for the Machine of Colton, for they were convinced that they could improve on it in a short period of time. The Russians asked themselves if the USA had worked on a secret weapon and had made such huge mistakes that it couldn't be disarmed, and a nuclear disaster was inevitable.

The press left Franks Knight. Only the disaster itself could surpass the news about the arrival of Jan Glas.

Jan hadn't spoken to the people of Franks Knight from the balcony. One day he'd had them enter the city hall in groups, where he had received them in the big council hall. There he had reassured them.

"Trust in me, then everything will be all right."

Wesley stood by the door of the council hall and gave instructions to everyone.

"Tonight it's going to happen. Prepare yourselves. Wait till there is a knock on your door and step outside then. Someone will be there to show you the way. Don't make any noise. Everything is taken care of, and there is absolutely nothing to worry about."

There were still yachts waiting near the fishing boats at the entrance of the harbor. One night, just before dark, one could see from the yachts how the chains had been taken away and how the fishing boats went back to the quay of Franks Knight.

Late at night, the fishing boats sailed out.

"Everything is just like old times again in Franks Knight," someone concluded. "They're out fishing again. The harbor is open to anyone."

The next morning, right before sunrise, the captain of a little freighter, who sailed close along the coast, saw a number of ships on his radar, which were so close to each other that he feared that they would collide. While he went up to them, he warned the coast guard.

The coast guard arrived with two fast ships.

The sun stood above the horizon now.

Soon they had identified the little fleet—it was the fishing ships of Franks Knight. The engines were off. The ships floated on the water, and some had already grazed another. It seemed impossible to make contact with the crews. There was no reaction on radio messages, and no one stepped onto the deck when megaphones were used.

"It seems to me that the ships are abandoned," opined someone.

Two rubber dinghies were launched, and a number of armed members of the coast guard managed to get on board the fishing boats. All the cabins were empty. The holds contained no fish.

Someone reported, "The fishing boats of Franks Knight are drifting!"

A motorcyclist, who was making a trip through Florida and has spent the night in Nacre Cove, had risen early and decided to take a look in Franks Knight before he took the highway to Perry. He had read different reports about the little place and had seen a commentary on television. The moment he passed the first houses, he knew something was wrong. The streets were quiet and deserted. This was not all that strange at that early hour, and he knew that the people there had no cars or other motor vehicles. The doors and windows of the houses were wide open. The broken panes in the shops on Main Street had not been replaced—someone had covered them with planks. Even the high front doors of the city hall were open. The man stopped and produced his cell phone. He had just started to dial 911 when two police cars entered Main Street. They stopped on the square in front of the city hall, and four police officers stepped out.

"I was just intending to sound the alarm," the motorcyclist shouted to them. "Have you noticed? All doors are wide open. You can just walk in anywhere, just like that!"

One policeman stopped, while the others ran up to two houses and the city hall.

"Yes, we've noticed. It's a very strange situation." "Did someone else already warn you?" asked the motorcyclist.

"A mention from the coast guard. Ships from the coast guard are on their way to the harbor of Franks Knight. One suspected that something was going on, so we came to take a look. You'd better leave now, sir. I think Franks Knight will be closed off from the outside world for now."

The motorcyclist nodded and drove away. The other policemen came back.

"There's probably no one left in Franks Knight," said one of them. "I've looked round in all rooms of that house there, from cellar to attic. The people have gone. But I don't think they've taken anything with them."

"Same thing at the place I checked," said another policeman. "No people, just a cat. Food is still on the table. They ate bread and had tea, but didn't do the dishes."

"No one in the city hall," said their colleague, a touch of fear in his face. "It gives you the creeps, walking through all these big rooms and climbing the broad staircases. You expect to find someone every moment, and you have the feeling that someone's looking at you all the time, from behind a cupboard or a door."

Many things happened during the next hours. The coast guard appeared in the harbor with a large number of ships, while other ships started a search operation. Helicopters were brought into action to search for drowning persons. Inquiries were made up and down the coast. Franks Knight was closed hermetically, and the streets and houses swarmed with policemen, army officers, and persons from different intelligence services.

The general command was given to Chris Lockhart, a special officer from the Bureau of Investigation, who had arrived strikingly fast—as if he already had been in the neighborhood for some time and only had waited for a sign to swing into action.

He looked like a well-dressed businessman who did office work, but his big fists and flat boxer's nose gave away that he had never avoided a hard fight. With his staff, he moved into a big room from the Center of the Heavenly Vision in the city hall and let himself be informed by anyone who could say something sensible.

"This city hall gives style to Franks Knight," he said, "but actually it's very exaggerated to call a little collection of houses a city. It's hardly even a village." He seemed to be well posted. "Many houses have been empty for a long time and complete streets have been pulled down. More than four hundred men and women left—there were no children. But good heavens, four hundred people cannot vanish into thin air, can they? I mean, if we have a sect here with an insane leader who has decided to commit suicide then you'd expect to find four hundred corpses. I know enough about the Raso insanity to know that they are capable of anything." He pointed at someone of his staff. "Divers! A little submarine! All of a sudden I can picture four hundred people jumping down from fishing boats with a block of concrete and a chain around their feet. We have to search the bottom of the ocean immediately!"

The man nodded yes and picked up a cell phone lying on a desk. After he had dialed a number, he said in surprise, "Even the telephone is still working."

"Maybe it's all a false alarm, and they'll come back," muttered Lockhart. "That would be a surprise!"

"That will probably not happen, Mr. Lockhart," remarked one of his subordinates. "There's every indication that they have left to never come back again. All those open doors and windows!"

"I know that, yes, I know that. It was just wishful thinking. You know, I might as well tell you now. Letters have been sent to the FBI, the CIA, a handful of other government departments, and even to the White House. They all have the same contents: A serious warning that the Machine of Colton actually exists and is so chock-full of energy that an explosion will be the inevitable result."

For a moment it was quiet in the office, until someone asked, "When?"

"Maybe today, maybe tomorrow, maybe the day after tomorrow, but within a week anyway. Another short question might be Where? And the answer can be found in all these letters, which all show the same text. In the USA! In the Ukraine! In China! And who knows where else. The machines aren't just in Mexico, but somewhere in one of our own states, and in other parts of the world as well. The explosion of one machine will cause a chain reaction. What has this to do with the theories about the Olmecs? It seems as if we have followed the wrong track all the time."

"Has someone any idea where these letters come from? Who sent them?" "There's absolutely nothing to find on them as if no one ever touched them at all.

Very frustrating. And now that the people of Franks Knight have vanished into thin air everything begins to get very serious—much more serious then I could ever imagine."

The man who had made the telephone call said, "The navy is on its way, with frigates and a little submarine."

"Fine," said Lockhart. "That completes it. We're searching along the coast, on the water, underwater, and inland. If they have changed ships somewhere in the Gulf of Mexico, we'll find them as well. It's just a matter of time—as far as we still have time!"

Having said this, he swore wholeheartedly and started to slam both fists on the desktop. His staff looked at him in amazement.

"We must learn to think things out," he said in an agitated voice. "All of us. What's the use of you if I have to do things all by myself all the time?"

"What do you mean?"

Lockhart took some deep breaths, which seemed to calm him down.

Then he explained, "There's a genius behind this all. Wesley Dunn, the Raso Priest?

Everything is prepared perfectly, and it could very well be possible that we have been led astray. We've drawn conclusions too fast. It might as well be that we don't need the navy at all. Listen. The fishing boats went to the harbor. We know that. After that, they sailed out again, and finally, we found them far away from here. Empty. You hear? Empty! But who can tell that people actually went on board? How many buses do you need to transport four hundred men and women? Ten? Or just eight?"

The man who had just called the navy reached opened the cell phone again.

"Understood, Lockhart. We'll have to give orders to search for a small column of buses. They may have gotten a ways away from here by now."

Lockhart banged his fists again on the desktop, and then he looked up to the ceiling in despair. "That's exactly what has to be done. But if they really have left by bus, they might have made use of another trick as well and—"

"And each bus went somewhere else, and after a long detour they'll meet up again," the man at the telephone filled in.

Lockhart stood up and waved his cell phone.

"I'm going to have a look in a couple of houses myself. You all know how to reach me."

He left the city hall and stepped at random inside one house and then another. When he opened the door to a living room, he scared two women trying to catch a cat.

"There are no dogs around," said one of the women, "just cats. Our colleagues took away the horses, which they used for their carts."

Franks Knight had become a ghost town. Every house looked as if the owners might return at any moment. Somewhere in a kitchen, a faucet was dripping. He turned it off. He didn't see a radio or a television set anywhere. In most living rooms hung a portrait of Manuel Raso. When he had left Main Street and passed Raso's mausoleum, he noticed that all the flowers in the park had been cut and put around the grave. Palm trees had stood around the mausoleum, but they had all been cut down and sawn into pieces.

The flowers have been put there as a farewell, thought Lockhart. I'm pretty sure now that the people won't be coming back.

He racked his brains, but he couldn't come up with any new ideas. He grabbed his cell phone and called someone from his staff at the city hall.

"Someone should check if there are hidden rooms under Raso's mausoleum. Maybe we'll find cellars there. Or under the city hall, or elsewhere."

He didn't expect the search would lead to interesting results, but on the other hand, he had to try everything.

"They're wiped out," he muttered. "By the big hand of the Olmec god Tacendo."

On his way back to the city hall he saw that the first television crews had already arrived. They went into the deserted houses, escorted by the police. It was not possible to refuse admittance to the press. This was world news. Lockhart wished he could surprise them all with a couple of smart remarks, that he could give the answers to all their questions, but when someone held a microphone under his nose and someone else aimed a camera at him, he was only able to rattle off the standard lines that made no one any wiser.

"It's too early to draw conclusions."

"I cannot answer that question just now."

"We started our investigation immediately, and we're doing our utmost to understand what's going on here."

He ended the conversation as soon as possible and hurried to the entrance of the city hall. When he looked up, he saw a huge rain cloud moving high above the roof, as if Tacendo actually reached out a dark hand. It was already raining over the Gulf of Mexico. It wouldn't be long before the rain broke here as well. Lockhart went back to the office at the Center of the Heavenly Vision and sat down at his desk again. All members of his staff were busy with cell phones and taking notes. This was the crisis center of Franks Knight, and he was in charge here. This was the place where all the results of the different researches came in.

How great it would be, he thought, if I only knew what I had to do.

Someone who was able to give the answers to many questions was Don Adler. But unfortunately there was a blind spot in his memory, and the things he did remember, he thought had actually never happened in reality.

He sat down at a little table on the wooden quay at the back of Restaurant Hernando in Nacre Cove, without recalling that he had been forced there, five years ago, by six men, Elmore, Doug, Pedro, Francis, Otis, and Raphael, to jump into the water, or that he had killed one of them, fat Doug, later with a single blow of a stick. He also wasn't aware of the fact that Arnold McKay had seen to it that he was sitting here right now and that he would spend a couple of nights in a hotel in Nacre Cove before traveling to Europe.

Arnold McKay himself sat at a window in the same restaurant, his left leg stretched under the table, the foot still in a cast, and looked outside through the little windows to reassure himself that Don actually didn't remember a thing at all. He turned a glass of whiskey between his fingers, and his face spelled trouble.

He, the great Arnold McKay, the genius, the manipulator, had been confident that everything would go the way he planned it. But something had happened that annoyed him very much. It had to do with compunction, with something that ran counter to his principles. He emptied his glass in one draft and ordered a second whiskey. He wasn't able to drive himself with his foot in plaster and had come here by taxi—and a taxi would bring him home again later as well.

It would be no problem at all if Don entered the restaurant and saw him sitting there, although he didn't hope that he would actually do so. As far as he was concerned, he would never see Don Adler again after today. And most preferably he would if he only was strong enough to do so, step upon the quay and give Don a couple of hard blows, kick him into the water, and step on his fingers every time he tried to climb back again. And the moment Don was almost exhausted, he would hoist him back upon the quay and call the police.

"Hello, this is Arnold McKay. Yes, indeed, the well-known scientist Arnold McKay. Do you remember the murder of a fat man in Nacre Cove, five years ago? Well, I'm sitting on top of the offender right now, on the quay at the back of Restaurant Hernando... "

He swallowed away his anger with the second glass of whiskey, which had been brought to him a moment ago.

Don looked to the left and didn't remember how he had once crept up to the stairs there, dressed in rags and starving.

Much had happened after Don had gone to Franks Knight and beat up the attackers of Wesley Dunn and Jan Glass. He had come to show the people the way...

After Jan Glas had talked to the press in the city hall, the people of Franks Knight, divided into groups of forty, got the opportunity to meet him. Wesley introduced everyone to Jan and called Don his helper. Jan told them about his vision and explained why he had come:

"Wesley Dunn is and will remain your leader-he is the great Raso Preacher who taught you to obey the old laws. But three men are needed to bring you to safety in time. Wesley, Don, and I. My vision was understood by Wesley, and he has done his utmost to find me and invite me to come over to Franks Knight. I'm going to follow the path of my vision, and everyone who follows me will survive the great disaster. Believe in me, that's all I ask from you."

Many people knelt down for him spontaneously; others made a bow. Everyone promised him implicit faith.

"Show us the way," they urged him. "Show us the way, yes, bring us into safety. Fear haunts us, and we want to be saved, as Raso has promised."

"You will be saved," said Jan. "Your Raso Preacher has done the right thing by inviting me. I'm just in time. Pretty soon we'll go away from here!"

That night the men of the city security went from door to door to spread the news.

"Wait till it is dark. Step outside. Leave your doors open, leave your windows open. Don't take anything with you. Possessions have no value anymore. Go to Raso's mausoleum for a last good-bye. Wait for new instructions there. Don't make any noise. No one may see us leave. It is very important that we not be followed by curious outsiders."

Wesley waited for the people and handed out flowers, which they placed at the foot of the mausoleum. A lantern was burning there—the rest of Franks Knight was pitch-dark.

They cut down the palm trees. The roots, which reached under the mausoleum, would die back. The symbolism was clear to everyone: the way back was cut off, and Raso could rest forever now. When everyone had gathered in the park, the lantern was put out. Three words sounded in the darkness:

"Time to go!"

After that, there was only the whispering shuffle of soles over cobblestones. Wesley went in front, followed by Jan and Don. Behind them came the men of Wesley's gang of heavies and the members of the council committee. The gang of heavies was mainly there to keep the people away from Jan. One saw him as a holy person, one wanted to be with him and, if possible, touch him. He had arrived, and now he took everyone with him on a journey to freedom. The crack of doom was near, but Jan Glas knew where to find the place where Raso's followers would be safe.

When they arrived at the harbor, they found the fishermen of Franks Knight there, their boats tied at the dock. The engines grumbled softly. Everyone found himself a place on board one of the boats. Looking back was of no use when the boats left the harbor— Franks Knight was invisible in the darkness. It was forbidden to make noise. Even talking in a loud whisper was not allowed. They would have preferred to sing, to express the feelings of this moment. Instead, one started to hum, while the words sounded in everybody's head. It was a hymn to the honor of the great Manuel Raso. Without knowing the others on the other boats were doing the same, each group knelt down on the deck of their boat. The tears ran down the faces of the people. Some of them couldn't help whispering the name of the man who once had predicted that they would survive the disaster as long as they behaved according to the rules.

"Raso...Raso!"

No one wondered about the fact that the engines were shut off after half an hour.

No one complained when they had to climb down rope ladders.

No one protested when they had to swim.

After some minutes they felt the bottom under their feet, and they stood up to their armpits in the water.

"Follow the light!" sounded over the calm ocean. "Please, follow the light."

Don Adler led the way now, holding a lantern high above his head. In the weak light, one could see that Jan Glas and Wesley Dunn waded along next to him. The engines of the boats started again. They turned and the rudders were fixed. The first mates climbed down the rope ladders and swam to the others.

The now unmanned boats sailed away over the ocean—there was, on special request of Jan Glas, little fuel in the tanks, and after some time the engines would stall so that the little fleet would float on through the night in silence.

Now one started to sing softly. It was an old song that had been passed on from generation to generation, and it was about Manuel Raso who traveled through America and worked wonders.

Women burst into tears. Some of them began to feel weak and let themselves fall as if they expected that the spirit of Raso should push them forward. They were picked up and carried along by the others.

The group reached a shallow, silted-up bay. Once there had been a river here.

When the last man crawled ashore, the light was already far ahead. The people walked along a narrow path in a long chain, between bushes and trees. They held each other by the hand so that they couldn't lose each other.

Don Adler dragged more than four hundred followers of Raso along with him this way.

He went on indefatigably, thinking of nothing else other than to reach his goal.

The helmet had provided him with information and given him orders, and he knew exactly what he had to do. He quickened his pace. The sooner they had left this forbidden, protected nature reserve, the better.

All of a sudden he could hear the splashing of water.

The spring! he thought. We're almost there.

At both sides of the spring was a fence, which marked the border between the nature reserve and the ground of Arnold McKay. Don had made a lockable opening in the fence and had the key to the padlock.

After everyone found himself on the other side of the fence, Don closed the opening again and threw the little key, which was evidence if anything went wrong, into the spring.

It was still a long walk to the big square.

Finally, in the light of the stars, the wooden office, in which he had lived for such a long time, loomed up ahead. He passed inside and let his hand slide over a wall, found a button, and pushed it. Lamps, hanging on contact wires between the trees, lit up along all sides of the square. There were also lamps burning at the round bar in the center and at the bandstand at the right corner.

The old tugboat, at the left side, was lit up by a single spotlight that made the black hull shine. Don led the people to it. When he arrived there he let go of the hand of Wesley Dunn, who, in his turn, let go of the hand of Jan Glas.

"Now we're safe," said Don. He spoke in a loud voice now. And then, even louder. "We're there! We've made it!"

The people cheered, knelt down, and kissed the stones of the square.

"Raso!" shouted Wesley. "Thank you so much!" "Follow me!" said Don. "Before mother earth goes down twitching!"

He climbed a chromium ladder, jumped onto the deck of the tug, turned around, leaned forward, and reached out a hand.

"If you're too tired to climb, I'll hoist you up!"

Wesley made use of the ladder. Don showed him a round hole in the floor of the open wheelhouse.

"You can climb down there. Go on."

But Wesley remained standing there, as Jan Glas joined him.

"No," said Wesley decidedly. "The others go first."

He placed two of his men by the opening to help the people to climb down. The first one who did so was a woman. As soon as she had placed a foot on the upper step of a metal ladder, lights lit up and showed a deep shaft. The people crowded around the shaft and looked down. They waited until the woman had reached the bottom, and then they heard her voice resound.

"Oh...so beautiful! This must be paradise!" She looked up and beckoned. "Come, come!"

The two men didn't have to help anyone—now they had to see that the people didn't push each other into the shaft.

The lights at the sides of the square went out again. The bar and the bandstand were dark silhouettes again.

Soon all the inhabitants of Franks Knight found themselves in the underground ships.

Only Wesley, Jan, Don, and Gerald and Buck—the two men from the gang of heavies—were still standing in the bare wheelhouse.

"Your turn," said Don and nodded three times in the direction of Wesley, Gerald, and Buck.

"Jan Glas goes first," decided Wesley. "He has all the right to set foot in this paradise earlier than I."

Don wiped his chin nervously and tried to control himself. He hadn't reckoned with this. All of a sudden the situation had become frightening.

He had received orders to take Jan Glas along with him. He wasn't meant to go down into the shaft. And then there was another order: In time of need, you must try to save yourself. Don't trust anyone but yourself.

He made an inviting gesture with his hand, waving it, palm up, from Wesley to the shaft.

"Just go..."

But Wesley wouldn't change his mind. He shook his head.

Avoid every form of suspicion, sounded in Don's head, and immediately he put a hand on the shoulder of Jan Glas and pushed him in the direction of the shaft. Jan tried to turn around. Wesley raised a finger and looked at Gerald and Buck. The men understood what he wanted and each grabbed Jan by an arm.

"Allow us to help you," said Gerald. "The shaft is deep, but the ladder seems strong enough."

Jan disappeared into the shaft and was followed by Gerald and Buck.

Don reached out his hand.

"Good-bye, Wesley Dunn. I've done all I could to help you. Now I have to go back. I have to close the shaft. You can open it yourself from the inside, but only do so when you know for sure that it is safe again outside. You will feel the earthquakes when the disaster has become a fact. After that, it'll take a long time before all the dust has come down and the sun is visible again. Success. You're all so lucky... "

"Stay with us."

"I'm not like you. Neither is Jan Glas... "

"I consider Jan Glas as one of ours. You're welcome here."

"I have to go back. Family, people I love. I cannot let them down."

It was as if someone whispered these words into his ears; he thought it strange to hear how he repeated them spontaneously.

"I understand," muttered Wesley, but at the same moment, he began to feel suspicious, although he didn't know exactly why.

He looked at Don searchingly.

"Wait a moment. I have to think."

He shook his arms nervously as if wasps had crept under his sleeves. Then he raised his hands up to the iron ceiling of the wheelhouse.

"Raso, give me strength!" Wesley didn't know what to do anymore. Why was he hesitating? This wasn't the time to hesitate at all. He was the leader of the large group. Raso had the best intentions towards them, Tacendo was watching over them. Wesley's world was not big. When he had traveled to England, it had brought him a heart attack. Now he felt how his heart beat too fast. He belonged to his people. Still, the doubt was there. Suddenly his eyes lit up.

"Don Adler. You have taken us here. Not Jan Glas. Isn't that strange?"

Don opened his mouth, and the answer came out automatically.

"We held each other's hands. Jan was pushing me in the right direction. His energy flowed right through me. I could feel your energy as well and from all the people who came behind us. Jan is a visionary, a man with great charisma."

"Well...Jan Glas said that you're his guardian angel and that you met in England. You followed him to Franks Knight... "

"His spirit penetrates deep into mine. With my help, he managed to save you from disaster."

Impatient voices sounded up from the shaft: "Wesley! Wesley! Come down, it's so beautiful here... " Wesley shook hands with Don and stepped into the shaft. "Thanks for everything. I won't look at you anymore... I find it horrible to leave you behind after all you did for us, for you won't live much longer."

Don kept silent. He watched over the edge as Wesley climbed down. The shaft went right through the hold, through the bottom of the tugboat, and then deep into the ground. Don pushed a button behind the metal ladder of the shaft. Somewhere deep under the bottom of the boat, the shaft was closed by a steel plate.

There was more to do. The hold of the tug had to be filled so that no one would discover the shaft. Don climbed down from the tug and ran to an annex of the office. Everything stood ready there to make cement. He used a wheelbarrow to bring the cement to the tug, and there he filled up the shaft and the hold with it. Then he covered it with a metal plate painted in the same white as the floor of the wheelhouse. Back in the annex he pushed an invisible panel aside and pushed a number of buttons.

Generators started up, which would provide the occupants of the subterranean ships with energy. He closed the panel and went outside. After he had checked everything one more time, he went away.

This time he knew that he would never come back again. It was useless to have a final look around—it was still dark, and there was nothing to see. And so he hurried to the house of Arnold McKay.

There he took a shower, prepared himself a meal in the kitchen, and then went up to a spare room and turned in.

There was no safer place to spend the night than in the impregnable fortress that Arnold McKay had made from his house, and Don Adler slept like a log.

Arnold peeped through the window at Don. He was thinking the same thing all the time.

"He has left Jan Glas behind! My God! This is disastrous!"

Don Adler should have taken Jan Glas to the house. Then he would have seen to it that Jan would remember nothing of the events, after which he would have put him safely on a plane back to Holland.

The master plan had failed, and not only did he blame himself for it, he also felt sick about it. Although he wasn't a man who easily panicked, he began to feel very nervous now. He didn't need the help of a psychiatrist to analyze himself.

He, Arnold McKay, was a genius. But this time his legendary intuition had let him down—and at a crucial point.

I should have expected this, he thought. A genius. He knew it himself. The people around him knew it.

No one had to tell him that he was also raving mad. He was busy taking revenge on the death of his parents and would let more than four hundred people die of hunger and thirst in their subterranean paradise. He felt no pity for them. The people from Franks Knight had deserved this. But Jan Glas was there, too, and if he died with the others, he really was a murderer.

It gnawed at him that he was doing exactly the same with Jan Glas now that the people from Franks Knight had done to his parents.

This could not be, this should not be—but for the time being, he had no idea how to redress this big mistake.

On the day that Arnold had drunk his first whiskey and left Joe Pendelton's grocery, he had made a decision: everyone who had been responsible for the death of Patrick and Susanne Martens would pay for it with their lives. They will die the same way, he had thought.

He saw Don Adler pay his bill. The waitress came back inside. She walked up to the telephone, and Arnold heard her order a cab.

To Perry, he guessed. He's going to the bank. Maybe he'll buy himself a couple of nice suits. And then he'll take the train to the airport."

"To Perry," he heard the waitress say.

He ordered another whiskey. After he had emptied his third glass, a cab driver came inside and the waitress showed him the way to the French doors that led to the wooden quay.

"He's sitting alone at a table, a broad-shouldered man."

Not much later Arnold could see Don rise to his feet and go along with the driver, down the stairs of the quay at the side of the restaurant, to the cab.

"There you go, Don Adler," muttered Arnold, while he raised his empty glass to attract the attention of the waitress. "Just praise yourself lucky that you're still alive."

And then he whispered all the curses he knew, which were quite a lot altogether. Two days later Arnold McKay found himself on the big square of Lost Harbor. He wasn't alone there. Every stool around the big stone bar in the center of the square was taken. Huge barbecues stood at four different places. Mexican musicians played in the bandstand. People walked up and down, eating, drinking, talking. Countless umbrellas gave shade on this hot day. Arnold had invited everyone who had been helpful with his searching for the Machine of Colton in Mexico.

True to his tradition he had also invited a number of business friends and there were also employees from his offices in Perry and people from the press. Everything had been arranged long before, and it should have been a big, exuberant party. But the band played quiet music and the panpipes cried with sad sustained notes and no one was dancing. For how could everyone be happy, when not far away from there, in Franks Knight, all inhabitants had vanished without a trace? The people of Franks Knight had everything to do with the Machine of Colton—the Raso sect had been convinced that the machine would set the world on fire. Now they all had gone, and no one could say what had happened to them.

"A party—as if we are celebrating the crack of doom," said Arnold in a wry voice to a couple of journalists. "But everyone was already on his way, I had already ordered rooms for everyone. There's no place to find in Nacre Cove, and besides, I had hired the entire Spring Tide Motel. We're not mourning, as long as there's still hope for the people of Franks Knight, but we're not in a merry mood either, because we fear that something serious has happened to them."

Arnold had planned the party long before. It would last for a couple of days and nights. He didn't even need his intuition now to understand that someone from the police or one or another official would come to visit him here and ask him a couple of questions. He wanted to receive that person here, on the square of Lost Harbor, while deep down under his feet more than four hundred people probably still believed that they found themselves in paradise and waited to feel the all-destroying earthquake, the end of the big world.

That was the way he played his game. Spectacular and full of risks.

It happened on the second day of the party.

Someone had rung the bell at the gate in front of the house. There were servants in the house now, and one of them opened the gate to let the visitor in. A nondescript Ford turned up the drive, and the chauffeur found a place among thirty other parked cars. Someone stepped out who introduced himself as Chris Lockhart from the FBI field office in Jacksonville. He wanted to have a talk with Arnold McKay. The servant called Arnold and took Chris with him to the back of the house. There stood a couple of four-wheel-drive motor vehicles. The servant took his place at the wheel, and Chris sat in the back. The servant drove at low speed over the winding, bumpy paths to Lost Harbor. Chris got off there and walked over the busy square, hands on his back, his eyes peering behind his sunglasses. He knew Arnold from pictures and television programs. When he saw him, he didn't go up to him immediately but observed him from a distance. Arnold had already seen him come with the servant and knew exactly who he was. Together with Sebastian Estanol, each holding a glass of champagne in one hand, he walked, leaning on a crutch, up to the newly arrived guest and said, "Still, it's a beautiful day, with all these people together. If there was only some news about the people from Franks Knight!"

Sebastian started to react to this, but Chris took a step forward and remarked, "If there's any news, I'll be the first to hear it. So if you stay close to me..."

His boxer's nose seemed to become even flatter when he grinned. He reached out his hand to Arnold.

"Chris Lockhart, Bureau of Investigation and Security Service—I'm conducting the investigation from the city hall in Franks Knight."

"Well!" said Arnold. "Pleased to meet you. My name is Arnold McKay. This is my friend and every now and then my business partner, for better or for worse, Sebastian Estanol from Mexico. Do you want to talk to the both of us or to me alone?"

"You alone, for the time being. As soon as you have time."

"But of course."

Arnold leaned heavily on his crutch and looked around, while Sebastian walked on. "Let me see. Where can we have a quiet talk? Ah. There. The old tugboat. Please come along with me."

They walked past big tables filled with all kinds of foods. Somewhere jugglers were stunting with balls and cones. The band played merrier music now. Arnold was addressed several times by people who wanted to tell him how much they were enjoying the party. Finally, they reached the tug and climbed on board, Arnold asking Chris to help him by hoisting him up and taking hold of his crutch.

Arnold limped over the deck with his guest and explained, "The tug is a reference to the harbor which once was here." He pointed straight in front of him. "There was a tributary river, which flowed into the Gulf of Mexico not far from here, but it was blocked by a dam, far inland. The harbor itself has never been anything special. Once there was a breaker's yard here, which couldn't make any profit. I bought all this ground when I had found the ideal spot to build a house. Lots of other things will change in the future."

"I'm impressed," said Chris, while he looked around. "Beautiful, such a big square, palm trees around it, and there a forest, oak trees...What an idyllic place this is. What more is going to change?"

"I'm always busy," said Arnold. "I only come here a couple of times every year. The offices and companies in Perry compel my attention, and I've always traveled around to keep myself informed about scientific developments, buy myself into interesting companies, and hive off other businesses. I want to build a few little but very comfortable holiday cottages on two sides of the square. Then I'm thinking of a big swimming pool and a tennis court. Friends and acquaintances can come here then to relax at my expense."

"And then do some business as well," remarked Chris.

"You understand it," said Arnold. He limped to the rail and beckoned a servant in a black suit. "What will it be, Chris? Champagne?"

"Mineral water, please," answered Chris. "Am I allowed to start my questions?"

"Of course. Come, we can sit in the shade of the wheelhouse; there are some comfortable chairs there. Tell me all about the developments of your investigation and, but no—you're the one who asks the questions... "

Not much later Arnold asked the servant who brought the drinks to remain standing at the foot of the metal ladder and let no one pass.

"It's surprising how close you live to Franks Knight, Arnold—am I allowed to call you Arnold?"

"Of course, Chris. It's not as surprising as you think. I have more houses. A penthouse in Perry, a little flat in New York and two houses in Europe, a bungalow in Italy and a chalet in Switzerland, to be exact. I was born not far from Franks Knight. My parents moved often, but we always came back here for unforgettable holidays. Soon after I had started to earn good money, I made up my mind to buy land here and build a house. I hope to spend more time here eventually, for I think it's beautiful here." "Well all right, but I have marshaled different facts and come to some striking conclusions. Jan Glas, who apparently disappeared together with the people from Franks Knight, was present at a symposium in England, which was financed by your magazine ParaPsycho. A magazine which was still unprofitable, so you must have put in money personally. And of all people it's Jan Glas who comes to Franks Knight, ParaPsycho paid his trip. This could be arranged, one tells me in England—I'm talking about editor-in-chief Pamela Mitchell now, with whom I had some lengthy telephone calls—because he could go to Florida for ParaPsycho as a journalist, but he'd had that miraculous vision and had become a man with a strange mission all of a sudden. Not exactly an objective journalist, if you ask me, he was kind of creepy! Probably should have seen a psychiatrist."

Chris looked at Arnold questioningly.

"I'm a scientist, Chris. I see things the way they are and when they appear to be different, we have come to understand them mostly thanks to the terrific research of colleagues. But, I also foster a certain interest in mysterious, unexplainable things. Just as I'm used to dining in the most expensive restaurants in the world but sometimes step into a joint where they sell nothing but junk food."

"What do you mean by that?"

"ParaPsycho is nothing but a hobby next to my scientific and technical work, next to my positions as manager, director, financier. I never thought that the magazine would become profitable, and I would have been satisfied with a small loss. Then, all of a sudden, all kinds of things happened—totally over my head. I had nothing to do with that symposium you mentioned, and I hadn't ever heard about Jan Glas either."

"But once again, you're living here close to Franks Knight. Did you ever come into conflict with these people?"

Arnold burst out laughing.

"Right! Of course! They troubled me, not knowing that I'm a great magician. I snapped my fingers, and they vanished on the spot. Is that what you want to hear? Are you accusing me of something? Why don't you just tell me then?"

"You shouldn't get angry at your own party. I'm sorry if I have offended you. For the time being, everyone's a suspect to me." Chris pointed at arbitrary party-goers "He there, in that blue suit, just as good as she there in her white dress. What I mean Arnold is that I know nothing at all yet. The investigation is stuck, and all I can do is question people. It's your turn now; soon I will be talking to someone else. About the people of Franks Knight— how well do you know them?"

"I've seldom been there. The first time I went to take a look, I was a boy of eighteen. I still remember well. No one was very talkative, except for a man from a grocery, Joe Pendelton. He told me about Raso. I found it shocking to hear that these people really believed in the crack of doom. Since then I have driven through Franks Knight once or twice, to impress curious business associates. They opened the car windows and leaned outside to take pictures of Raso's big mausoleum. I only became really interested in what happened there when I was busy setting up ParaPsycho, and Pamela Mitchell—you mentioned her yourself a moment ago—told me about Jan Glas, who had come out with the sensational history of Captain Adriaen Kalf. That is to say, Pamela wanted to write an article about that and invite Jan Glas to the symposium. No one could have suspected then that the Machine of Colton should lead to Franks Knight— to my very own neighbors!"

He shook his head and added, "I could laugh heartily about it, but that doesn't seem very nice as long as all these people are still missing."

"Maybe you have a theory about it? Do you have any idea what might have happened to them?"

"I've thought about that. Well, to be honest, I think about it all the time. For, however you put it, this is a unique situation. I myself think that they have found a place to stay somewhere, where they think that they are safe when the earth explodes. They have prepared themselves very well; maybe they have worked for years and years on their plans. Jan Glas came to tell them that their time was almost up. Now they have executed that plan and managed to leave their homes without a trace. There obviously were no witnesses. No one has seen them leave."

"I agree with you so far. But where have they gone to? Do you have ideas about that as well?"

"Yes. Let me tell you about it. But first I'll give you some well-meant advice. Guard Franks Knight day and night, see to it that nothing gets stolen. Give the bill for all the efforts to Wesley Dunn, after he has come back with his people. For believe me, as soon as the waiting for the disaster takes all too long, they will decide to return to their homes. They are extremely fanatic followers of a theory that is wrong from all sides, and it won't take long before they find out about that. Second, search for book-keeping; there might even be a double-entry book-keeping record in the city hall or somewhere else."

He stopped talking as the band raised the volume at the end of a number. Chris took the opportunity to ask in a loud voice, "What does book-keeping have to do with it?"

"They've found a shelter somewhere. They must have paid for it. They're not in a hotel or something, take that from me. It has to be a secret place, something like a bomb shelter. They must have all kinds of conveniences at their disposal. They need gas, water, electricity, but also an enormous food supply, for so many people. Do you understand? I would look for papers or computer files and put a couple of good accountants to work as soon as you have found something. On the other hand, you might as well do nothing at all and wait quietly for their return."

"I choose the double-entry book-keeping," said Chris. "And further?"

Arnold shrugged his shoulders.

"I see those fishing boats as I see the open windows and doors. We've seen all about that on television. The ships float away, the houses are open. In other words, the people of Franks Knight show to the world that they have need of nothing anymore. Franks Knight will get destroyed, the ships will sink. But they have reached a place where the spirit of Raso, with the help of the great god Tacendo, will save them!"

He leaned over to Chris, his elbows resting on his knees, and said in a conspiring voice, "I had such a great time in Mexico. That is to say, before I broke my left foot. We have discovered some special constructions, and in the meantime, I did some interesting business with different people who had come with me to the hacienda of my friend Sebastian Estanol. We didn't find the Machine of Colton. But what we met on our path was an avalanche of publicity, and ParaPsycho, that marvelous magazine, has sold extremely well worldwide and yields a profit instead of the expected loss. Take it from me, Chris, that no one will ever find the Machine of Colton, and the people of Franks Knight will soon live in their own houses again."

"Are you telling me that it has all been no more than hype? What do you think then about everything Captain Kalf wrote and what Mary Landock has shown? And where has that mysterious Mary Landock gone to?"

"Three questions in a row. Kalf, the Cape of Good Hope, long ago. Who can tell? Maybe he was telling lies in order to save his skin. History doesn't tell if he succeeded in that or not. He might as well have gone completely mad or committed hallucinations to paper after having smoked lots of opium. I know almost nothing about Mary Landock. I never met her and only heard about her from Pamela Mitchell. Pamela has talked to her long and often. Well, if the entire population of Franks Knight can disappear from the face of the earth, surely a single scientist can do the very same."

"How did the people leave Franks Knight?"

"You have to make inquiries about that, Chris! And I'd take a chance on trucks. As far as I know, no one in Franks Knight ever had a driver's license. They used horses and carts there. A couple of big trucks drive up to Franks Knight, the people climb in, and there they go!"

"Very well possible. Trucks take them to something like a bunker. You've been of great help to me. Also where that book-keeping is concerned."

"Perhaps they've gone to another state," said Arnold. "Think of a rocky territory, think of caves, deserted mines. Chris, let me order another drink for us. Would you like to have a glass of champagne now?"

"Please. One glass can do no harm," said Chris. "Caves, mines, ideal hiding places..."

Arnold called the servant who stood leaning against the ship's plating and asked him to bring a bottle of champagne. The men went deeper into the situation, and both of them came up with new theories. When Chris received a call, he stood up, pressing the cell phone to his ear, and left the wheelhouse, Arnold sat there alone and stared fixedly at the metal floor, as if he could see right through it to what happened deep down under the boat. He wondered how more than four hundred people would react when they started to suspect that Jan Glas had trapped them all and that they would never be able to leave their subterranean paradise. Would they kill him? Jan couldn't give a satisfying answer to any question. Who had taken all this trouble to receive them into a little Shangri-La like this where there was plenty of foods and drink? The spirit of Raso? The Olmec god Tacendo? Or a man of flesh and blood with bad intentions? For how long would it remain quiet down there under his feet?

The feeling of guilt that had nested in his head began to grow like a malignant tumor.

Chris entered the wheelhouse again, put his cell phone in front of him on a solid wood coffee table and produced a second cell phone, which he showed to Arnold on the flat of his hand.

"In Franks Knight, they had only one telephone." In Joe Pendelton's grocery, thought Arnold, but he said nothing. "It was in a grocery," said Chris. "Jan Glas had a cell phone. Look, it's this one. He left it behind in the city hall. A pity, yes, such a pity. Otherwise, we would have been able to locate him."

Don Adler was instructed to take it away from him, Arnold thought. He was the one who left it in the city hall.

The conversation went on for another thirty minutes. Then Chris stood up and shook hands with Arnold.

"I have to go back to the city hall. There's a lot to do. Yes, I hope as well that the people will return to Franks Knight after some time."

"That will happen," Arnold assured him. "Like carrier pigeons who always return to their base. The world will not explode, and the people from Franks Knight will not settle down in their new shelter. No matter if they find themselves deep underground now or on top of a hill—one day they will decide to go back home."

Chris left the wheelhouse and climbed down. Arnold saw him on the square, talking to Sebastian Estanol and different other people. Then Chris caught a ride back to his car with one of the servants.

Lost in thought, Arnold remained sitting in the wheelhouse for a while before he went back to his guests.

For the time being there was no one in the belly of the subterranean boats who felt caged or in panic. They seemed to be in paradise. Don Adler had created a shelter for the people of Franks Knight that could hold its own with a five-star hotel. He had connected six coasters to each other with high metal cylinders. First, he had made big round holes in the ship's plating with an oxyacetylene torch, after which he had welded the cylinders, which had been made to measure beforehand. A solid wooden construction had given two extra stories to every ship's hold. There were huge bedrooms, two enormous kitchens, twelve bathrooms, supply closets, launderettes, a fitness center, various community halls, and smaller living rooms. There was an easy chair for everyone.

The energy was produced by generators—Chris Lockhart had not discovered them during his visit to Lost Harbor, but if he had seen them he would have understood that Arnold McKay used them for the lighting around the square and the equipment of the bar and other facilities.

The water supply had been no problem at all. Don had discovered a little well not far away from the harbor and he had laid in underground piping. It was easy to turn it off with a tap near the well.

The only one who made use of the fitness center was Jan Glas. The people of Franks Knight spent their days mostly meditating. Every coaster was provided with wall clocks, and they lived according to the principles of day and night - at eleven o'clock at night all lights went out, and at six in the morning they went on again.

Jan could not give an answer to the question, Who had made this safe shelter available to them?

"It must be providence," decided Wesley Dunn. "A miracle we'll have to accept as a gift. For this had been predicted by Manuel Raso! The big world is going down, and we will all stay alive!"

Everyone was content with this for now. The underground life was pleasant. The supply closets were well filled. No one was hungry, no one was thirsty, and no one took it into account that their stay here could last for a very, very long time...

10

The House of Arnold McKay – Present Day

One night Arnold came back from Perry, where he had been living in his penthouse and working in his offices. The cast around his foot had been removed at the hospital. He still walked with a crutch, but he was able to drive a car now.

During his absence helicopters had flown above the territory around Franks Knight, and soldiers had combed the neighborhood and had also set foot on Lost Harbor.

Chris Lockhart had visited him in his office at Arnold M. Tech Tactic Labs Inc., where Arnold M. Holding Inc. was also established. Without realizing it, Chris had given him information that had made Arnold feel a bit calmer.

"We found nothing. Not a single clue. Your Lost Harbor looks so nice from the air; I looked down on it when I went along on a flight."

Heavy showers right after the disappearance of the people of Franks Knight had washed away any tracks, and Arnold was only too glad that no one had come up with the idea to bring in tracker dogs and take them to the mouth of the dried-up river. No doubt they would have found the tracks of more than four hundred walkers there, despite the rainfall.

He hoped that Chris wouldn't ask him to loan him the advanced equipment he had used during his searching through Mexico—a flight over Lost Harbor with that would show the subterranean coasters as if they were only covered by a layer of translucent glass. But the police, the FBI, and different security services relied on their own equipment, which wasn't as good as Arnold's.

Behind his hand, Arnold had permitted himself a little, arrogant, superior smile, after which he had asked Chris for the purpose of his visit.

Chris didn't beat around the bush.

"I'm here to invite you to dinner in a good restaurant. Then we can talk at ease. You're still one of the main suspects because your name keeps on turning up everywhere. There are many things I just don't understand. You went to Mexico to search for the Machine of Colton, but you never took the time to go to your neighbors in Franks Knight to ask for information there."

"People who give no answers to your questions are not worth a visit," said Arnold.

"All right. That sounds reasonable. It's very well possible that I'll scrap you from my list, or put you somewhere on the bottom of it anyway. In the meantime surely you have a couple of new theories for me, which will be just as useful as the former ones. For you have—"

Arnold interrupted him, "I don't like the words suspects and lists at all, and it irritates me that you say them in connection with me. The Raso followers believe fanatically in their bizarre theories, and now they have left. Out of their own free will, we may assume. You only speak of suspects when there's talk of aggression—or worse, murder. And in this case, there's no talk of that at all."

He added to this in an authoritarian voice, "I hope I have been clear enough." After dinner, Chris had become none the wiser, and Arnold still didn't know how high he stood on the list of suspects. Chris went back to Franks Knight. Arnold could have driven along with him because he wanted to go to his house at Lost Harbor. But he'd had enough of the conversations with Chris, during which he had to stay on the alert constantly and had to mind his words. In the parking garage under the building of his penthouse stood a little sports car, and he used it to drive back himself.

Now he was sitting in his living room with a glass of whiskey in his hand, staring at the clock on which the silver Raso stood, ready to swing around his scythe.

After the party, everything in Lost Harbor and his house had been cleared out, and now he was alone.

For some time already he had been thinking about setting everyone free and telling everyone that it had all been a joke, but he understood only too well that he would get heavily punished for that; there was a chance that he would spend the rest of his life behind bars.

Besides, he wasn't able to do that all by himself. The coasters lay too deep in the former harbor, and under the square was a thick layer of concrete. There was no way out. He had let go of that idea every time—and his hatred towards the people of Franks Knight was so immense, that he wanted to leave them to their fate.

They would run out of food. Soon there should be no more fuel left to keep the generators running so that there should be a permanent power failure. And then he would go to the little well himself and turn off the water, which would make his revenge complete.

The clock struck eleven. Raso swung his scythe around wildly. Arnold drank whiskey and started reflecting upon everything that had happened after he had left Joe Pendelton's grocery as an eighteen-year-old boy, to check if he hadn't made a mistake that could bring him into trouble after all.

First of all, he realized that he'd had a lot of patience—he was forty years of age now—and that it would be absurd to change his strategy after such a long time.

He had put them deep underground, all of them! He had been judge and executioner at the same time, and soon it would dawn on them that they had done the same to Patrick and Susanne Martens.

He cursed wholeheartedly, and then he cried out in despair the name of the Dutchman.

"Jan Glas!"

Then he stared into his glass and began to marshal the facts.

He had never told Louis and Emmy McKay that he knew that they were not his biological parents. He had gone to Florida with Micky Sharpe because he wanted to pay a visit to Franks Knight. There in the grocery, he had found out the truth, which he always had kept silent from Louis and Emmy.

Arnold had vowed vengeance against the people of Franks Knight and started brooding on plans. In the meantime, he plunged with wild enthusiasm into his studies. He was a young man of genius and wanted to know as much as possible about as many subjects as possible because, as he said to himself often, "Who can tell what I'll need to know later, to give the murderers of Franks Knight what they deserve!" Next, to his textbooks, he devoured literature. Wherever his parents moved, he found the way to the library immediately.

One day he got hold of an old, thin book, written by a certain Jason Fournier. The man had run away from the suffocating Franks Knight long before Wesley Dunn had seized power and kept the people together by using strong-arm tactics. The title of the book was The Heavenly Vision of Manuel Raso. That way Arnold came to know that Manuel Raso actually had existed and that he must have been a special man. He read everything about the vision and the horrible thing made by the Olmecs and their god Tacendo. The book ended with the fearful suspicion about the future of the world and Franks Knight. Arnold knew all about the fanatical attitude of the people from Franks Knight where the teachings of Raso were concerned, and he understood that the madness had come to a head under the leadership of Wesley Dunn—it had resulted in the death of his parents.

Arnold wanted to see something of the world and decided to go to Europe during his summer vacation. Because he had done his best at the university, his father gave him sufficient money for the flight and hotels. He landed in London, went on to Paris, and finally ended up in Amsterdam. Everywhere he came he kept his eyes open, and he started to hatch plans. He was very interested in the imposing history of old Europe, and when he went back to America, he knew that he was going to use something from the past for his retaliation.

He had time enough.

For now, it was important to study hard, increase his knowledge, and amass a fortune. Knowledge plus money was power. Arnold wasn't someone to devote his attention to books only; he loved to put everything he had learned into practice. At a very young age, he was already an engineer who made computers obey as if he had put a spell on them. He was a master in improving other men's inventions and was hired by big companies to fiddle with their latest products. He worked in the car and aircraft industry and made a fortune there. Next, he came up with new designs for complicated medical equipment, which gained him fame. He became acquainted with a team under the management of another young genius, the Mexican Sebastian Estanol, which worked on the interesting interaction between brains and computers. Here he had something with which he could further his long path to revenge.

He entered into a cooperation with the team, and that turned out to be a lucky strike. In a short time, he learned much about the working of the human brain, and he saw countless possibilities for coupling it with advanced hardware. Together with Sebastian he put new products on the market, especially meant for hospitals and mental institutions. Sebastian was contented with what he had achieved and wanted to work fewer hours and buy himself a hacienda in Tabasco. Arnold said goodbye to the team and went on by himself. The business he and Sebastian had together was sold. In the course of time he had set up many businesses and sold them again, and he worked together with people in the USA, Europe, and Japan.

Arnold developed his helmet, which made it possible for him to penetrate into the mind of any arbitrary person.

Hatred was still his motive, revenge his goal.

He built up his plan, slowly, patiently, and precisely, just as his father once had built his clocks.

When he found himself in the Netherlands for quite a long time again, where he advised different companies in Amsterdam, Leiden, and Delft, he started to execute his plans. In an antique shop in Leiden, where he searched for beautiful paintings, he met an old man who stood leafing through old books and negotiated nervously with the owner. Although Arnold wasn't able to understand everything, he understood that the man would like to buy a certain book, but found it too expensive—he simply couldn't afford it. Arnold addressed the owner in English and asked with a smile what this was all about.

The owner pointed at the old man and said, "This is Adam Drost, my oldest and most troublesome customer. He's an expert where our history is concerned, a well-respected man of learning who..." he turned circles with his forefinger at the height of his temple, "gets more absent-minded every year. And he's still living in a far past himself because he thinks that my books cost no more than a handful of small change. He has an imposing library at home, and he simply can't stop collecting books."

Adam understood English as well and was also able to speak it. While he clutched a book as though he would never let go of it again, he said, "He overcharges me on purpose every time, because he prefers to exchange. One book of his for two or three of mine. But I never dispose of any book, and I just haven't enough money to make new purchases." There was Arnold's intuition again.

Not much later he had bought the book for Adam Drost and walked to his home with him to admire his library. Adam thanked him time after time, and as they went through the old town center, he said, "The book you bought for me was written in 1777, and it's all about the hunting rights in our country. It is dedicated to the Prince of Orange-Nassau. In fact, it doesn't matter what books tell about—they always give interesting information. Listen... "

He stopped and opened the book. He obviously wasn't as absent-minded as the owner of the antique shop had said, for Adam translated the Old Dutch directly into English:

"The right to hunt, that is to say, being allowed to catch and slay wild animals, is due to everyone according to the natural law... "

He looked up with sparkling eyes.

"Isn't that beautiful? The author, a certain Master Joachim Rendorp, goes against the rules of the nobility. For the nobility claimed, of course, that all the wildlife belonged to them and not to the common man. Joachim uses the entire history of the country to prove that he's right, and I'm convinced that he will come up with some important details in this. I'm going to read this book frontward and backward. It was published by a bookseller from Amsterdam, Petrus Schouten... "

He rattled on, rambled from one subject to another, relating that Rembrandt was born here in Leiden, in 1606, and described the castle of the city, which was built in the twelfth century, until Arnold interrupted him.

"Do you know about old texts? I mean, can you read all Old Dutch texts?"

"But of course!"

Arnold's heart beat faster.

"Would you be able to write it as well?"

"Faultless," said Adam proudly.

"I also mean the handwriting itself. It should look totally real."

"That's an art in itself, and I know the job."

"Then I have a task for you, which will bring you a lot of money."

"What is a lot of money?" Adam wanted to know.

"You know what I paid for your book. It seems reasonable to me to give you a thousandfold of that in exchange for a little friendly turn."

"A thousandfold?" Adam Drost's mouth fell open. He had no trouble at all with mental arithmetic.

At his home, in a living room full of books, Adam passed a proficiency examination.

Arnold made a deal with him and went back to his hotel. He called off all his appointments, and then he sat down at a small desk and began to write.

He wrote in English and made use of a ball pen and a scratch pad.

Two days later he went back to Adam and read the text to him. Adam asked him to leave the text behind with him and give him one day to think.

"And an advance, could that be possible?"

Arnold paid him a nice sum beforehand and made him swear that he would never talk to anyone about this project.

When he came back, Adam had worked out his plan.

"It wasn't all too difficult, for your story is clear—although it seems very fantastic to me."

"Go on."

"The East India Company was a good idea. I suggest that it all enacts round the year 1745. I chose the Cape of Good Hope as the location. One made an important intermediate stop there to take in fresh food and water and bring the sick ashore. I have filled in the names as well. I would like to call the captain Adriaen Kalf and his ship the Starfish. In a tavern, the Mutineer, he meets the Englishman who I would call Colton, eh..."

"Samuel," said Arnold determinedly, thinking of Raso, "which is very much like Manuel. A little joke you wouldn't understand. Go on... "

Together they brought the story to perfection. Then there was another problem.

"The ink," said Arnold. "The paper... It all has to be real. Faultless text in the right ink on the right paper."

"No trouble at all," grinned Adam, who would do anything to receive the promised money. "I have the ink. Indian ink is called Chinese ink as well, and it has existed for a very long time— more than two thousand years! In fact, it is a carbonaceous watercolor which becomes as good as indelible by an oxidation process. And where the paper is concerned..." He stood up and walked up to a cupboard. He took a green cardboard file out of it, which was closed by green ribbons. The file contained sheets of paper with letters and figures on it.

"This is part of a book-keeping of a brewery of Leiden. Drawn up in 1745, that's why I mentioned that date already. For look here...only the first ten sheets have been used. Under it, I have some blank sheets!"

Arnold looked at him in rapt admiration.

"Splendid. This is just what we need. You have so much paper now, that you could even permit yourself some mistakes."

Adam didn't share his enthusiasm.

"I always work precisely, I'm not intending to make a single mistake."

"Even better," said Arnold. "Get cracking!"

The time hadn't come yet to make it public, but Arnold was a patient man and put the document in a safe.

He had to find someone who did journalistic work and would understand that he had gotten ahold of something very special. At a later stage, he would make the same person believe that he'd had a spectacular vision—thanks to the helmet that would be placed on his head!

Years later, when Arnold had set his eye on Jan Glas and had arranged for a bookseller to sell him the atlas that contained the report of Adriaen Kalf, Adam Drost had already passed away.

The origin of the document had become untraceable.

When the big work in Lost Harbor was almost done, Arnold had gone on a business trip to Holland again. One afternoon he was present at a party of a company that had become so big with his help that it had to build a new office. When they had started to dig into the new location, they found a deep waste pit from an earlier age. Once, there had been houses standing there and the pit contained many objects that had been thrown away then but were of historical value now. There were tin jugs, stone plates, forks, and a broken stone pipe. Everything had gone to a museum, except for a tin jug, which had been given a place in the hall of the new office building.

Arnold watched the manager of the company pose for a photographer, standing next to the tin jug. There were two other men standing there as well, and Arnold was fascinated by the looks of one of them. He was young, in his early thirties, and slender, and his dark hair fell down at the sides of his narrow face. There was a dreamy look in his green eyes. Arnold was not the first person to call him a mystic in thought. He asked an employee of the company who he was.

"Oh," she said, "that's Jan Glas, a publicist. The other man standing there with our manager is the archaeologist who emptied the pit and did some other excavations as well. Jan Glas is interested in everything that has to do with history; he wrote some little articles about the finding in different newspapers."

Arnold knew enough. This was the man he needed. Everyone would believe someone with such eyes. In Franks Knight, they would believe everything he said. He kept on observing Jan. After some time he saw Jan take a business card out of his pocket and give it to someone. The man took it and put it on a high table between empty glasses and an ashtray.

Arnold walked past and, while Jan and the man were talking to each other, he snatched the little card from the table and put it in his inside pocket.

When he entered the lobby of his hotel, he took it out again and asked a receptionist if she could translate the text for him.

She read, "Jan Glas, Publicist, Translator," followed by his address and the different ways to contact him, and then, "Look here, in small letters. Looking for interesting old books, all kinds of subjects. Do you want me to call him for you?"

"No, thank you," said Arnold, as he took the card from her again. "Thank you very much for your kind help."

In his room, he called one of his offices in Perry, where a publishing company was established that brought different scientific magazines onto the market. It was time to carry out one of his ideas.

"You can start with the first number of ParaPsycho...."

In London, he did business with the Maximum Axion Laboratory Ltd. in East End. He went from there to Soho one night, where he visited a restaurant and stepped into a pub for a glass of whiskey. There he met a special young woman. Two stand-up comedians had already left the little stage opposite the bar under lukewarm applause when she was announced:

"Ladies and gentlemen, all the way from Australia, tonight here with us in The Cooler—Deborah Farner!"

Deborah entered the stage via a door. Under the vivid light of the spotlight, she looked vulnerable. She looked around nervously, with her big blue eyes almost hidden behind her long, blond curls.

Arnold found her very attractive, and it cost him a great deal of trouble to avert his face in order to see if others were gazing at her with the same admiration—as if such a finding would make him jealous instantly!

Deborah wore a white T-shirt, white trousers, and white sneakers. Without looking at her audience, she took the microphone from the stand and straightened her back. Then she stepped to the right of the stand and said something in the affected voice of an English noble lady. The next moment she stepped to the right and reacted in cockney, the language of the London gutters. Stepping to the left again, she made use of a Scottish accent, and then moving to the right she spoke like a Texan. The complete repertoire of English accents was linked to just as many characters—from lady to drunkard, from an unemployed person to the queen—without a hitch. But no one laughed. There was no humor in her texts. She remained standing there for another while after she had finished, put the microphone back on the stand and said, when no one applauded, "This was my first gig in England and probably the last one as well. It doesn't matter, I'm only a backpack tourist, and tomorrow I'll leave London again."

Then she made a bow, turned around, opened the door at the back of the stage, and disappeared. Everyone at the bar started talking again, except for Arnold. He slid down from his stool, stepped upon the stage and walked up to the door. He entered a little storage space, where the stand-up comedians sat down on casks and empty crates. They looked up at the little man, who seemed bigger than he was because he radiated so much personality. Arnold decided to keep his stay as short as possible.

With a self-introduction of "Lucas, agent," he attracted everyone's attention. He said, "Could I have a word with you in the bar, Deborah?"

He didn't wait for her reaction but went back to the bar. Fifteen seconds later she was standing in front of him.

"If you're an agent, then I'm a motor mechanic."

"How can you say a thing like that?" he asked in surprise.

"A real agent would ask for one of the talented men, but you choose me instead.

"Tell me what you would like to drink," said Arnold. "Tonight you'll have money, and you'll sleep in the luxury suite of an expensive hotel."

"I like dark English beer," said Deborah. "And I like luxury suites as well. Although, I must admit, that I am content with the room I have right now; which I have to share with several cockroaches. I don't feel much like sharing a suite with one very big cockroach."

Arnold grinned. Shrimp or Cockroach—what was the difference?

He ordered a whiskey and a beer and beckoned Deborah to follow him to a little table, sitting opposite to each other, Arnold got down to business right away.

"You'll sleep all by yourself in your suite. I sleep in another hotel myself. No, I'm no agent, but I do need an artist. An actress. You have to do something for me, and I will pay you well for it."

"Let me guess," she said.

He couldn't keep his eyes off her beautiful face.

Deborah shook her head.

"No, I can't make up anything, I just don't know… "

"Tell me about yourself."

"All right. My name is Deborah Farner, as you already know. I'm really from Australia, from Gosford, between Newcastle and Sidney, and I'm also really a backpack tourist. I'm good for nothing, all I can do is imitate some voices, and until now, I've never been lucky with anything. There's an Australian constant loser sitting here right in front of you. How about you? Who are you, and what's your real name?"

"What do you wish for yourself?" he reacted, ignoring her questions.

She took a sip from her beer, placed the glass back on the table, and leaned backward.

"Freedom," she sighed. "And freedom is only for sale for a lot of money. I'm dreaming of a house of my own, not in Gosford at the coast, but somewhere inland where one can be all alone. And a car—a pick-up—and some money in the bank." She sat up straight again and added to it with a smile. "A man to share my lazy life will turn up automatically then, don't you think?"

"Pretty soon you'll be able to buy yourself that house, with a brand new pick-up in the garage. And there will be money for you in the bank. Maybe you'll have to stay in your suite for a week, maybe for a month or longer, I just don't know. When the time has come, I'll let you know, and then you have to go to Harwich, where you will say some nice words at a symposium. You're someone who can pass perfectly for an attractive scientist, and you're bold enough to bring it to a good end."

"You're serious," she said. "I can see by looking at you."

He stood up.

"We'll take a cab, pick up your things, and go searching for an expensive hotel."

Arnold left the pub the way he had also left the storage behind the stage—without waiting for her. She followed him immediately, and in the street, she took his hand.

"This sounds very exciting," she said. "Do I get another name?" "Yes," said Arnold. "Remember it well. Mary Landock."

She repeated it a couple of times.

"It is etched in my memory," she said, and then she changed her voice and spoke quiet and well-mannered English from the highest circles. "I have always loved to study, but it is even nicer to mean something special to science now. All the gentleman here next to me has to explain to me now is what kind of profession I practice."

"You'll get the text from me on paper," promised Arnold. "Soon. As soon as I have written it down. The way you said that was perfect. I think you're also someone who knows when to keep silent about things that shouldn't get passed on."

He felt the pressure of her fingers in the palm of his hand.

"You can count on that. I mean it. But then I must count on that I've already received a nice advance before I go to Harwich."

"Of course. We trust each other. Wait, before we take a cab, I'll show you my passport. Then you'll know who I am which is something you won't tell anyone."

"You're an American, that's for sure," she laughed. "Unless you can imitate voices just as easily as me... "

Arnold took a swig and wiped his mouth. He screwed up his eyes when he looked at the clock his father had built. Listening to the ticking, he started to analyze the events he had reflected on in detail. Everything had fit together as perfectly as clockwork.

The four most important people were Adam Drost, Deborah Farner, Don Adler, and Jan Glas—the forger of the document, the woman who played Mary Landock, the man who worked in Lost Harbor, and the man who received the heavenly vision. Then there were various helpers, who had received big tips for little, but nevertheless, important services. Like the Amsterdam bookseller who saw to it that Jan got the atlas from 1901 with the Kalf document between its pages. Or the stuntman who had grabbed the purse from Mary Landock and jumped through a window; he had been awarded a brand-new BMW for his short performance. Arnold understood that everything would go as well as the value of the presents he gave. He had enough money. He had hired someone to cause the explosion in the barrack near Southend-on-Sea so that everyone would think it had been a hidden lab where Mary Landock had worked on secret projects.

Deborah Farner had ridden along with Jan Glas from London in his car. She had made him drunk and had put the helmet on his head when he was fast asleep—the way Arnold had shown her. When Jan woke up, he had looked round in surprise and didn't seem to know where he was or who she was. She had brought him to his car, where the man who would later burn down the barrack, waited. He had worked for Max Ax once and still had the key to the barrack and had furnished it according to Arnold's instructions. He would be generously rewarded. He wanted to escape the rains of England with his family and settle down in France. Arnold had bought him a nice house in Burgundy.

The man slipped behind the wheel of the Volkswagen and Jan sat in the back seat, where he promptly fell asleep. When he woke up again, he found himself sitting on the grass not far away from his car and saw the flames shooting out from the barrack.

The first thing he remembered was his vision...

Deborah was already sitting in the plane by then, on her way home to Australia. She had a lot of money with her, and there was also a great amount in her bank in Gosford. During the flight, she thought back to her successful performance at the symposium in Harwich. She had especially enjoyed showing the mysterious form of life to the audience. It was nothing more or less than an ordinary magic trick, brought to perfection by Arnold, who had put a minuscule appliance inside the kneadable plastic. The little Machine of Colton looked impressive, but the only thing that really worked was the light behind the little ruby red eye, fed by a little dry cell.

Arnold turned the bottle upside down above his glass and noticed that not a drop came out of it.

"Jan Glas," he whispered, "I'm so sorry... "

He had made up his mind. The generators of Lost Harbor would keep on running for quite some time before the fuel tanks ran dry. There was undoubtedly still enough food and drink in the subterranean ships. But he would close off the main at the well, and after that, he wouldn't return for a long time.

This decision implied that he was going to sacrifice Jan Glas.

There was no way out of the comfortable subterranean prison; it was impossible to escape. Arnold would close off the main and leave everyone to their fate.

The solution to his personal problem—compunction—was obvious. The helmet, which had worked perfectly for Jan Glas and Don Adler, should help him as well. Programmed the right way, it would wipe the death of Jan Glas from his memory so that only the glorious feeling of revenge on the murderers of his parents would remain. Don Adler had put the helmet into the steel safe in the office building in Lost Harbor. After he had worn his great invention, the helmet, for a couple of minutes, he would feel relieved and would be satisfied with himself and the things he had done during all these years.

He was delighted at this idea. This was the perfect solution in his drunken mind—it would be as if Jan Glas had never existed at all and someone who didn't exist couldn't perish of hunger and thirst.

He jumped to his feet, ignoring the shooting pain in his left foot.

All lights in the house were still burning when he went outside through the back door. The code for the lock on the gate was the same as that for the locks in and around the house and even for a drunk man easy to remember. It was a numerical code. The first four figures formed his year of birth, the next string his year of birth in reverse order, and then again the four figures of his year of birth in the right order. The fence opened, and he closed it behind him again with a kick of his right foot. Then he started to follow the path to Lost Harbor. It was a hot, humid night. The moon, almost full and high in the sky, gave enough light to see where he went. But his drunken head concentrated least of all where his feet touched the ground and several times he stumbled, swearing wholeheartedly each time. He favored using his right foot, to spare his left foot as much as possible.

He reached the square and immediately went up to the bar in the center, fetched a bottle of whiskey and a glass and hoisted himself onto a stool. He gasped for breath, filled his glass, took a swig. The sweat ran down his face, his back and breast were wet. Slowly but surely he calmed down. He straightened his back and looked around. He had to grin when he realized that this was the ideal place for hobos who loved a drink. Lost Harbor was an untraceable place.

Never before had he sat here all by himself at such a late hour. In the light of the moon, he could see the tug and the bandstand, the dark shapes of the palm trees, and behind them the oak wood like a black wall. Between the bandstand and the tug, he could see the wild ground that joined the nature reserve in the distance.

A man should be able to sit here forever, without any worries, without ever getting drunk.

"Jan Glas," he muttered. "Am I a murderer? Jan Glass. Am I just as bad as all these people right here beneath me?"

He jumped from the stool and started to kick his feet on the stones until he was screaming with pain. The alcohol hadn't made his left foot insensible to pain yet—he would need to drink a lot more for that. After a while, he went up slowly to the wooden office. When he had reached it, he could hear immediately that one of the generators had stopped. Something had broken down; perhaps something had come loose. He decided to let it be, entered the office, and reached for the light switch. Nothing happened. He groped his way to a cupboard, opened it and rummaged around. He found what he was looking for, a flashlight. With that, he went back outside again and stumbled past the wooden building over a narrow path that led up to old oak trees and ended at a little well. He moaned, sank down on his knees, and bent deep forward. He shined the flashlight under a big, twothousand-pound stone and put his hand into the cold water. His fingers slid along a tube and found the main faucet. He turned it off and aimed the beam of light at the moon so that it seemed as if he made the dark satellite visible.

Looking up at it, he burst out laughing and cried out, "This is the beginning of all misery! Only one generator left—and for how long? And no more water!"

He went back to the square and sat down on the bar stool again. He filled his glass to the brim. He had to bend forward to take a pull. One generator left no more water. That wasn't enough. Before he took the helmet from the safe, he wanted to do more, although he didn't know yet what that might be.

"Let me think," he whispered, and then he sat there for a long time, staring into the darkness. His gaze lingered on the dark silhouette of the tug.

"The tip of the iceberg," he grinned. "Everything that's under it remains invisible."

He thought automatically of Chris Lockhart—from the FBI, from the Secret Service, from the police, what did he care—with whom he had sat down in the wheelhouse, and he remembered Chris showing him Jan Glas's cell phone.

"That's it!" he muttered and reached for his glass to celebrate his discovery with a couple of swigs. "Communication! The revenge is not complete if I haven't made my voice heard to those bastards down there! If I could only reach them and explain to them why they are there!"

He had not taken this into account when he had ordered Don Adler to build the subterranean prison. When he poured more whiskey outside his glass than in it, he decided to drink straight from the bottle.

He nodded thoughtfully as an idea materialized in his befuddled brain like a magician on a misty stage.

Don had installed a number of air shafts, which swirled underground like giant snakes and opened their muzzles wide under the sloping edge of the square—invisible to everyone. Their length and a cleverly contrived system of partitions had made the shafts soundproof. They had a diameter of about six inches, but there were also two bigger airshafts that led to the two enormous underground kitchens. They emerged far from the square between the oak trees, and Arnold knew where to find them. The tubes had a much wider diameter, but the last sections, close to the kitchens, were narrow and also provided with partitions so that the people from Franks Knight couldn't use them as escape routes. Arnold thought that he would be able to get in from the outside and crawl down to the constriction. From that position he might be able to talk to the occupants if he called out to them at the top of his voice, they might understand him and answer him.

This thought obsessed him. He let himself slide down from the stool and staggered along the square. When his foot hurt him too much, he started crawling. He knew that one of the big airshafts was not far from the well. He used his flashlight to find his way. Although he was convinced that he was doing everything quickly, he was actually moving very slowly. There was a big difference between what his brain charged him to do and what his body did, and in reverse order, what his body did and what his brain registered. He got back up on his feet and trudged along past the well and stopped abruptly when his left foot sank into the water. It felt refreshing. He went on. Finally, he found one of the two big airshafts. It stuck out four inches above the ground, and a metal cap was placed above it to prevent rainwater from coming in. The cap looked like a dish turned upside down. Don had covered the top with glue and strewn it with earth and little twigs- anyone who didn't know that the airshaft was here would pass it unnoticed.

Arnold stretched his length on the ground and looked under the cap. He saw that it was held above the shaft by four metal strips so that there was enough space for ventilation. The strips had been fixed with bolts and nuts.

"Tools," muttered Arnold. "A wrench."

He could have taken the shortest way to the wooden office, but he went back to the square first and took a bottle from the bar. Staggering and finally crawling again, the bottle in his hand, he reached the office. In a cupboard full of tools he found what he was looking for and went back to the airshaft.

There he sat down with his back against an oak.

Every time he brought the bottle to his mouth, he looked up to the moon that shone through the leaves and blinked his eyes as if he stared into the headlights of a car. Then he put the bottle on the ground and slid on his belly to the shaft.

The moon had made a long journey through the sky when he finally had managed to unscrew two nuts and take away the bolts. Don had tightened them fast and it was difficult to loosen them. Arnold knew that he had no strength left to remove the other two bolts as well. He sat on his heels and placed his fingers under the cap. Then he stood up slowly. His arms stretched, but he didn't let go of the cap. The two metal strips that were still connected started to bend, and more space opened between the cap and the brim of the shaft.

Arnold sank down on his knees and shone into the opening with his flashlight. If he widened it a bit more, he should be able to slip through it. He bent the cap some more. Then he stuck his head under it and cried down, "You're all going to die, just like Patrick and Susanne Martens!"

He realized that no one could hear him, sat down again, and reached for the bottle. After he had polished it off, threw the bottle away as far as possible. He heard the rustle of the leaves, the dry crack of a twig, and a dull thud.

He lay down on his belly and slid back to the shaft. Suddenly he had to fight against an urge to sleep. He let the wrench fall down into the shaft and listened to the sound. The wrench clattered against the metal and landed deep down against a partition with a loud bang.

If I manage to get that far, they'll be able to hear my voice, he thought.

In the beam of the flashlight he saw that the shaft went down perpendicularly over a length of six or seven feet, and then it bent.

Reckless as he was now, he ventured into the shaft and slid down. He stopped with his calves behind the twisted cap and dangled with his arms down in the airshaft. As if this was the ideal position to think, he started to whisper the order of the coming actions.

"I'll scare them all. Wesley Dunn has to come to the kitchen, and I'm not going to tell him at first who I am. Only after I tell him that I'm the son of Patrick and Susanne Martens, will he realized slowly but surely that he's trapped. Maybe I can hear panic break out down there. Then I'll ask for Jan Glas and apologize to him. Then I'll go back up to search for my helmet and adjust it so that I can wipe everything that has to do with Jan Glas from my memory. That's the way I'm going to do it!"

He stretched his legs some more and slid down until he had hooked his heels to the cap. He hung from his feet with his full weight now and felt a pain as if his bones had been broken again. Crying with the pain he bent his feet forward. His stomach contracted and pressed whiskey into his gullet. He started to throw up. He came loose and slid through the shaft. Seven feet down he slipped on his belly through the curve and then sheer down again, to the left, to the right, down, faster and faster. He couldn't slow down on the smooth metal. He let go of the flashlight, and all of a sudden it became dark. The shaft narrowed. Arnold held his hands out in front of him, and they clashed against a metal partition. The bones in his fingers cracked and broke. His body came to a stop with a shock, and his body was pressed together in the narrow tube.

Arnold McKay was stuck like a cork in a wine bottle.

As if the shock had sobered him up on the spot, he was able to think clearly now.

The first thing he asked himself was Why didn't I realize that I would never be able to turn round again once I had let myself sink down?

Then he threw up for the second time.

It was ironic to think that he had been sitting down safely in his living room only a couple of hours ago; it would have been better to kill a bottle of whiskey and just go to bed. He would never sit there again, he would never again watch the silver Raso swing his scythe about on top of the clock his father had built.

In the dark, he couldn't check if he was still able to move his fingers. They had gone numb. His foot, on the contrary, hurts more than he could bear, and he started to sob, trying to spit out the dirty taste in his mouth and feeling a growing pressure build up in his head because he was hanging upside down.

I'll die sooner than Wesley Dunn and his people, he thought.

Hot air struck his face. He smelled food—somewhere deep beneath him, someone was busy cooking. He had to throw up for the third time, but this time his stomach was empty and he spit gall, which burned in his throat.

"Hello!" he began to shout. "Hello! Is there anyone who can hear me?"

He waited for an answer.

It remained quiet.

The pressure in his head was still growing. It was useless to hope for rescue. No one would miss him. He had his offices and companies and had arranged different appointments, but he was known to be a fickle man, and it had happened more than once that he was unreachable to anyone because he had caught a plane to visit someone in a faraway country who didn't expect him at all.

A business was like a medieval town: the serfs under the noblemen, the noblemen under their king—the employees under the office managers, the office managers under the owner and the general manager. Arnold was the owner and general manager, did what he wanted, and never gave account to anyone. It was lonely at the top indeed, as it was said so often, so lonely that no one would go out searching for him when he had become untraceable one more time and didn't answer the phone.

The pressure in his head increased even faster now. The blood sang in his ears and he heard himself pant.

I've lost, he thought. But I've won as well...

Then he lost consciousness, and his body relaxed.

11: The Netherlands, England, USA, Present Time

Robbert Goudriaan had followed the events in Mexico on television and the Internet and had bought all the papers and weeklies that reported about it. He had enjoyed everything where Mexico was concerned, but the disappearance of all the people from Franks Knight in Florida and Jan's vanishing into thin air as well—this news gave him the creeps. He wished that he was able to do something for his friend, that he could do a heroic deed that would bring him back again. He was angry at himself and thought that he hadn't used enough arguments to keep Jan from going to England and America.

Several times already he had walked to Jan's small apartment to take his mail from the mailbox in the communal hall and bring it upstairs. Each time he opened the door of the apartment and stepped inside, he hoped to see Jan sitting in his favorite armchair. But today, as on the other occasions, the living room was empty. He put the mail on the table and opened a window to air the house, and then he started pacing up and down aimlessly. He never stayed there for more than half an hour before beginning to feel too bad.

On Jan's desk, he found the telephone number of ParaPsycho among other notes. He copied it, and after he got home again, he decided to make a call. A receptionist put him through to Pamela Mitchell. She was shocked by the events and was happy to be able to talk with someone who knew Jan well.

"In a certain way I'm feeling guilty," she said. "I asked permission from Mr. McKay, our big boss in the USA, to send Jan to Franks Knight. Now he has disappeared, together with all these people, and no one has any idea where they've all gone to."

"I should like to come to London," said Robbert. "It'll give me the feeling that I'm at least doing something. I want to move, talk..."

"You're always welcome," said Pamela. "Although I can't imagine that I can help you with anything. On the other hand, I would really like to talk to you, so I leave it all up to you. If you wish, I can ask Hellen Derringer from the Third Eye Association to drop by as well; then the three of us can sit together and discuss what might have happened. Hellen is cut up by it, too."

Robbert felt relieved after the conversation. He decided to go to London first and then travel on to America. He wanted to see Franks Knight with his own eyes. Without another moment of hesitation, he plucked a painting from the wall, tucked it under his arm, and walked outside.

It was a little painting, a Dutch landscape under a cloudy sky, made at the end of the nineteenth century by someone of the Hague school. It was a valuable piece of art from someone who had worked in the style of Josef Israëls. He had been able to buy it at a good price from a colleague historian, who told him that it would never become valuable because it was not signed.

"It might very well be from Israëls himself, and if so it's worth a fortune. Now it's something you give away to a good friend like you."

Over the course of years, the painting had increased in value. Every painting from the Hague school was in demand by rich collectors.

Robbert dropped in on an antique dealer who lived on the same street and had asked him often if he was willing to sell the piece of art to him. The man was surprised to see Robbert standing in front of him now with the painting.

"Can I buy it now?" "You know the price. Let me tell you why I'm doing this."

The man knew all about the tragedy in Florida. He knew Jan personally and understood that Robbert couldn't hold out any longer in Amsterdam.

"England and Florida. With the money I'm going to give you, you can travel around the world several times."

"Then I'll have something left when I return," said Robbert. "And if Jan is with me, we'll go on a pub-crawl together—until all the money's gone, and we'll have to get cracking again with a thick head. And believe me, I mean it... "

"You'll get your money, Robbert. Are you taking a plane to London?"

"Yes, this very day—that is to say if you can arrange the money."

"More than that, I'll drive you to Airport Schiphol!"

Robbert slept in a hotel in London that night, and the next morning at ten o'clock he was sitting opposite Pamela in the office of ParaPsycho. It was in a big building that also housed the offices for the scientific magazines published by AMP.

Hellen Derringer was there, too. Pamela showed them a series of pictures of Jan Glas and Mary Landock, which were taken during the symposium.

"Jan was delighted with her," said Robbert. "It wouldn't have surprised me if he had fallen in love with her. She's very beautiful."

"And now they've both disappeared," sighed Hellen. "One would almost think that they have cleared off together, but then you would be forgetting about more than four hundred other people who disappeared as well."

Pamela told everything she knew about Jan. About his vision, his stay in the hospital, and their conversations with Jack Parker, the police inspector in Southend-on-Sea. Robbert listened attentively and often shook his head.

"It all sounds so implausible," he said. "How about the documents of Adriaen Kalf?" Pamela wanted to know from him. "It was those documents which involved Jan in this affair; without them, we would never have heard of him here in England. You worked together with him. Are they really so old?"

"Yes. Even the paper has been studied properly. I'm convinced of it that Adriaen Kalf wrote his report round the year 1745."

"But what to think of it? The Machine of Colton,...the little version which Mary Landock showed us, the stories about Manuel Raso..."

One theory after the other was suggested and brushed aside again. They talked together for more than two hours. Then Hellen had to leave, and Pamela had a meeting with her team of editors.

"We can talk more later," she promised Robbert. "Meanwhile, please stay right here in my office, and I'll see to it that someone brings you coffee and sandwiches."

Robbert devoured the sandwiches, for he had been too nervous that morning to have breakfast in the hotel. Pamela's desk and the table were covered with papers, pictures, and magazines. Robbert idly read a letter that had been sent to ParaPsycho. It lay on top of a pile of more than a hundred other letters. Quite a lot, he thought, taking into account that Pamela had said that most letters arrived via e-mail. The letter on top was written by someone who wondered how the Machine of

Colton worked. He laid it aside and reached for a second letter; it had to do with the same subject. Robbert chose some more letters at random. More recent letters were about the disappearance of the people from Franks

Knight. Jan Glas was mentioned several times. Someone had written a ten-page report about Olmecs, which he found very interesting. It contained information he had never read before. The next letter was very short; it contained one handwritten line only. When Robbert read it, his fingers began to tremble, and he felt dizzy with emotion. The words had been written by an attentive reader from Oxford. Robbert folded the little piece of paper up and put it in the inside pocket of his jacket. He neatened the pile of letters on the table and poured himself another cup of coffee from the thermos someone had brought him with the sandwiches. His fingers still trembled as he added milk and sugar to it and started to stir.

"If what I think is true," he whispered, "I haven't come here for nothing."

Then he picked up a copy of ParaPsycho from a pile of magazines. Mary Landock was on the cover. He opened the magazine. Page three contained a column written by Pamela, and under it stood all the information about ParaPsycho— Pamela, as the editor-in-chief, was listed on top, and then followed the names of the editors, freelancers, and photographers; the address; and information about the publisher.

Robbert nodded yes.

"Maybe the writer of that little letter loves to solve crossword puzzles," he thought, "or anagrams. Just like me."

He decided to keep the little letter and not show it to Pamela. He was sure that she wouldn't miss it—maybe she hadn't read it attentively at all—and it didn't seem wise for him to confront her with the contents.

Pamela came back. He talked with her for another thirty minutes. Then he said good-bye to her and went back to his hotel. The next day he took a cab to Heathrow, west of the town, and stepped on a plane, which would bring him to Florida within ten hours.

Chris Lockhart received Robbert Goudriaan in the city hall of Franks Knight on the second floor of the building and suggested they sit out on the big balcony. It was a hot afternoon, and the balcony had already been in shadow for a couple of hours. The main reason for Chris to talk with Robbert was to drive away boredom, for the investigation was stuck, and all he did during the day was wait for news from his men, who were still searching the houses and asking questions of the people of Nacre Cove and elsewhere.

They sat down on cast-iron chairs. When they looked over the balustrade they could see the square and the houses on the other side of Main Street.

"You're a friend of Jan Glas, a historian by profession, and you have worked with Jan on different publications about Captain Kalf. Am I right?"

"Yes. Jan is a good friend of mine."

He started to tell his story. Chris listened to him. As he listened, he looked at Robbert searchingly.

"So here I am. I just couldn't stay at home."

"But there's nothing you can do here, can you? You've made a long journey, from Amsterdam to London, from London to here—"

"I tried to make Jan change his mind. I blame myself that I gave up when I didn't seem to succeed. What has happened to him? What is your opinion? Did your research yield any results?"

Chris grinned.

"Robbert. Can I call you Robbert?"

"Sure, it'll make me younger than I am."

"Of course I understand that you're worried about Jan. We all are. Don't forget that this is a very complicated affair. Hundreds of people have vanished! I'm not at liberty to give out any findings. It may have been better for you to stay home."

But Robbert was not a man to be easily daunted.

"I've followed everything possible," he said. "I watched television until late, especially the English stations that gave the best information. As far as I see it, Chris—am I allowed to call you Chris, then? The entire inquiry has led to nothing yet. The days grow into weeks, soon the weeks grow into months—"

"Tell me, did you come empty-handed?" asked Chris with something of unexpected hope in his voice. "Do you know something we don't know?"

"I think so. I discovered something by accident, and I think that it is interesting. On the other hand, it is very well possible that you will consider it a false alarm."

Chris was curious. "All kinds of information are welcome. All right, all right, very welcome! And you're right, I have to admit it, our inquiries have led to nothing. Tell me about your discovery."

"Give me the time to explain it to you."

Even outside, in the shade, it was hot. Robbert pushed back his pair of glasses, which had slid down along his sweating nose.

Chris smiled apologetically. "If I had received you in my office in Jackson, we could have stayed inside and kept cool, but things are quite different here. In Franks Knight, they don't know what air-conditioning is."

Robbert gave a deep sigh. "Being a historian, I know as no one else that the world's most important men lighten the pressure of heavy decisions by permitting themselves little jokes. They have their personal oddities, like the cruel Nero who let himself be admired as a poet and singer. And in these days this hasn't changed, I believe. Take the quality of wealthy people who never have any cash in their pockets and always make another person pay for little things like a meal, a drink, or a souvenir. Artists who refuse to get on stage if their dressing room doesn't meet their requirements. They even—"

"I got it," said Chris.

Robbert nodded.

"Yes, yes, so far the introduction. It's just that I want you to understand what I mean. Very well then. I went to London, and in the office of ParaPsycho, I had a talk with Pamela Mitchell. While she had a meeting to attend to I was sitting there all by myself, I found a pile of letters from readers. I read a short letter. Very short indeed. One single line, with a name and an address under it. A reader from Oxford..."

Chris held his hands at the height of his chest and turned them around and around to urge Robbert to go on.

Now Robbert asked a question that made Chris lean back irritated and look up to the blue sky.

"Do you know what an anagram is?"

"No, I'm afraid I don't."

"I'm talking about the transposing of letters. You take all the letters from a word and make another word out of it. That's an anagram."

"I understand."

"You can do a thing like that with a name as well. I wouldn't know directly what I could make out of Chris Lockhart, for that I should have to write your name down first, and—"

"Please..." the voice of Chris sounded both despairing and begging. "Let me show you the little letter," said Robbert. "For I've taken it with me.

Remember what I told you about important persons and heavy decisions, see it in that context, and you'll agree with me that—"

Chris reached out his hand. Robbert took the letter from the inside pocket of his jacket and gave it to him. Chris unfolded it and read aloud,

"Mary Landock is an anagram of Arnold McKay. Best Wishes, D. K. Cooper, Oxford." He studied the line. "Mary Landock. Eleven letters. Arnold McKay. Eleven letters." "The same letters. An Anagram. "Okay, I understand that. What's your conclusion?" "I really would enjoy my discovery, if I wasn't so concerned about Jan, Chris. I've looked at that little piece of paper for hours, in my hotel room in London and on the plane, as if it was a book of a hundred thousand words. It seems impossible to me that this is sheer coincidence. You don't find two names just like that consisting of the same letters, from people who have nothing to do with each other—"

"Your conclusion..." urged Chris.

"A little fact has big consequences. Pay attention, I'm going to make large leaps now—Arnold McKay makes up the name Mary Landock. So the woman at the symposium used a false name. She played the role of scientist Mary Landock. If so, the life form she showed wasn't real either, the same as the little Machine of Colton was a fake. I even dare to say that the report of Adriaen Kalf might be a hoax."

"Could that be possible?"

"Everything's possible. Master forgers painted works that were attributed to famous artists like Johannes Vermeer and Frans Hals and bought by big museums. All one needed in the case of Kalf was paper from the middle of the eighteenth century and someone who was able to write faultless Dutch from that time. I confidently believe that Arnold McKay has fooled everyone, although his motives remain totally unclear to me. His name is in every number of ParaPsycho—Arnold McKay Publishing, and much was published about Mary Landock in the magazine. Her picture was even on the cover. That of Jan as well. And by the way, who introduced Mary Landock to the symposium? Hellen Derringer of the Third Eye Association? Pamela Mitchell of ParaPsycho? I think it must have been Arnold McKay himself. In short, I think that Arnold McKay has something to do with the disappearing of the people from this place and with that of Jan."

Chris remained silent. He had produced a little notebook and wrote down the two names: Arnold McKay, Mary Landock. With a pen, he crossed out the letters one by one.

"Small causes produce great effects," he finally said. "It is very possible that you're right. I've been convinced of it all the time that McKay played a central role in this bizarre game. I've talked to him several times. As a matter of fact, I wanted to ask him some more questions, but it seems impossible to reach him. No matter which office I call in Perry, I always get a laconic answer-

McKay comes and goes as he pleases, and sometimes he's trackless for a couple of weeks."

He repeated his last words and jumped to his feet at the same time.

"Trackless for a couple of—"

Robbert didn't know what else to do than to stand up as well.

Chris leaned over the balustrade and looked down at the deserted square and Main Street.

"Yes, this might be important. You know what, Robbert? Come with me. We're going to the house of Arnold McKay. If he's not there, I'll show you Lost Harbor, which is part of the land he bought. I can't sit still, and you've given me something to do. Together we can think up theories and work them out. Come, let's go right now."

First Chris led his guest through the streets of Franks Knight. Every now and then he opened a door for him so that he could take a look inside. They went past Raso's mausoleum, and Chris took him along to the stables and coach houses.

Robbert shuddered with fear time after time. It was so unreal to walk through a little ghost town like this. Every now and then a police car drove through the streets, but for the rest, it was deadly quiet everywhere.

Back on the square in front of the city hall, Chris stepped into a car, and Robbert sat in the passenger seat.

"McKay's house is not far from here."

On the way, they talked on about what might have happened to the people of Franks Knight. Robbert could see in the right side mirror that they were followed.

"Four of my own men," said Chris, who had noticed him checking out the mirror.

There was no reaction when Chris rang the bell at the gate in front of the house of Arnold McKay.

"Someone has made an opening!" shouted one of his men, who had stepped out of the other car and stood on the walkway near the fence. Everyone went to where he was standing. Two bars of the fence had been bent, one to the left and one to the right, so that a wide opening had come into being. A grown man could easily slip through it. The opening was right behind a thick oak tree that stood in front of the fence so that it was not easy to discover. Not far away stood an old, rusty van at the side of the road, with license plates from Georgia. Chris produced his cell phone, explained the situation, and asked for reinforcements.

"The house is watched constantly," he said. "And still the fence was forced open. The police are coming. I've told them to come to Lost Harbor, too. I wonder what we'll find there."

He stepped through the opening, followed by Robbert. The four men, who wore short-sleeved shirts and were armed with revolvers, came behind them. The group walked past the house, which looked like an impregnable fortress with all its shutters down and showed not a trace of burglary. They discovered a second opening at the back, not far from the gate. They slipped through it and came upon the winding path that led to Lost Harbor.

"Maybe it wasn't a good idea, after all, to take you with me, Robbert," said Chris. "If it gets dangerous, I trust that you'll remain passive and not stand in the way."

"It's far too hot for me to perform heroic deeds," responded Robbert.

Wet with perspiration the six men reached Lost Harbor and looked out on the big square from behind the bushes.

"There," said Chris, pointing out in front of him. "Four young people. At the bar. I'm pretty sure that they've watched television recordings made from a chopper, which showed the house of McKay and Lost Harbor, where a party was going on. Now they've come to take a look themselves, and now they're having free drinks. In retrospect, it's a wonder that only four people have managed to find this place. Come, let's go to them."

His men ran up to the bar. As soon as the gatecrashers caught sight of them, they jumped to their feet and took flight.

Chris strolled up to the bar and said to Robbert, "Sit down. What are you having?"

"How can you remain so calm in circumstances like this?"

"I don't have to worry about this situation. Soon my men will come back with two drunken and scared boys and two girls who are just as drunk and scared. It's so damn hot, that all I want to do now is check if the fridge is working and if there's enough mineral water."

"Mineral water..." mused Robbert. "I could do with a nice glass of beer."

Chris's men came back with the fugitives.

"A bar stool for everyone," said Chris, and pulled a beer as if he were an accomplished barkeeper. The inspector observed the four young people. He put a big glass of beer in front of Robbert and said, "Georgia. That's where you come from. Are you on vacation?"

"Yes," said one of the boys, looking at Chris with fearful eyes. "We have a room in the Spring Tide Motel and—"

"And you saw Lost Harbor on television and wanted to take a look there yourselves," Chris filled in. "Am I right?"

"Yes," said the boy again. "It had made us very curious—"

"Listen. We're not policemen but the police are on their way. I can see to it that you don't get arrested. You trespassed and stole liquor, but it's too hot to get excited about that. Just give me an honest answer to my next question. Did you use drugs?"

All four of them reluctantly nodded yes.

"Hard drugs? I'm sorry, but I have to tell that to the police."

"No, no hard drugs," said one of the girls. "Marijuana, that's all."

Chris reached out his hand.

"Give it to me."

"We threw it away," said the other boy. "When we ran. We threw it in a shaft."

"A shaft?" Chris pointed at one of his men. "Go with them to the shaft." And to the four youngsters. "If hard drugs are found, I'll hand you over to the police. If it's just marijuana, you've told me the truth, and I'll see to it my men bring you back to the Spring Tide Motel—for none of you is allowed to slip behind the wheel of that van of yours."

Robbert looked around. He was impressed. The big square, the bandstand, the tug, the palm trees, the oaks, the heat, the tension, the strange sensation of being so far away from home and immersed in the fantasy world of someone he had never met—this was Lost Harbor, Arnold McKay's hidden paradise.

And while he was sitting there, at the bar in the center of the square, enjoying his beer, all kinds of things happened around him.

Five policemen appeared. The boy and the man who had gone to the shaft came back. Chris listened to what they had to tell and decided, "Someone's going into the shaft. I want to know what was thrown down there."

To Robbert, he said, "What a strange story. It's an airshaft. The was covered by a metal cap. Two bolts have been taken away and the cap has been twisted off. Why is that airshaft there? Who unscrewed the bolts?"

He looked at the two girls and the two boys, who had heard his questions and shrugged their shoulders.

Ten minutes later one of his officers came up to the bar to tell about the results of their investigation.

Robbert couldn't believe his ears. "Mr. Lockhart. We have taken a body out of the shaft. It's Arnold McKay!"

Chris swung into action immediately. He sent two policemen away with the drunken boys and girls. "Drive them to the Spring Tide Motel in their van. They have to get out of here right away."

Then he took his cell phone and gave orders.

"Send a chopper with the right people and the right equipment. We have to search deep underground. Taking into account that we might have to drill right through concrete."

Robbert stayed out of it all. He remained sitting there on his stool at the bar and watched the activity on the square increase.

Two big helicopters landed.

Men in uniform and plain clothes swarmed over the square like ants.

Some searched for hidden spaces under the square with special equipment.

Some started drilling, cutting, and digging; a hole was made right behind the tug.

"The gates to hell will open!" he heard Chris Lockhart shout.

It became even more crowded on the square as more than four hundred people appeared from the depths. They were all silent and moved like zombies, with drooping shoulders and downcast eyes—as if risen from the grave and too surprised to realize that they just had been saved.

An anagram had led to their freedom.

Robbert Goudriaan couldn't believe his eyes.

And those same eyes filled with tears when he suddenly recognized Jan Glas among all those people. * The people of Franks Knight were back home again. They even had their horses and cats back.

But the riddles hadn't been solved yet, and Chris Lockhart had found no answer to all his questions. Jan Glas maintained through thick and thin that he'd had a heavenly vision, and a lie detector confirmed it.

Perhaps Sebastian Estanol could bring light into the darkness; he was on his way from Tabasco to Florida to study the helmet found in a safe in the wooden office in Lost Harbor.

Sebastian had said he had certain suspicions. "Arnold McKay was far ahead of his time. I'm sure that the helmet contains hardware that influences the brain. I'll gather a team of scientists, and together we'll figure out the possibilities of the helmet. If Jan Glas was brainwashed, we'll know it soon enough."

The people of Franks Knight had taken up the thread of their existence again. They still believed in the crack of doom.

"Tacendo has put us to the test," said Wesley Dunn to the press. "He led us away from our houses and brought us to a subterranean paradise. He will do that one more time. Then the prediction of Manuel Raso will come true, and we will survive the greatest disaster mother earth has ever known."

Jan remained, at the request of Chris, in Florida to wait for what would be discovered about the hardware inside of the helmet. Robbert and he both had a big room in the house of Arnold McKay. The house had become headquarters for Chris Lockhart and his men after they had to leave the city hall because the people of Franks Knight had returned.

One afternoon Jan, Robbert, and Chris were sitting down in the big living room of the house when a visitor was announced.

"Someone from Franks Knight wants to have a talk with you, Mr. Lockhart. He insists on a word with you, but I wonder if you're willing to listen to him. For he's rather drunk. He was standing at the side of the road, staggering on his feet, and waved down a police car on patrol."

"I doubt he could be from Franks Knight," reacted Chris. "The people there take no alcohol, but let him inside- you've made me curious."

The man who entered the room was as thin as a rake and wore threadbare, old-fashioned clothes. He looked around in surprise, like someone who had been unexpectedly brought from a deserted isle to a museum—and then he saw the big clock with the silver Raso and his scythe.

He fell down on his knees and put his hands flat on the floor.

"It's true," he mumbled. "It's true!"

Chris summoned him to stand up again.

"Who are you?"

"Joe Pendelton. Grocer. I'm looking for Mr. Lockhart, and I believe that's you. I recognize you from television."

"Yes, I am. Sit down, man, before you fall down. You have been drinking. Isn't that odd for someone from Franks Knight? And I thought none of you had television. I haven't seen one in any home there."

Joe Pendelton sat down on the couch next to Jan Glas.

"I'm an alcoholic. I won't lie about that. Sometimes I watch television in the office of Al Corbetta of the Spring Tide Motel. I was already buying whiskey there when he was still a toddler and his father Sammy was the boss."

He took a deep breath, three, four times.

"There's something I want to tell you. I saw a commentary about Franks Knight. In Al's office. I saw you, Mr. Lockhart, but not just only you: I also saw the owner of this house, Arnold McKay. He gave me my first glass of whiskey, long ago."

Chris raised his eyebrows but remained silent. After a while, Joe continued.

"Yes, long ago, a young man stepped into my shop. He showed me a picture of that clock there. I told him who made the clock. Patrick Martens. Mr. Lockhart, I recognized Arnold McKay on the spot, when I saw him on television. He was that young man who came to visit me. Patrick Martens was married to our doctor, Susanne. She got pregnant. Pregnant! That was forbidden, that was against all of Raso's rules!"

He started to cough. He beat himself on the chest with both fists and retched as though he were going to vomit. After some time he pulled himself together and said, "I'll tell you something now that should have remained a secret. Susanne and Patrick had a child. A son. We never saw the baby. Wesley Dunn didn't find it necessary to track the child down. Susanne and Patrick had left Franks Knight and returned without their child. There was a public meeting. We, the people of Franks Knight, made a decision. Susanne and Patrick had to be punished for this. They were locked up in the cellar of the city hall. They finally died there of hunger and thirst... I'm convinced that Arnold McKay was the son of Susanne and Patrick. He almost managed to kill us all. He wanted to punish us the way we had punished his parents."

Joe wiped the tears from his eyes, let himself fall onto the floor, crawled up to the clock, and whispered, "We're guilty, we're all guilty."

Jan Glas, Robbert Goudriaan, and Chris Lockhart looked in silence to the man on the floor, and slowly but surely they began to understand what had happened.

Robbert Goudriaan was the first to speak.

"Life is an accumulation of coincidences."

THE END

The Author – Koos Verkaik

Koos, a 'Dutchy' with spunk and an inexhaustible drive and fathomless imagination, is one of the most prolific authors of sci-fi and children's books in The Netherlands. His novels, *All-Father* and *Wolf Tears*, earned him the moniker, the Dutch Stephen King.

He wrote his first sci-fi novel, *Adolar*, in one weekend when he was 18 years old and the manuscript was published shortly thereafter.

Koos has published over 60 books, both children's books and novels, hundreds of comic scripts, and he has worked as a copywriter. He is currently working on several screenplays and new novels.

To read more about Koos and his work visit his website at www.koosverkaik.com or follow him on Facebook at https,//www.facebook.com/koos.verkaik.5

Also by Koos Verkaik

Novels in Dutch

Adolar

Terug naar het Dorp

Conflict Afrika

Mana, en Toen Brak de Hel los

De Meesterparasiet

Grapstad

Psycho Park

Alvader

Wolfstranen

Neanderthaler Dromen

De Dans van de Nar

Children's Book Series

Saladin Series

Saladin het Wonderpaard

Saladin en Silver

Silver en het Spookpaard

De Nar van Nottingham

Slimmetje Series

Het Konijn uit de Hoed

De Boze Beer

Schipbreuk

De Hoge Hoed is weg

Ridder Joris

De Schat van Kabouter Bollewijn

Professor in Paniek

De Tovertrein

De Verdwaalde Walvis

Sneeuwmannen in Kabouterland

Otto de Otter

Krimpende Paddestoelen

Wolpertinger series

De Monsterherberg

De Onderlanden

Het Land van Franje

De Drakentuin

Roest IJzervreter

Drie Dolle Prinsen

Koning Leo Lawaai

Alex de Grote

Heros de Haas

Novels in English

The Nibelung Gold

All-Father

The Dance of the Jester

HIM, After the UFO Crash

Heavenly Vision

Children's Book Series

Wolpertinger Series

The Monster Inn

The Downhills

Uncle Balloon

The Land of Fringe

The Dragon Garden

Rusty Iron

Three Mad Princes

Saladin Series

Saladin the Wonder Horse

Saladin and Silver

Silver and the Ghost Horse

The Jester of Nottingham

www.ingramcontent.com/pod-product-compliance
Lightning Source LLC
Chambersburg PA
CBHW061257170626
46813CB00012BA/2388